PARAMOUNT PICTURES

Presents

A Rosenfield production from ANJA Films

BANG THE DRUM SLOWLY

Starring

Michael Moriarty
Robert De Niro
Vincent Gardenia

Screenplay by
MARK HARRIS
based upon his novel

Produced by
MAURICE AND LOIS ROSENFIELD

Directed by
JOHN HANCOCK

Music scored by
STEPHEN LAWRENCE

COLOR   A PARAMOUNT RELEASE

BANG
THE DRUM
SLOWLY

~~~~~~~~~~~~~~~~~~~~~~~

MARK HARRIS

A DELL BOOK

Published by
DELL PUBLISHING CO., INC.
1 Dag Hammarskjold Plaza
New York, New York 10017
Copyright © 1956 by Mark Harris

HE wiped his face with the towel again. "Old man, a book can have Chicago in it, and not be about Chicago. It can have a tennis player in it without being about a tennis player."

I didn't get it. I probably looked it, for he went on, "Take this book here, old man—" and held up one of the books he had swiped from some library. Along with the numbers I could see Hemingway's name on the spine. "There's a prizefighter in it, old man, but it's not about a prizefighter."

"Is it about the sun rising?" I said. I knew that was part of the title.

"Goddam if I know what it's about," he said . . .

WRIGHT MORRIS, *The Huge Season*

SPECIAL SOUVENIR SCORECARD

NUMBERS AND POSITIONS OF ALL THE PLAYERS
(AT BOSTON, OPENING DAY, APRIL 12, 1955)

NUMBER	POSITION
2 GEORGE GONZALEZ	*3RD BASE*
42 PERRY SIMPSON	*2ND BASE*
5 PASQUALE CARUCCI	*RIGHT FIELD*
4 SID GOLDMAN	*1ST BASE*
3 "CANADA" SMITH	*CENTER FIELD*
6 VINCENT CARUCCI	*LEFT FIELD*
7 "COKER" ROGUSKI	*SHORTSTOP*
18 JONAH BROOKS	*CATCHER*
44 "AUTHOR" WIGGEN	*PITCHER*
1 "UGLY" JONES (CAPT.)	*SHORTSTOP*
12 WILLIS TYLER	*INFIELD*
14 "WASH" WASHBURN	*INFIELD*
15 HARRY GLEE	*OUTFIELD*
19 "LAWYER" LONGABUCCO	*OUTFIELD*
20 REED McGONIGLE	*OUTFIELD*
9 "GOOSE" WILLIAMS	*CATCHER*
10 BRUCE PEARSON	*CATCHER*
16 "BLONDIE" BIGGS	*PITCHER*
17 JAMES VAN GUNDY	*PITCHER*
21 "HORSE" BYRD	*PITCHER*
22 JACK STERLING	*PITCHER*
23 GIL WILLOWBROOK	*PITCHER*
24 HERB MACY	*PITCHER*
45 LINDON BURKE	*PITCHER*
46 F. D. R. CASELLI	*PITCHER*
48 KEITH CRANE	*PITCHER*
36 CLINT STRAP	*COACH*
37 JOE JAROS	*COACH*
38 "EGG" BARNARD	*COACH*
39 "DUTCH" SCHNELL	*MGR.*

BANG
THE DRUM
SLOWLY

CHAPTER 1

Me and Holly were laying around in bed around
10 A.M. on a Wednesday morning when the call
come. I was slow answering it, thinking first of a
comical thing to say, though I suppose it long since
stopped handing anybody a laugh except me. I
don't know. I laugh at a lot of things nobody ever
laughs at except her. "Do not be funny," she said.
"Just answer it." But I seen her kind of listening
out of the corner of her eye.

"Triborough Bridge," I said.

"I have a collect call for Mr. Henry Wiggen
from Rochester, Minnesota," said the operator.

"I do not know a soul there," said I, "and I do
not accept collect calls under any circumstances." I
used to accept a lot of collect calls until I got wise
to myself.

Then behind the operator I heard this voice saying, "Come on, Arthur."

Well, there is only one person in this world that
calls me "Arthur," and the first thing I thought
when I heard it was I got this picture of him in jail
in Rochester, Minnesota. Do not ask me why jail,

13

but that was the picture I got, and I said to Holly, "Bruce is in jail in Minnesota," and she sat up in bed, and I said to the operator, "Tell him this better be important."

"Arthur, Arthur," said he, "you must speak to me," and I said I would.

And then it was like speaking to him always is, where all he can say is this one thing his mind might be on, like he might get up in the morning saying, "I must write a postcard home," and says it while dressing, and says it at breakfast, and says it maybe 3 or 4 times all morning, or he says, "Arthur, I must have $20," and says it again all the way to the park and all the time dressing and drilling, and then might say it in the middle of the ball game when you are trying to keep your mind on what you are doing until you finally give him his 20 and he stops saying it and becomes silent, and he said, "You have got to come and see me."

"What did you do?" I said. I still thought he was in jail.

"You have got to come and see me," he said. "I am in the hospital."

"With what?" I said.

"You have got to come and see me," he said.

"I cannot afford it," I said. "I am up to my ass in tax arrears." This was the statement of a true rat, and you can imagine how it must of sounded to him. But I knew nothing of the circumstances at the time. If he had of hung up on me then and there he would of had a right to do so. Yet who could he of called besides me? There was a silence, and I personally cannot stand silence on long distance, especially if I am not sure how deductible it will be, and I said, "Say something! Do not just stand there!"

"You have got to come and see me," he said.

"All he says is I have got to go and see him," I said.

"What did he do?" she said.

"He is in the hospital," I said.

"Then you have got to go," she said.

"I will come," I said.

All we threw was one change of clothes in a bag because we naturally had no idea, plus my Arcturus kit, figuring if I done some business along the way we could call the whole trip deductible. "He would not be in Rochester, Minnesota, if it was not serious," she said. "I do not like the look of it."

"He has got North Pole coverage," I said. When I am trying to sell a total policy I say, "This policy covers everything except sunstroke at the North Pole." It is good for a laugh. However, I never wrote such a total policy except the one I sold to Bruce, $50,000, the first I ever sold, and the fastest, selling it to him in 5 minutes flat in the hotel in Boston one night, not even trying to sell it to him but only just tuning my line you might say, the seal not yet even broke on my kit and my license scarcely dry because only that afternoon I polished off this course I took. I took the course bit by bit all that summer, every time we hit Boston. I said,

"Leave me point out just a few advantages of protection of this type," and he said, "Arthur, show me where I sign." I did not write another policy for a month. I have sold about 70, all to ballplayers except one to Mr. Jacob Epstein, my former English teacher at Perkinsville High. The reason they call it "Arcturus" is because Arcturus is the nearest star, or else the brightest. I forget which. Maybe both. They told me in the course but I forget.

"Surely his coverage is not all you can think of," she said.

"No," said I, "naturally not," though it was. First you think about money. I used to pee away money like wine until I got wise to myself.

We made a fast stop at the bank, and then she drove me to the depot. "Take care of 600 Dollars," I said, which was what we kept calling him before she was born. She was 3 months pregnant at the time. She said she would, and I kissed her and said I would be back in a couple days. I was not back for 6 months.

I flew through a snowstorm from Albany to Chicago, the stewardess going up and down the isle smiling with her big white teeth and singing, "Trala, this is nothing but a snowstorm." She said we were over it, but it looked to me like we were *in* it. It got very dark inside the plane, and I started getting these flash pictures of the whole goddam machine coming to a dead stop 30,000 feet over Indiana or somewhere, and the stewardess said to me, "Are you *the* Henry Wiggen?"

I said I was. It made me feel pretty good, for it been some time since anybody asked me that in just that way, not selling me anything, only asking. In the summer of 52 I was the toast of New York, but 2 years later I couldn't of got a traffic ticket squashed. She said, "I bought a copy of your book at the American airport in Cairo, Egypt." She had very big white teeth and quite a lovely smile and all, and right away my X-ray eye started seeing through her uniform and down to the girl herself. You know how you do. One minute you are picturing yourself dead in Indiana and the next minute a girl glides in view and gives you a smile and a little thing like a snowstorm at 30,000 feet don't seem to make much of an impression any more.

The upshot of it was we wound up over coffee in the airport in Chicago. She told me what a lonely and gloomy city Chicago was on a snowy night. "I will probably just lay on my bed curled up with a magazine," she said, and now I begun getting pictures of her curled up like a girl does.

"No doubt you have got a roomie for company," said I.

"Oh yes," said she, "but she is on a flight to Mexico City," and she yawned, and I started telling myself it was insane to go on in a snowstorm, besides which what could I do when I got there and how much more sense it would make to get there in the morning fresh as a daisy, and on and on. But then I said to myself, "Henry, what a louse you are with a wife 3 months pregnant that you kissed goodby not 7 hours ago!" "I have got to make a couple phone calls," I said.

I called Goose Williams. I could not of sold Goose anything, and I knew it, but if I didn't at least try I wouldn't of had the nerve to list the trip deductible. He used to hate me. His wife said he went out for a loaf of bread Sunday and was never seen since. "I do not know which is worse," she said, "having Harold home or having him away."

"I wish to speak to him concerning insurance matters," I said.

"Harold already cashed in all his insurance," she said.

"He should not of done that," said I.

"Harold should not of done a lot of things," she said, "and a lot more things he should of done he never quite tended to. Tell me, Henry," she said, "is Harold at the end of the trail?"

I could not get used to her calling him "Harold." "Goose?" said I. "At the end of the trail? That is the most ridiculous thing I ever heard of."

"Tell me the truth," she said. "He is at the end of the trail. He has not got as much as one full season left in him. He has got only his wife and his debts and his children, and all of them a pain and a burden to him," and I held the telephone away from my ear and looked out through the glass at the stewardess. She was twisted around on the stool, studying the seams of her stockings. "He will be 35 come August," she said. The stewardess twisted her body first one way and then the other, and I said to myself, "It is true that you have got a wife back home, but it is also true that you only live once, and furthermore she practically as much as invited you up." "I wish you was Harold," she said, "and Harold was you. How old are you, Henry?"

I do not even think I answered. She begun crying a little, and I eased the phone back on the hook and slid the door open and started out. But right away I got these further pictures of Holly back home worrying about me and probably following me on the clock and no doubt picturing me rushing in one plane and out the other, and I quick closed the door again and called Joe Jaros and spoke to his wife. It was Joe's wife later left the cat out of the barn. Usually I do not hang with the coaches much, but me and Joe become fairly friendly on account of Tegwar, The Exciting Game Without Any Rules, T-E-G-W-A-R, which nobody on the club can play but me and Joe because nobody can keep a straight face long enough. I will be hilarious on the inside but with a straight face on the outside, and I was smiling while his phone was ringing while poor Goose's wife was probably still crying in a dead phone at her end which shows you the kind of a thoughtless personality I have. Joe was out baby-sitting his grandchildren. His wife give me his number, but I did not even take it down. "My Lord," she said, "Joe has got insurance with 3 or 4 different out-fits."

"You do not have insurance," said I, "unless you have got Arcturus."

She laughed. She asked me how long I planned

to be in town, and I said I did not know. There
were the pictures of Holly and the pictures of the
stewardess curled on the bed plus more pictures
now of Joe Jaros baby-sitting his grandchildren, all
cozy warm with a snowstorm outside, not tramping
the streets like Goose nor with girls in a number of
towns, not drinking up all his credit in the saloons
until all of a sudden one day the girls and the
credit begin to give out at once. I seen it happen. I
seen too many old-time ballplayers hanging around
clubhouses telling you what a great game you just
pitched (though you might of just got the hell
shelled out of you) and could you by any chance
loan them 5 to tide them over, which I used to loan
them, too, before I was in so damn deep I was
playing winter ball and hitting the banquet circuit
and *still* getting in deeper with every passing day
until Holly took a hold of things. I said, "Henry,
look at Joe. He did not flub his life away chasing
after every pair of big white teeth he run across,"
and I slid open the door again and circled around
and went out a side door saying "Positively No
Admission" and listing a number of fines and pen-
alties and prison terms you could get for passing
through that one door, and out in the snowstorm
and back up in the air.

The only time I was ever in Minneapolis before
was in June of 53 for an exhibition in St. Paul, the
night Red Traphagen split his finger and walked
in to the bench with the nail hanging off and said
to Dutch, "That is sufficient," and stepped out of
his gear and never even went back east with us but

went to San Francisco and taught in the college there.

I fell asleep in the hotel wondering what I might of missed not following through with the airplane stewardess in Chicago, kicking myself for not having took a stab at it, yet knowing that I would of kicked myself all the harder if I done the opposite, laying there thinking how life was one big problem after the other and feeling sorry for myself and I suppose actually thinking I had any problems, not knowing what a real problem was.

I hardly knew a soul in town. I called Rosy Ryan in the morning, general manager I think they call him of the Millers, once a right-hand pitcher for the Giants, the first National League pitcher to ever hit a home run in the World Series, which he done in 1924, but he was out. I personally never hit a home run in 4 years up. The TV said, "Today's high, 15 below zero." I figured I heard wrong.

I called up Aleck Olson, the Boston outfielder, and he come rushing down, and we had coffee and gassed and talked about annuities, which he was very interested in and bought one off me later in the summer. I did not wish to sell him one on the spot but told him check around and compare Arcturus with the others, because I knew he would find nothing better, besides which they never do check around anyway, and he went with me to The Dayton Company and I bought a storm coat with a fur collar and earmuffs and gloves, $70, all deductible, business. I would not of needed them if I was not in Minneapolis and would not of been in Minneapolis except on business. Holly says the same. Me and him started floating around town like a couple old buddies, which handed me a laugh. All summer a fellow is just another ballplayer on somebody else's ball club until if you run across him in the winter it's a horse of another color, and he laughed, too, not knowing why, like Bruce does, laughs when you laugh without knowing why, which I bawled him out 500 times for but never made a dent.

Well, you know me, if I get to a place hungry the first thing I do is eat. When I got down to Rochester, Minnesota, I stumbled across this kosher restaurant, being very fond of kosher food, and when I was done I went to the hospital. He was not in the room. Yet I could tell it was his by the smell of this shaving lotion that he uses about a quart and a half of every time he shaves. And for who? For a prostitute on 66 Street name of Katie that he thinks he is in love with and goes around telling everybody he is about to marry. A nurse popped her head in the room and said, "Are you Mr. Wiggen at last?" and I said I was, and she left, and soon I heard the sound of his shoes racing along the hall and finally sliding the last 6 or 8 feet like we used to slide in the hallway in Perkinsville High, and in he come, all dressed, all fit as a fiddle, looking as tip-top as I ever seen him, and I said, "This is sick? This is why I dropped everything back home and risked my life in a snowstorm and went to the expense of a new wardrobe in Minneapolis?"

"Hello, Arthur," he said.

"And do not call me "Arthur." If you would trade in these gallon jugs of shaving lotion on a bar of soap and wash out your ears you would hear something."

"Do not be mad," he said. "They do not wish me to leave without a friend."

"Then stay," said I.

"I was even here over Christmas," he said.

"For what?" I said, and right about then 3 doctors walked in, and the head one spoke, saying, "Sit down, Mr. Wiggen," and they all begun to smile, first smiling at Bruce and then at me and then at each other, and one of them offered me a cigarette, though I do not smoke and did not take it. "How will things be going with the Mammoths?" said the doctor. But he did not really care. You could tell. He started flipping through papers on a clipboard, and then he turned the whole thing over and did not look at them, and he said, "Unless we have made a terrible mistake somewhere Mr. Pearson is suffering from Hodgkin's Disease." He then begun telling me what it was. It was bad.

"Exactly how bad?" I said.

"It is fatal," he said.

I could not think what "fatal" meant. It is like a word like "cancel" or "postpone" that for a couple seconds I can never think what they mean but must ride with them, or like being told an X-ray is "negative" which always sounds bad to me until I remember that it is not bad but good. "What is that?" I said.

"It means I am doomeded," said Bruce.

"You goddam fool," I said.

Then I closed my eyes, and time passed, and when I opened them he was standing in front of me with one of those little tiny hospital cups, and I drunk it down all in one gulp, and he took the cup and run back across the room and filled it again from a pitcher. He kept running across the room like that about 4 times, too stupid to bring the pitcher over. But I couldn't say anything. I couldn't talk, and I seen the doctors there like 3 bumps on a log. "3 phonies," I said. "3 monkeys that I doubt could cure a case of warts. You are the boys that send me 50 letters a day looking for contributions for your rotten hospitals. What do you do with the contributions I send?"

"We done many great things," said the first doctor. "We are only human and cannot do everything."

"I will never send another penny," said I.

"This is not a pleasant occasion for us," said the doctor, "no more than it is for you."

"It is some world," I said. "I say turn the son of a bitches loose and leave them blow it up," and I got up from the chair but sat down again, very weak in my knees.

"Anyhow, Arthur," said Bruce, "I am covered by North Pole coverage. It is all paid right down to the end."

"I doubt that you have even got what they say," I said.

"We are naturally hoping we are wrong," said the doctor.

"You never looked better in your life," I said. "What do you weigh?"

"185," he said.

"That is your weight," I said. "Why do they not put you on a scale? I suppose that would be foolish, however, since I doubt that these knucklehead individuals could read a scale."

"Be calm, Arthur," said he. "You must be calm and listen to what they say, for they know best," and I sat back and listened without believing them. It was all too impossible to believe.

CHAPTER 2

We pushed off in the morning, and I really mean pushed because his car wouldn't start and Bruce pushed it, leaning into it from behind and moving it out about as fast as any tow truck could of done. This was in the police garage, for when he come up to Rochester he parked it in the street, and he wound up paying an enormous amount in fines and charges. The man said, "I hate to take your money because I am a Mammoth fan from way back," but he took it all the same. We filled it up with anti-freeze, the kid in the station saying, "This will last you a lifetime."

You would be surprised if you listen to the number of times a day people tell you something will last a lifetime, or tell you something killed them. or tell you they are dead. "I was simply dead," they say, "He killed me," "I am dying," which I never noticed before but now begun to notice more and more. I don't know if Bruce did. You never know what he notices nor what he sees, nor if he hears, nor what he thinks.

* * *

One thing he knew was north from south and east and west, which I myself barely ever know outside a ball park. We drove without a map, nights as well as days when we felt like driving nights, probably not going by the fastest roads but anyhow going mostly south and east. "Stay with the river," he said.

"What river?" I said. "I cannot even see the river."

"You are with it," he said, and I guess we must of been. He traveled according to rivers. He never knew their name, but he knew which way they went by the way they flowed, and he knew how they flowed even if they weren't flowing, if you know what I mean, even if they were froze, which they were for a ways, knowing by the way the bank was cut or the ice piled or the clutter tossed up along the sides when we ever got close enough to see the sides, which we sometimes did because he liked to stop by the river and urinate in it. He would rather urinate in the river than in a gas station. Once a couple years ago I caught him urinating in the washbowl in the hotel in Cleveland. I bawled the daylight out of him. "I wash it out," he said. Maybe he did and maybe he didn't. For a long time I kept an eye on him.

Moving south he noticed cows out of doors. "We are moving south all right," he said, "because they keep their cows out of doors down here." He knew what kind they were, milk or meat, and what was probably planted in the fields, corn or wheat or what, and if birds were winter birds or the first birds of spring coming home. He knew we were south by the way they done chicken. "We ain't real south," he said, "but we are getting there. I can taste it."

He did not talk about it. It was OK with me either way. I was getting so I could talk about it or not by now, for the first shock wore off. It was his business and up to him to say the word, which a number of times he was just about set to do, opening his mouth and looking for the words but then not saying them, maybe shoving in a chew instead. He chews this Days O Work. Mostly he watched the country go by, now and then rolling down the window and spitting out and rolling it up again, maybe pointing at something, saying "Look there," and I looked and said "Well!" or "What do you know about that!" without really knowing what he was pointing at. When he drove he drove slow, slouched down a little, only his one middle finger hooked around the wheel, maybe studying the car ahead for a long time and then suddenly taking a notion to pass, and swinging out no matter what was coming, and sometimes if the passing looked tight he would stop his chewing, and when I seen him stop I closed my eyes a little and waited for the big noise in case that was what was in store. He had no science, then nor ever, but drives like he plays ball, on hunches, which in some ballplayers pays big dividends because some ballplayers are natural and their hunches usually never go wrong. But Bruce is not a natural.

We drove maybe 24 hours at a stretch, never

calling a halt for sleep until he said so, doing whatever he said because I figured that was up to him, too. I had more time, and it did not seem fair to stop and sleep until he wished to, even as tired as I sometimes got, and then he would say, "Leave us hunker down," saying right afterwards, "I am sorry, Arthur," because I never could stand him saying "Hunker down." Yet it did not seem to make much difference if he said "Hunker down" or not any more, and I said, "Go ahead and speak any way that suits you because to tell you the truth probably a lot of things I say ain't the King's English neither."

I called Holly the first night out from a little town in Iowa name of South Cedar Rocks, Iowa, where there was only one telephone. The girl put the call through and then got up from her chair so I could sit. Usually I call Holly every night, person to person, asking for some phony party like Mr. Frank Furter or Mr. U. R. Madd or Mr. M. Y. Love, and she says he is out in the ice-house and cannot be bothered or sprained his leg climbing the wall or down in Perkinsville buying striped paint, and that way she gets to hear my voice, and me hers, and no cost to anybody except the company. When things went sour on me around in June of 53, when every time I worked I lost if it didn't rain, the club got wind of these calls and brung her down and set us up in the apartment on 66 Street downstairs from the whorehouse, thinking I was worried about her, which I was not. All that was wrong with me was the club wasn't hitting, and soon she went back home and I went back in the hotel with Bruce. I could not tell her what was up. I meant to, but the telephone girl was standing there with her ears a mile wide and all I said was I was going home with Bruce and would fill her in later. "OK, Henry," she said, "if that is what you must do it is what you must do. I have faith in you," which made me think of the airplane stewardess, and I lifted up one foot and kicked myself, which set the telephone girl off in a fit of giggles.

"What word from 600 Dollars?" I said.

"No sign of life as yet," she said.

Driving along I couldn't think why in hell I didn't tell her, nor why I shouldn't, and I kept writing these letters in my head, breaking it gentle, and then tearing them up and finally calling her when we hit St. Louis and busting right out with it, saying, "Holly, Bruce has got a fatal disease."

She always liked him. She always said, "Add up the number of things about him that you hate and despise, and what is left? Bruce is left," and she did not scream nor faint, though why I should of thought she would I do not know because she never done so in my life. All she said was "Oh?" and I said, "Are you there?" and she said, "Yes, I am only pulling up a chair and collecting my thoughts."

"Well, sit on your thoughts awhile," I said, trying to be funny and take the sting out of it a little. Actually you get over it fairly quick. You might not think so, but it is true. You are driving along with a man told he is dying, and yet everything is going on, the gas gage getting lower, the speedometer registering, cows nibbling in the field, birds singing, chickens crossing the road, clouds moving across the sky, and the sun coming up and going down. It is still 27 miles to this place and 31 miles to that, and you keep getting hungry and you keep getting tired, and then you eat and then you sleep, and everything begins all over again. You cannot go on staggering from the first blow of it. You take it full, but you come back in.

"How can you be in a joking mood?" she said.

"Bruce been cheering me up," said I.

"Where is he?"

"Right now," said I, "he is just outside the booth playing the pinball machine."

"How unfair is life," she said.

"Yes," I said. What else could I say? It was true. One chap will get knifed whatever way he turns while others they keep falling down on dollar bills, and she said call her tomorrow, which I done for about 3 days running until she could get it out of her, and by the third day she was joking a little herself, back off the floor. It happened that way to everybody.

Still in St. Louis I called Dutch, meaning to tell him because I thought he should know for the sake of the club and lay his plans according. I couldn't find his number in the book and the information wouldn't give it out, so I called "The Globe." They said how in hell did they know I was who I said I was. They asked me what was the name of Red Traphagen's wife, and who signed my pay-check, and what hotel did St. Louis stay at when St. Louis was in New York, and I told them, and they give me Dutch's number, and then after all that waltzing I did not have the nerve to tell him. He does not like bad news and does not like the person that breaks it. I pity his letter carrier and his tax man. He likes things to go smooth, no headaches, and hates the man that ruffles up the smoothness of it, never forgetting nor forgiving but only keeping his hate in his head. He remembers raw calls an umpire made 20 years before, and he hates that man though he made 50,000 right calls since, hat-ing everybody then because everybody some time or other crossed him, players, coaches, writers, the Moorses, all the world, admired by millions and loved by none, hated by his closest friends. If he wasn't the greatest genius in baseball he would be out of a job, buying and selling when the moment is ripe, now gambling, now playing safe, always fig-uring, playing his own strength one day and the other fellow's weakness the next, now juggling, now standing pat, always driving and never letting up, and almost never wrong. He has finished out of the money only 5 times in 24 years. When he dies they will need 5 men to hold him down while the other clamps the lid. "When I die," he says, "the paper will write in their headline THE SON OF A BITCHES OF THE WORLD HAVE LOST THEIR LEADER, yet many a boy might shed a tear or 2 that I brung to fame and greatness."

When he answered he said "What!" and I jumped, and I could not speak, and he said "Whatwhat!" fast, like that, like a gun, like those rapid repeaters we used to shoot off on the Fourth, and I said, "Howdy there, Dutch. This is Henry."

"Where the hell are you?" he said, and I quick held the receiver off a ways and said, "Up home. Can you hear me?"

"How is the insurance racket?" he said.

"Fine," said I. "I am tip-top and will have a great year."

"Do not squawk to me about it," he said. "Call the office. You had a bad year, Author. Have a good year and they will make it back to you in 56."

"I am not squawking," I said. "It did not even come yet."

"You are squawking in advance," he said.

"No," I said, "I am only calling to wish you a Happy New Year. Money is nothing to me," and I told him how we come out in court against the United States Bureau of Internal Revenue, and he got quite a laugh out of that.

But he stopped laughing. "There is something very fishy here," he said. "I can not imagine you running up a big phone bill gassing over nothing."

"Well, I will see you in Aqua Clara," said I. "How is the weather out there?" It was clear and warm, not a cloud in the sky.

"Miserable," he said. "Just miserable."

We crossed the river at St. Louis and went down the other side, down through the bottom of Illinois and chipped off a corner of Kentucky and Tennessee. We seen kids playing ball in a field down around a town name of Opelika, Alabama, because I remember we stopped there and got the car greased and walked around some and stood watching these kids whacking a ball around with the cover coming loose. "The first field I ever played baseball in," Bruce said, "was in a field of peanut hay."

He said nothing more. He never tells you anything much in a bunch, only a little now and a little later until over the long pull you will find out a lot that he will never tell in one day or one week. He will just leave things eat. Coming across the bridge out of St. Louis he said, "Yes, it is best to say nothing to Dutch," and I said yes it was, and then maybe down around Murphysboro, Illinois, he said, "Dutch would can me for sure," until along around Paducah, Kentucky, he said, "I would hate being canned if he did." Then he did not say another word about it until the other side of the Tennessee line, and then he said, "I always give him my best," which was true. Dutch never asked much of Bruce, and what Bruce give him was not always perfect, but it was his best. "Dutch knows I always give him my best," he said, and then he said it 2 or 3 more times, fixing it in his mind, saying it the last time like he was more sure of it than ever, and dropping it cold and thinking new ideas.

We were a pretty good ways out of Opelika, not far from the Georgia line, and he said, "It was my granddaddy's."

"What was?" I said.

"The field."

"The peanut hay?"

"Yes it was," he said, and then 10 miles later said, "It was warm on your feet," and little by little he told it, the smell of it when it was wet in the morning, and the smell of it when it dried, how it stuck to your feet wet and then crumbed off, and how a baseball picked up the color of the field until soon you could not hardly see the ball against the ground, and you took it and taped it in white tape until the tape, too, was the color of the field, and you taped it again, and then maybe again until the ball was too big and you all got a hold of nickels and dimes that you hid in the mill and went over to Bainbridge, 6 or 8 of you because you never trusted any one kid with the money and bought a new white baseball and tried for a long time to keep it off the ground. He remembered the names of the kids, this one now doing this, and that one that, one dead in the war, one the father of triplets, except here and there a name slipped his mind and he doubled up his fists against his cheeks and leaned forward and closed his eyes, saying, "I can see that goddam kid as clear as day."

"Probably some morning when you wake up his name will be right there on your tongue," I said.

"Or it might be too late," he said.

"That is true," I said. "It might. We will all of us die with things never remembered."

"His hair was parted in the middle," he said. "I will ask my old lady, for she never forgets a name."

Soon we hit the line. I kept watching for it on

the speedometer, and then when we hit it it was not much, just a little wormy sign that might of said "Apples For Sale" or "No Fishing" but instead said "Entering Georgia" that probably been stuck in the ground years and years before and left to rot, half hid by the bushes by the side of the road like nobody was particularly proud of this part of Georgia and just as soon you thought you were still in Alabama. Bruce never seen it, but he knew. He knew the whole country around in there, the names of all the little rivers we crossed and the names of all the railroads. Every train we seen he knew if it hit Bainbridge, and if it did what time. To him Georgia is a special place, different than all the others, and Bainbridge a special town, and Mill more special yet. Me, I believe one place is like the next. I been in 43 states and 4 countries, Mexico, Canada, Japan, and Cuba.

CHAPTER 3

Bruce Pearson was born on June 4, 1926, in Bainbridge, Georgia. He has one sister, Helen, now of
Seattle, Washington, and either one other brother
or one other sister, I forget, that died when but a
child. I never met Helen.

His father farmed on a farm about 300 yards up
the road. I seen the farm and also seen where their
house was, the well still there and the crapper out
back, but the house moved down now, same house,
different spot, that Southern States U dug up from
its roots and hoisted on a flat-top truck, the farm
rented out now to a colored man name of Leandro,
Gem's brother or brother-in-law. I do not know.
Gem is their hired girl. Leandro also barbers on
the side, cutting colored hair, or maybe barbers
first and farms on the side. I do not know that
neither. The number of things I do not remember
or maybe never knew or am only in the foggiest
haze about is quite amazing.

He played all sports in high school, and in his
junior year he won a scholarship to Southern States
U. However, he quit school after the football sea-

son of his senior year at high school to help his father farm. Southern States U got wind of this and rushed a man down to talk Bruce into going back and getting his diploma, which Bruce said he would be glad to get but asked, "How will my father farm the farm without me?" and the man from Southern States U went back and sent down an experimental tractor for Bruce's father to farm with. They sold their horse, and Bruce got his diploma.

By now the war busted out, and he went. It was something to do, and he thought he would like it better than college. He trained in Virginia and invaded France, sometimes in the thick of things and sometimes just laying around until one day he found himself in the middle of a hole in a field and nobody around that he knew. He figured just lay low and see what happens, and with his spare moments he dug his hole deeper, every so often peeking up over the top and seeing what he could see, and if he seen anybody he shot him. Then he hid down in his hole again, and when he could not keep his eyes open any more he spraddled out like he was dead, and when he woke up he dug some more and give a look around every so often. When he was out of bullets he tied a white hanky on top of his gun and walked back towards England. He was picked up by Americans or Frenchmen and shipped either to England or straight back to the U.S.A., and he was discharged in Virginia and went home.

That summer he played ball for various towns, catching mostly but also doing some pitching, these deals where towns pay 3 players, their battery and one other, and he made maybe 40 dollars a week-end and helped his father the rest of the time. Soon Southern States U got wind he was back, and the man come, and Bruce said he would be happy to go to college only how would his father farm without him again, and the man said, "Did we not send you a tractor some time ago?" But Bruce said his father needed more help than only a tractor, and Southern States U sent down some college boys wishing to learn farming. They helped Bruce's father, and Bruce went up.

He was partly used as a defensive line-backer. I don't know exactly what you call it, for I personally give up football when a kid and do not read about it and never look at it. If it flashes on the screen in the newsreel I go take a leak. He roamed up and down the line, too fast for anybody to go around, and anybody with a football come near him he tackled him. On the offense he whipped off these short little passes, 5 and 8 yards, very deadly and very accurate, and now and then reared back and flung a long one, and Southern States U lost only 2 games the first year Bruce was up, and none the second, and they played in a Bowl somewheres the second year, and won that, too, and it was easy work, no pressure.

He roomed with a fellow name of Hut Sut Sutter way up over the gymnasium, Sutter now with Green Bay. I run across him 2 winters ago on the banquet circuit at a Youth Jamboree in Baltimore where we both spoke, the only time I ever laid eyes on him, a short, wide fellow, and he told me he would show me some fine whorehouses in Baltimore. But I had a train to catch and anyhow was never interested in whorehouses to begin with. All winter they horsed around in the gymnasium, shooting baskets and swinging on the ropes and swimming in the pool, and once a month they took off in a college car and hunted up whorehouses, Sutter a regular expert in this matter. They played baseball for Southern States U in the spring, and when their season was done they went and played in the Alabama State Amateur Baseball League, though it was actually more Mississippi and Louisiana than Alabama, back and forth along the Gulf all summer, 8 and 10 ball games a week to make it pay, and never carrying more than 10 or 11 men on a club for the same reason, a League without a schedule and without records, so you might of been in first place or last, you never knew. You hit a town and hooked up with another club and went from town to town across Alabama and across Mississippi and into Louisiana until you played all the towns, and then you looked around for a new club to play against, and you started back, and maybe you stood with your own club and maybe not, because if one club was short a man you swapped shirts and joined it.

He was still pitching and catching, both, about half and half now because he liked to pitch, though he was all speed and nothing more. People told him he would never be a pitcher without more variety, but he did not care. He liked to pitch. He was not interested in going any place in baseball, then and maybe never, playing only for the kicks and what little cash was in it. A League where it never mattered if you won nor lost was the kind of a League he liked. What difference did it make to him if boys with "Mobile" on their shirt beat boys with "Biloxi," or the other way around, especially when you were just as libel to wear "Panama City" next week and "Baton Rouge" the week after? If somebody had wore "Bainbridge" on their shirt it might of made a difference, or if it been a league in Georgia, so he wore whatever shirt anybody threw at him, and he pitched when he could and caught when they needed a catcher, and he hit hard, loving more than anything else to stand up there swiping away at a baseball. In parks with short left fields they told him don't hit too hard because they could not afford lost balls, and he done so because he is the kind of a fellow that does what anybody asks him to, probably loaned his last dollar to anybody he knew 2 days in a row, anybody that give him a long, sad story, though no matter if he loaned it or not he would of went home broke anyways because him and Hut Sut Sutter kept the whorehouses showing a net profit from New Orleans to Port St. Joe. He caught the clap in Phenix City and cured it with miracle drugs in Birmingham. He grew and added weight. He was only a kid, just turned 20.

One day him and Sutter were hanging in the pool at Southern States U, and Bruce said, "Think of all that water, and my mother and father with none."

"Tell the University move your house over on the town side," said Hut Sut Sutter.

"We do not own no land," said Bruce.

"Tell them buy you a hunk of land," said Hut Sut, and him and Bruce went and seen somebody, and Hut Sut said, "This boy will not lay his hand on one more football until the University buy him a piece of experimental land, and move his house, and pipe his mother and father in on the town supply."

The University said, "We already bought him an experimental tractor and sent him down some experimental labor, but I suppose we can do the rest as well," and they done so.

Bruce was latching on to the idea by now, and every couple weeks he went and told the University what they needed, and they sent down a pickup truck and an air-condition until when Bruce could think of nothing more Hut Sut Sutter said to him, "Why not just put in for some experimental money?" and he done this, too, and he got it, probably not much, but some.

He got along pretty good as long as Sutter was around, but Sutter graduated and his ideas went dry. He went on living in the high room up over the gymnasium, and he sat by the window spitting tobacco juice down, watching it incurve and outcurve. He run with the college girls, but what they wanted most was dancing and being seen at the college spots, which was not what Bruce wanted. I suppose what many a girl was saying was, "Take me dancing and show me off at the college spots, and then we will go up in your room high on the top of the gymnasium," not saying it but only supposing he would understand how that was how the system was, never knowing how he could not figure systems, how he can never speak with his tongue but only with his strength, and what he done he took to the professionals, and they called him "Honey" and "Dearie" and loved him and left themself be loved, so for 20 minutes at a crack he could always have what passes in his book for love. I suppose if you have none a-tall 20 minutes looks good, even if it keeps you poor, and God knows it kept him poor until I took a hold and grabbed his check and put it in the bank and paid his insurance, only twice a month giving him 20 to go blow at Katie's.

How he found his way around the second summer in the Alabama State Amateur Baseball League I do not know, for Sutter was off to greener grass, until in July or August, somewhere in there, he run into Ray Pink, formerly of Pittsburgh, now a Mammoth scout. I called him "Roy" by mistake in "The Southpaw" and got 40 letters. Pink seen him pitch and said, "Why kill yourself for peanuts playing this slow ball when with teaching and training you might win big money and glory?" and he give him a new 47 Moors and a hunting gun, telling him he could now drive home in style and hunt all winter and not be bothered with football, shipping him then to the Mammoth farm at Appalachia in the Ind-O-Kent League, Class C, where he finished out the year pitching and catching and generally playing slow ball for peanuts but believing he was better off than he been.

He drove home in his Moors and hunted with his new gun all winter until a couple days before he left for Aqua Clara the Cushion-Gear in his 47 Moors fell apart or blowed up or only laid down and died, whatever it is that happens. Everybody that ever owned a 47 has a different tale to tell. He hopped in the pick-up and drove down to the Moors plant in Tallahassee, Florida, and bought a new Cushion-Gear for $145 and come home and put it in, and when he was done he had no money to get to Aqua Clara, and the City of Bainbridge staged a Night for him, public on the main drag with flags and speeches and a collection box in the shape of a baseball bat. I seen the clips, part of the papers he later burned, and photos of citizens large and small dropping in their buck or 2, and they said in their speeches, "Bruce Pearson will bring fame and glory to Bainbridge," and turned the box over and wrapped the cash in a baseball stocking sewed closed at the top by a lady of the town, and Bruce stowed it with his gear and was off to Aqua Clara.

Bainbridge never had a ballplayer got anywhere near the big-time since a fellow name of Mr. Randy Bourne that had one spectacular month with Boston in 1930. At least 6 times I sat in his barn and heard him tell of the month of May in 1930, when he was with Boston, of the home run he hit in Cleveland and the triple in New York, the base he stole in Pittsburgh and the barehand stop in St. Louis until the story simply ends because after once around the circuit the pitchers found him out. I could not listen. I shut my ears. I knew Bruce would of give most anything to settle down forever on a farm near Bainbridge, never mind the fame and glory, only give him time to live. Yet his face showed nothing. He only slouched against the wall and listened.

And when he left for Aqua Clara he felt the pressure, for the town would be watching, all eyes, and the more he thought about it the greater the pressure weighed him under, and instead of going straight to Aqua Clara he cut across to Jacksonville, Florida, and he drunk up his money and threw the stocking away in the ocean and wound up sleeping it off in jail until word got down to Aqua Clara, and the club sent up Bradley Lord, official ass-kisser of Old Man Moors and The World's Only Living Human Spineless Skunk. I am Player Representative for the Mammoths and sat in on many a winter meeting with the owners, and I guess I ought to know, and Bradley fetched him back down. That was the spring of 48. He was not yet 22.

Mike Mulrooney took him back to QC with him in the 4-State Mountain League, AA, trying him at several spots. Then he said, "You are a catcher," and Bruce believed that if Mike said he was a catcher he was, because he believed in Mike and was crazy about him. Did you ever meet anybody that was not?

He played good ball for Mike, and he went up in the September stretch of 48, or maybe late in August, and the pressure buckled him, and down he went again. He come up once more in the middle of the following July, and he stood. Dutch had no catching worries then, for Red Traphagen and Goose Williams were enough, more than anybody could ask at the time, and Dutch used Bruce when they needed a rest. He pinch-hit some, when the wind was right, and pinch-run now and again, and warmed pitchers and carried jackets and I guess run back and forth between the bullpen when the telephone broke down. It always does. I don't know, the field crew forget to roll it up when it rains. It's a wonder it *ever* works. And I suppose the big reason Dutch kept him, then and after, was because here was a boy that could belt a ball a mile and run like a dear and throw like a rifle, one of the nicest arms in baseball, bar none, if he only didn't have to stop and think, never a natural but always a powerful promise. Probably Dutch said to himself 49 times, "Why do I not turn Pearson loose?" and then never done so but hung on to him and carried him along like you might start pawing through your drawers and come on a batch of receipts and bills and say, "Why do I keep these?" and then throw them back in because some day they might turn out important, do it 49 times and every time throw them back. In September of 49, the Mammoths fifth, out of the money and headed neither up nor down, Bruce was busting down walls and picking men off base, and Dutch was no doubt saying, "Aha, at last my chicken is coming home to roost." Then all winter he figured Bruce in on his plans until in the summer of 50 Bruce was Bruce again, a marvelous 2 o'clock hitter and the dandiest looking batting-practice catcher in the business.

I myself joined the organization in the winter of 49 and was at Aqua Clara the spring of 50. I do not remember Bruce there. He was not a fellow you noticed, and anyhow my eye was on the big names, and I kept busy trying to walk like them and spit like them and get close enough to hear them talk, many of them my golden hero since I was no higher than a grasshopper, and I went back west with the QC Cowboys and pitched for Mike 2 years, winning 21 games the second year, not even the full year at that, and I come up in September of 51, and I stood.

I won 26 in 52, my best year and damn near my ruination, for between the Series money and the book I owed the United States Bureau of Internal Revenue $876 which I busted my ass over playing winter ball in Japan and Cuba and hitting the banquet circuit and selling annuities to ballplayers, my mind on too many things, my strength drained away, and my bill with the United States Bureau of Internal Revenue now hiked to $1,125. I wrote them and said, "It is no use. Come put me in jail. I will work it off at a dollar a day hammering rocks." They wrote again, saying, "Please remit," and they dragged us through court, and Holly showed cause to the Judge why the bill should of only been 37½% what it was, $421.89, and the judge said, "Yes, and this will learn you, Henry, that the way to make more money is to make less, and the way to go broke is to get rich." He was a Mammoth fan from way back, and read my book, but the damage was done because I could not deliver the goods with my mind full of lawyers and hammering rocks, my strength all wasted away, and 15 pounds over my weight from the banquets.

I roomed with Perry Simpson most of 52. Then Keith come up, a colored fellow, and they naturally juggled him in with Perry, and me with Bruce. I wrote in "The Southpaw" that "I figured I could put up with Bruce for a month," page 295, 300 in the quarter book. I am sorry I wrote it now, though he will never see it. He never reads. It was long more than a month. It was all 53 and 54 except a couple months when the club took me and Holly the apartment on 66 Street, and we hit it off pretty good once I got used to the stink of shaving lotion and this filthy chewing tobacco called Days O Work and spitting incurves and outcurves out the window and urinating in the sink and calling me "Arthur" and calling the bellboys "Ballboys" and never flushing the goddam toilet until every time he forgot I made him stand there and flush it 5 times, and sending home postcards with nothing wrote on them, all of it getting me down when it should of never bothered me a minute, or if it bothered me I should of went and flushed it myself and not made a speech because if I had the sense to look in my own goddam book I would of seen where his guts and his heart were being eat away. I should of knew it the first time I ever took any notice of him, in the spring of 52 at Aqua Clara. Red Traphagen says the same, saying "Slap it all in," and finding it for me, page 139, 142 in the quarter book—

"All except Bruce Pearson. Bruce is the third-string catcher. He might catch 5 or 6 games a year, but mostly he warms pitchers in the bullpen. Every year he comes 2 days late to camp because he ties one on on the way down. He don't drink except once a year, and then he goes the whole hog and drinks for 2 days in Jacksonville and Dutch has got to send Bradley Lord, and Bradley has got to hunt around for Bruce and find him and wait till he is done. Then he puts him on a bus to Aqua Clara, and when he gets there Doc Loftus works him over awhile and Mick McKinney works him over some more, and after about 6 hours Bruce is as good as new.

"The sad part is that there is never much work for him. Yet a ballplayer has got to play ball like a singer has got to sing and an artist has got to draw pictures and a mountain climber has got to have a mountain to climb or else go crazy. That's the way it is, and that is why things look so dark for Bruce every spring.

"You never seen such a sight. I could scarcely recognize him, for he did not look a-tall like the ballplayer that I had throwed to in the bullpen the September before. He is blondheaded, and it was pasted down over his eyes now, and there was blood in it, and the way I remembered him he was meek and mild and never said a word unless he was spoke to. But now he was ranting and raving. He had Bradley Lord by the back of the neck, and he called Bradley every name in the book plus a few that I suppose is special to Bainbridge, Georgia, and his shirt was tore clean in 2 and the fly of his pants was wide open and all the buttons gone. Bradley Lord was screaming at Dutch to take him off his hands. Dutch just laughed. "He will quieten down," he said.

"Then he begun to cry, and it was pitiful, and he cussed out Bradley Lord some more, and he cussed out the Grayhound Bus Company and the City of Jacksonville and the whole State of Florida and the game of baseball and QC and all the cities in the 4-State Mountain League, cussing and crying all the while. Dutch said he never seen him quite so bad before, and he sent Bradley Lord out for Doc Solomon and for Mike Mulrooney, Mike being over working with the rooks.

"After a little bit he stopped. He was sobbing and shaking, but he seemed better, and he rose and went over to the fountain and took a drink and come back rather wobbly and sat on the bench in front of the lockers. He seemed deep in thought, and then he rose and went very deliberate to the water again, and he filled his mouth and shot a stream across at Red, and it caught Red square in the face, and Red wiped it away.

"2 men come in for the empty crate of milk, and Bruce begun to give them hell and call them all sorts of foul names, "nigger" and such, and some of the boys made him quieten down and chased the men out of there so as not to cause any more disturbance than was necessary, and then Bruce begun a torrent, running down the colored people and milk companies and Bradley Lord. He dove for the bottles and would of upset the crate but me and Lindon pulled him off. He got hold of one bottle, however, and looked around for someone to fire it at, but by this time the clubhouse was cleared out and there was nobody left but me, for all the boys was eating their lunch on the grass outside. Bruce smashed the bottle on the floor, and I finally got him under a shower, and he shivered and shook and vomited something awful. Doc Solomon come then and said leave him vomit. I said there was little else you could do, for you can not give a man an order not to vomit. Doc Solomon left, and Bruce shook and shivered and vomited, and between times he laced into Doc Solomon, calling him a Jew and what not else.

"He was at the heights when all of a sudden

in walked Mike Mulrooney, and it was Mike that calmed him down, handing out the sweet talk and saying what a great ballplayer Bruce was. He went right in there under the shower and turned it off and crouched down on the wet floor with Bruce, and they talked about the good times they had back in QC. Soon Bruce come out just as calm as if he was sober, and Mike talked to him some more and held his hand and patted his shoulder.

"Then Dutch yelled 'Back to work!' and I went.

"That night I seen Bruce at the hotel, and he was as nice and polite as ever, and quiet, and when he spoke he spoke soft, and you could hardly believe it was the same man. From that day onwards he settled down and done his work, like he was told, and you never heard so much as a peep from him the season through."

CHAPTER 4

On the main drag in Bainbridge quite a few people give him a wave, and we slowed, and they said, "All fixed up?" and he said "Yes," and we moved on through town. The roster lists him from Bainbridge, but actually he lives in Mill on the road to Climax, which got its name on account of an old mill there that long ago broke down. You can see it from his window, and every so often you might see somebody come along needing a board and cut across to the mill and rip one off. This been going on for years and years until one day there won't be any mill left a-tall. One night I said, "That is one mill that ain't milling around much any more," and Bruce's father said, "Yes, Arthur, and that is an old joke, too." Bruce clumb all over that mill as a kid and still knows all the places for your feet. He goes up the top of it in about 15 seconds flat, and down again as fast, and he knows 100 secret little corners where they hid money and tobacco and letters from girls and other things they weren't supposed to own, and we went on through Bainbridge and down the road to Mill.

We got there before I realized it. I was looking for a town. He give me the impression they lived in a town, and then it wasn't a town a-tall but only a house off the road, white, with the sun hot on it, and his folks on the porch swatting flies, not knowing he was expected. On the nail by the door they keep these fly swatters. When you come out of doors you grab one. You get to do it automatic, like grabbing a bat when your swipes come, and then when you go back in you loop it over the nail again.

They didn't much stir when we pulled up, only sat and waited, and he jumped on the porch, never mind the steps, and kissed them and said, "This here is Henry, call him Arthur," and his father went in the house and dragged out 2 more chairs and 2 more swatters, and we all sat. All their business is done on the porch. After awhile the girl brung out 2 more glasses and laid them on the rail, and she said, "Howdy, Mr. Bruce, are you all better now?" and he never turned around but said "Yes." He might turn around for a white person sometime, but hardly ever for a colored one, and she poured water in the glasses. They wobbled a little, but they never fell, not then or ever all the time I was there, just sat balanced on the rail.

Such business as they do they do it slow, first a little sip of water and then a word or 2, and then no answer for a time until a word or 2 from someone else. It gets very restful, just sitting looking at the road and drinking water until when the water was gone his mother shouted back over her shoulder "Gem!" and the girl come out pretty soon again with more water.

"We were worried," his father said. One of his suspenders was always hanging loose, and I kept getting these terrific urges to get up and pull the hidget tight. Then everybody pulled on water awhile.

"I was in good hands," Bruce said. He balanced his hat on the rail, and curled up his tie and laid it on top of the hat. His mother took a sip of water and reached for the tie and uncurled it and smoothed it out and laid it straight on the rail. She was quite fat, with these extremely enormous breasts. When she was young she was quite thin and pretty. In their old photos she was thin and her husband heavy, but when times become easy for them she put on and he shed. She died last summer and never knew the truth, heart failure, 100 pounds over her weight, which maybe was what killed her, plus the excitement of the race.

"I bet it was cold up there," she said.

Everybody thought these various matters over, and then all of a sudden they all stood up and picked up their chair and went back in and hung their swatter up and shoved in at the table and ate. Do not ask me how they knew it was time, but they always did. Night after night I listened for some sign or signal, thinking maybe there was a certain shadow fell a certain place, or a certain car went by, or a certain train whistle, but I could never figure it. I just ate, and it was good, too much of the same too many nights in a row maybe, but very good, and after we ate we picked up our chair again and grabbed a swatter and went back out of doors.

"Not too damn cold," he said.

We sat awhile and swatted awhile, and it begun growing dark, and every now and then a car come past and stopped and said, "We seen where Bruce is home," and they said, "He sure is," and told me who was in the car. "That was Wilkies," "That was Johnsons," and Gem come out with 4 glasses and laid them on the rail and poured, all in the dark, and she gathered up the swatters because you couldn't see what you were swatting at any more anyhow, and right about then a car always drawed up and sat and waited for her. The same car brung her back in the morning, and she got out and took the glasses off the rail and went around the house and in, 7 days a week, every goddam day. The glasses were all wet with dew in the morning.

"What was wrong?" his father said.

"Nothing," he said. He only sent them post-cards, picture but no message, all different views of Rochester, Minnesota, but only 3 words, "Pearson, Mill, Georgia," and the rest only a white space. Sometimes he picked up a card and studied the picture, squinting close and looking for something in it that nobody else could find, like maybe a man might sit studying moving pictures of a particular ball game and trying to figure out what he threw wrong to a particular hitter, and wishing he could back up the film and have another try.

"There was a kid I played with with his hair parted in the middle," he said.

She told him the kid's name and where he was now and what doing, and he told it to me though I was sitting there and heard it myself and couldn't of cared less, and soon they begun yawning, and one of them would say, "It is about time to hunker down," and then another would yawn and say it, and later another, and then his mother dragged her chair in and made me up the bed in the guest room and afterwards come back in her robe and slippers and said through the screen, "It is about time to hunker down," and then we all got up and dragged our chair in, Bruce last, leaning his chair against the door, not locking it, only keeping it from rattling.

There was a table by my bed that every night I laid out on it 2 pages typewrote by the doctors in Rochester, the first page headed "Until the doctor comes," the second "Instructions for the physician." On the back I wrote down the numbers of the doctors in Bainbridge. In the morning I always stuck it back in my pants.

I never slept much the first night, only laid waiting. He kept his light on a long time, though what he done there I have no idea because he don't read and don't listen to the radio much. In the hotel he likes to sit in the dark and look down in the street at the traffic or across the way at lights in another hotel, and he likes to watch the flashing signs. Sometimes he spits and gets up on his elbow and watches how it floats, if it incurves or outcurves, and whatever way it hooks he turns and tells me, and probably 9,000 times I told him, "Who gives a good goddam how your spit hooks?"

About 2 days later Holly sent down my contract in the mail. His was there when we got there, $7,540 or 7,860 or 7,695, always some crazy amount like that every year which give him the idea the club sat around all winter figuring out exactly what he was worth, boiling it down to the penny, and he signed it and stuck it back out in the box. You always see in the paper what contracts are back and signed, and somewhere amongst them you might find his name. Or then again you might not. There are writers that don't even know he is with the club, and ballplayers on other clubs the same that call everybody by their name but Bruce because if they once knew it they keep forgetting, shouting at him maybe for a stray ball, "Hey, catcher." There was never much to keep them remembering. He been up there a long time, yet nobody every really knows him. I doubt that anybody even keeps a book on him. Between times they forget, and then sometimes I suppose they wish they did, for he will bounce a pitch off a fence now and then, if it was the kind of a pitch he was looking for. He decides ahead of time what kind of a pitch is coming, and if it comes it is his meat. If it don't he is lost. He cannot guess a pitcher, cannot remember what that same pitcher threw him the last time. He cannot hit to the opposite field, only to left, and will stand up there driving pitches to left no matter if a 100-mile tornado is blowing in, or at least he would if Dutch ever left him try. But Dutch will never use him with a wind in from left.

I opened it and looked at it and wrote a little note across the top saying I was taught in school where slavery went out when Lincoln was shot, and I stuck it back in the box, never signing it, and the letter carrier picked it up on his way back to town, saying, "My lands, Wiggen, you sure answer your mail prompt."

Waiting for the mail was a big operation. It took the 4 of us, beginning after breakfast until he angled in beside the box so as not to have to reach across, and some days he got out and gassed with us, and some days not, saying "I am running late today," though I don't believe he ever did because he never come more than 5 minutes one way or the other. You could tell time by him if you ever cared what time it was, which you never cared because it never made much of a much down there if it was 6 o'clock or half past 2. And if he did come up and gas did he bring the mail up with him? No, he did not. He left it in the box, like that was as far as his duty went, and when he left he said, "There is mail," and Bruce went down for it, twirling the swatter around on his finger. I never seen such a man with a fly swatter. His eye was awful quick, and he never went after a fly but once, never dizzied it first and polished it off second but always nailed it square the first try, even the tricky ones that me and his mother and his father all give up on before it wan-

dered over Bruce's way, and he brung the mail
back up and passed it around, and they opened it
and read it and laid it on the rail, shuffling it back
and forth until they all read everybody else's, and
then they talked about it, the bills, church notices,
ads, and the letters from their relations until I
knew every piece of their business from the taxes
they owed to what his sister Helen was planning to
wear over Easter in Seattle, Washington, and after
the mail was hashed over we always took off, me
and Bruce, and I think that was what he liked the
best.

For a place where there was really nothing to do
we sure kept busy, and the time went. We clumb
around in the mill a lot. It was dark and cool, and
it stirred up a lot of old remembrances, and he
talked in there, stringing together whole long sen-
tences, which he usually never does, running off
regular histories of the boys that hung in the mill
with him so long ago, what they looked like, where
they went, who they married, and we sat high up
on these various boards slung across from place to
place, and now and then he bit off a chew and said
"Arthur?" and when he said it like that, with a
question mark after it, I knew what was coming,
and I said, "Do not ask me questions that I cannot
answer." But he asked them all the same, saying,
"Arthur, tell me why in hell I clumb to the top of
the mill a million times and never fell down and
killed myself, and why I never drowneded in the
river, and why I never died in the war, and why I

was never plastered by a truck but come clean through it all and now get this disease?" I said I did not know, which I did not and still don't. I said why does one airplane go down or one ship, or why does some poor cluck go tramping down the street and get struck by lightning. "Lightning I could understand," he said. "Arthur?"

"Ask them little," I said.

"How do you play Tegwar?" he said.

I told him.

"Arthur," said he, "if I tell you something do not laugh."

"I am not libel to laugh for some time," I said. "My wife has not answered the telephone in 3 days, I owe 40 quarts of blood to the United States Bureau of Internal Revenue, and I am libel to never play baseball again rather than play for slave wages."

"I been handed a shit deal," he said. "I am doomeded."

"I am falling off this board laughing," said I.

"But the world is all rosy," he said. "It never looked better. The bad things never looked so little, and the good never looked so big. Food tastes better. Things do not matter too much any more. Like you take I used to wash my car all the time. I used to worry about it. Sometimes I laid in bed at night thinking about my dirty car and could not sleep."

"It sure needs it," I said. I kept trying to bring him back into living again. He stood a chance of living a long time yet, not too long but long enough, and I tried to keep him thinking of things yet ahead.

We visited around. He knew some boys that he once played ball with down at the crate and box plant in Bainbridge, and he hung there once or twice a week when they were on their lunch, and he knew people up and down the main drag. Everybody always asked him 2 things, how did he come out in Minnesota and where would the Mammoths finish. It was a Mammoth town, Mammoth pennants in the sporting-good stores, Ugly Jones gloves, Sid Goldman bats, and these little plastic statues of various Mammoths that some crook sold all over the country that none of us ever got a penny for, plus Sam's book, called "Sam Yale —Mammoth," and Dutch's, "Dutch Schnell— Mammoth," both wrote by Krazy Kress, plus my own, "The Southpaw," wrote by yours truly and nobody else, $3.50 or 35¢ in the quarter book (39¢ in Canada).

And we must of sat in 45 barnyards talking about crops and hogs, crops and hogs, crops and hogs, until I probably knew more about the situation in south Georgia than the United States Bureau of Internal Revenue knows nor ever will, Bruce not talking much but only listening, though then not really listening neither but only looking and nodding and smiling, liking the sound of their voice without caring what they said.

In church the same. He begun going to church. His mother thought I was a great influence on him. "In days gone by," she said, "I could not of dragged him by the hair," but now he went, slouching in the seat like he sat slouched against the barnyard fences, not listening but only liking the sounds. He was very fond of this preacher, Reverend Robinson, the first person except me and Holly to know the truth. Bruce wished to tell him, so we done so, and I liked him quite well though I never been very regular at church, in fact never went a-tall, and he liked the singing, too, and always hummed the songs a couple days after, maybe through Wednesday.

We played golf at the Bainbridge Country Club, 9 holes, and I probably stunk up the joint pretty bad. They did not have very good left-hand clubs, and then I'm not too goddam interested in golf anyway but only done it for him. I'll shoot 78 keeping my own score, but he is very good. He does anything good when there is no pressure on, and there was none, for we just played for the kicks, maybe 4 or 5 times, and we started hunting the same number but never got there, turned back. I do not hunt. I never fired off a gun in my life and was just as glad, nor never fish neither, or at least never done so before but went with him down by the river and spent the whole first afternoon taking off the winding reel and putting it back for the left hand while he sat on the bank and caught weeds. Several times a man come along and said, "No fishing here," and Bruce said, "I am not fishing, only weeding," which I thought was pretty quick for Bruce except I soon seen it was his father's joke, and probably *his* father's before that, back and back. They was always from Georgia. He caught quite a few, and I caught some myself, the only fish I ever caught and probably ever will. Golf, fishing, hunting, these were never my dish of meat.

The river was like the old mill for him, stirring up 10,000 remembrances. Many an hour he was not fishing a-tall but only watching the river wash by, the Flint River they call it, dangling his shoes in it, sometimes kicking at the water with his toe, or spitting in it and watching it travel on, or flipping little stones in it and watching the circles get bigger, and maybe 3 or 4 times in an afternoon, more times than he could possibly of had to, he laid his line down beside him and stood and urinated in the river, and watched that, too, watched it all mix in the with the water, and disappear.

Also, we played Tegwar. Mrs. Pearson would not hear of card playing on the porch, so we moved back in the kitchen, which we should of done long ago. It was air condition, and no flies, and his father dragged over a chair and watched, and then he said, "Deal me in, boys," and I dealed him in, 17 cards apiece plus one in the middle. "You have not been putting one in the middle," his father said.

"It is the fish-fly card," I said, and me and Bruce took all the tricks the first 2 deals until his father dealed and threw the fish-fly card in the middle, a 9 or something, and I swooped them up, saying, "That will be 6¢ to me and a nickel to Bruce."

"You lose your deal when the fish-fly card is a 9," said Bruce.

"How come 5 to you and 6 to Arthur?" his father said.

"Rules," said Bruce.

"You see," said I, "it was not a double-birdie. Probably you been playing Southeastern Tegwar all your life, but the boys all play Western Canadian style, which for my money is much faster and leaves you free for a butchered hog most any time."

"It keeps you from dropping dead on the board," said Bruce.

The old man looked up quick, and I knew. Or at least I think I knew. The Reverend Robinson told him. I would of suspected anyhow because he went on playing Tegwar 3 nights, shoving his money across at us, never knowing the rules and never caring, but seeing how much it pleased Bruce for once in his life to be in on a gag that somebody else was still out on. Nothing give Bruce as much of a kick all summer as Tegwar.

One night in the middle of Tegwar Holly rolled in. She simply could not stand it up home without me. The snow and the ice got her down, for she loves sun and heat, and so do I. She was nervous, not knowing what to expect nor what to say nor who been told what. Bruce's father practically fell over backwards getting out of his chair in a hurry. They are extremely polite to white women. She shook hands all around and was one of the family in no time.

Another chair was dragged on the porch, another swatter looped on the nail, and Gem brung 5 glasses instead of 4 now. Also, there was a fan for her, covered with designs of roses like the one his mother used, because it begun getting warm down there, and everything you said it took twice as long getting an answer out of anybody because there was now not only swatting and sipping but also fanning. You kept busy.

I seen the first sign of 600 Dollars now, nothing much, only a little rise in her belly that you would of never noticed except sideways in a slip or less. She was tip-top and felt fine, her weight right, the 2 of us parading in the bathroom the last thing every night and stepping on the scale, Holly where she ought to been, me maybe a shade over. I consider 200 right but do not worry if I hit 203 or 4 in February.

I briefed her, telling her only me and Bruce and the Reverend Robinson knew, probably the old man but not his mother, and that was all. She herself told nobody in the beginning, only Pop, but finally busted down and told the Epsteins. She could not keep it in.

It was 66 Street all over again. When we lived on 66 Street Bruce was always there and we were never alone, coming mornings until time to go to the park, coming after the ball game, or staying all day when it rained, wandering in because he knew nobody else, and because nobody else he knew would of stood him, settling down wherever we were, or following us around the house, never speaking much but only listening, or at least looking like he was. He met Katie on the stairs one day and fell in love with her and wished to marry her, and I told him go ahead and marry her, anything to get him out of the house, but she would not.

What did she want with $7,000? She must of paid half that much in taxes, for I know she paid her tax man $300 just to file, and him not nearly the expert Holly is. I seen her hold a $100 bill in her hand fishing in her purse for keys and throw it back in like any girl might throw a single back.

After awhile you got used to him, and if he didn't show up you begun to worry and look at the clock, and then when you heard him on the steps you said, "Damn it all anyhow. Here he is again." But once he stepped in the door you could not heave him out. He was so happy to see you, and he might of brung flowers or a slab of meat or a basket of fruit or a box of candy, always something, never nothing, something for you and something for Katie that he took upstairs and handed to her between customers and kissed her on the cheek like she was 16 and not yet been to her first dance. So we were never alone down there, for there was always Bruce, slouching, like in the barnyards or in church, listening without listening, looking from me to her and back again like the world never seen 2 people so smart and so good. Any other man you would of said, "Take your eye off my wife like that," but not Bruce.

He never left until we said, "Well, sack time," and she popped open a button or zipped a zipper. He took off fast then, afraid he might see some part of Holly he believed he should not see. It even embarrassed him if she wore a low neckline, which she sometimes does, having a good neckline and wishing to show it off. Why not? And then when he was gone, and we could of talked, there was nothing to say, and what we done we laid there and heard him paddering around in his room, or maybe heard him open his door very quiet and go on tip-toe down the stairs and out, and then a long time later back, though where he went I never knew and never asked. Sometimes he drove, but mostly he walked, and in the morning he was up before anybody, fresh, like he slept his full 8.

The last night he stood up until morning. He packed his suitcases and loaded them in my car, and his gear, and he drove his own car out back and parked it there, the one they give him when he signed and the one we drove down from Minnesota in, a 47 Moors with Cushion-Gear, probably the greatest flop in the history of the business. In his car he loaded his golf clubs and his remembrances from the war, his fishing poles and his guns. Then he burned some papers. We seen him from the window dropping papers one by one on the fire and raking the fire together to keep it burning, now and then reaching down and plucking a paper out and reading it, even while it burned in his hand, and then leaving it flutter down until all was burned. That is my best picture of him, standing there all black against the light of the fire and leaning on the rake, and Holly's, too, and then we went to bed but could not sleep, and in the morning we shoved off for Aqua Clara.

CHAPTER 5

The talk of the camp last spring was a kid name of Piney Woods, a wild and crazy catcher out of a place called Good Hope, Georgia, that the writers all called "Dutch's good hope from Good Hope" until it become obvious that he could not last. Back he went to QC in April, and we went into the year with the same 3 catchers we finished 54 with, Goose and Bruce and Jonah Brooks. Jonah come up from QC when Red split his finger in St. Paul, Minnesota, that time, a fine boy, just fine, always singing. 13 runs behind and he will be singing, calling "Wing her through, Author, wing her through," and then after a good pitch singing, "Author wung her through, he wung her through," except when now and then he thought the call was wrong, and then sung, "Oh-o-o-o Lord my big black ass," his jaw always going and his mind always working, his eye everywhere, a natural catcher if ever I seen one, except he could not hit.

For a time it looked like Piney Woods might be the answer. He can hit. But he is no natural. He is too wi'd and crazy. He drives in motorcycle races in the winter. Dutch was looking for a combination of a natural catcher like Jonah and a hitter like Piney, and still is. I guess there is only one Red Traphagen in a lifetime.

The first few days me and Lucky Judkins sat in the stands watching the drill and lying about money, telling each other how much we were holding out for. I don't know why you lie about money. I guess you figure people figure you are lying, so you might as well. One morning Ugly Jones clumb up from the field and said, "Author, leave me give you one piece of advice. Do not hang in the park because your eye gleams and your hand itches. You are becoming anxious to play ball, and this will cost you money," which was true. I mean it was true I was becoming gleamy, I guess. Ugly is a wise old hand, veteran of many a holdout, and I went back to the house, and we swum and laid on the beach and played badminton and waited for the te'ephone to ring, and every time it rung I said, "This is Old Man Moors meeting my price," but it never was, and to myself I thought, "This is Bruce. The attack come." But it was never Bruce neither. It was writers, or one of the boys, or Joe Jaros wishing to play Tegwar. The boys phoned a lot, or dropped by, and I kept in touch. My weight kept going up something awful.

The real bomb burst was Lucky getting swapped to Cincinnati for F. D. R. Case'li, a right hand pitcher and a good boy, a cousin by marriage of

Gussie Petronio, the Mammoth catcher before Red, leaving me the last and only holdout. I might of went out of my mind a little if there been any left-hand pitching in camp, but there was none, 90 boys that threw with their left hand maybe, but none that threw very hard or very smart, and I sat tight. The boys were all with me, down to the last penny.

It all dragged on so long I said to Holly, "Am I a baseball player or only a man living on the beach at Aqua Clara?" and she said, "What difference?" Everything you said to her any more she said, "What difference?" meaning lay in the sun and enjoy life. She was happy. I never seen her so still before. She is usually always running around doing 77 things at once, hanging with the wives, reading books, studying taxes, cleaning the house, gassing on the phone, but now she done nothing only laid on the beach and looked at the waves. Now and then she took a dip and flipped over and left the waves wash her in, and then she laid on the sand again and browned up, and nights she got all dressed for Bruce.

He come down every night after work. You could see him from far off, walking along and looking at the waves and whistling "Come Josephine In My Flying Machine," which the boys all sung in honor of Piney and his stupid motorcycle. Piney himself sung it every time you asked him, closing his eyes, not laughing, thinking you loved hearing it for the singing, when the reason you loved it was he took it so serious, singing—

Come Josephine in my flying machine,
Going up she goes, up she goes.
Balance yourself like a bird on the beam,
In the air she goes, there she goes.
Up, up, a little bit higher,
Oh my, the moon is on fire.
Come Josephine in my flying machine,
Going up, goodby, all on, goodby.

He always dragged a stick in the sand behind him. He parked it by the door and come in and ate, salads for me mostly, and lean meat and no bread and butter and this disgusting skim milk, my weight at 209 by now and climbing a mile a minute, and when we was done we sat out back, out of the ocean breeze, until along about 10 he went around the house for his stick, and I drove him back to the Silver Palms.

In the hotel we shoved his bed around near the phone, and I wrote my number on a piece of paper and tacked it on the wall, and he said, "I hope if it happens it will not happen at a bad hour," and I said, "It might or might not probably never happen. I have no faith in those cockeyed doctors up there. But if it happens do not stop and check the time, just call me," and he said he would.

I began selling policies to kill the time. I drove down to St. Pete every couple days, and Tampa and Clearwater, and over to Lakeland once, never pushing, only chatting with the various boys and leaving it sell itself, which it does once you put the idea in their mind. All spring they see too many old-time ballplayers floating from camp to camp and putting the touch on old friends, maybe giving a pointer to a kid and then saying, "By the way, could you advance me 5 until the first of the month?" which kids often do, probably writing home, "Oh boy, I just had the privilege of loaning 5 to So-and-so," until after they loaned out enough 5's it did not seem so much like a privilege any more.

I drove Lucky down to Tampa the day he was traded. Lucky was the second person I ever sold an annuity to, and he said, "Well, Author, one day we will all be done working. We will just fish and look in the box once a month for the checks, me and you and Bruce and all the rest," and I almost told him, for it was getting hard to carry it around. But I smothered it back. Once you told somebody everybody would know, and once Dutch knew it would of been "Goodby, Bruce." "It is hard picturing you in a Cincinnati suit," I said. In the lobby of The Floridian I got to gassing with Brick Brickell, the manager of Cincinnati. "You are holding out serious," he said. "For what?"

"$27,500," I said.

"You will never get it," he said. Then he looked around to see if anybody was listening. "*We* would pay it," he said.

"I doubt that," I said.

"Try me," he said. "Hold out long enough and we will buy you, and I give you my verbal word we will pay you 25,000 at the least. I been trying to buy you already."

"What are they asking?" I said.

"A quarter of a million dollars and players," he said.

"What will they take?" I said.

"150,000 and players," he said.

"What will you give?" said I.

"Now, Author," he said, "I cannot reveal a thing of that sort. The trouble is that they want Sam Mott. Dutch is worried about his catching."

"Does he not worry about his left-hand pitching?" I said.

"Brooklyn will sell him Scudder," he said, "but only if you are gone, not wishing to cut their own throat."

I drove F. D. R. Caselli back with me, jabbering all the way, him I mean, and all the time he jabbered I kept making up these little conversations where Old Man Moors called me on the phone, pleading with me, "Come on and sign. I will meet your price," until I was just about ready to call him myself. But then again I told myself, "No! Do not sell yourself short!" F. D. R. had blisters on his hands, and he kept asking me what was good for them, and I told him something or other. I forget what.

All spring the wives kept pumping Holly full of miserable stories about babies born with this or that missing, and mothers suffering, which if she ever believed any of it she would of went wild. But she never believes what people say, and all that happened I kept getting as fat as a pig until what we done we bought a badminton set and played badminton all day, deductible, for my weight is a matter of business. By the middle of March I was probably the world's champion heavyweight left-hand badminton player, and still no call from the boss.

One day the club said it was definitely closing a deal with Cleveland for Rob McKenna, saying this on a Friday night for the Saturday paper and leaving no chance for anybody to deny it on Sunday, for they have no Sunday paper in Aqua Clara, and putting all the writers a little bit on the spot since they hated calling Cleveland all the way out in Arizona to check on the truth of what they already probably knew was the bunk. This scared me, though, and I went to the phone, and the instant I touched it it rung, and a voice said, "Do not touch that phone!" It was Ugly Jones. "Author," he said, "you are doing fine."

"I am fatter than a pig," I said.

"Good," he said. "That is the way to convince them, for it worries them more than it worries you. It might not even be a bad idea to show yourself around. Leave the brass see how fat you are."

What we done we went out the park the following Wednesday and sat in the stands behind first. There was about 6 left-handers warming, a few wearing QC suits that been up the spring before, the rest wearing Mammoth shirts, one kid wearing my number, 44, kids, all kids, and all full of hope.

Old Man Moors and Patricia and some automobile people up from Miami strolled in and sat down, Bradley Lord joining them soon after. Patricia said "Hello" and asked Holly how she was. Her and Holly gassed awhile, and then she went back. Old Man Moors glanced up my way, pretending he was looking over the paint job on the park, and I called for peanuts, which fat you up about a pound for a dime, and I begun munching away.

The first left-hander set George and Perry down 1–2, and the peanuts went dry in my mouth a little. Pasquale then took 2 strikes and belted one out amongst the palms, and I give a little look down at the Moorses and scarcely had time to look back when Sid hit one that fell not 4 feet from where Pasquale's went, back-to-back homers from the power factory, always a nice sight, and Canada shot a single into left, and Piney one into right. Dutch shouted, "I seen enough of that one," waving the left-hander out of there and bringing on a new one, a tall, thin kid with a dizzy habit of wearing his glove with 3 fingers out. He walked Vincent and Ugly and hit Herb Macy on the butt until when he finally found the plate George blasted one back at him that bounced off his knee and blooped out over second base, and the poor kid was lugged off on a stretcher. Another one went out the same way the same day.

Once Dutch looked up at me, and I waved. He did not wave back. He takes it as a personal insult. Behind your back he tells you, "Sure, sock it to them for every nickel you are worth," but when you do he does not like it, though he himself was a holdout more than once in his playing days, and anyhow he was quite busy waving one left-hander out and a new one in, about 5 of them before a kid come on in the sixth and struck Sid and Canada out. The Moorses begun shaking their head "Yes" between themself, Bradley Lord shaking his, too, as soon as he seen it was safe, The World's Only Living Human Spineless Skunk. This newest kid was rather fast, but no curve whatsoever, and I said to Holly, "The boys see that he has no curve by now," which they did all right. Piney and Vincent singled. Ugly stepped in, looking up my way and giving me a kind of a wink and taking a couple and then lacing a drive down the line in right that the whole park busted out laughing over because it slammed up against the fence and stuck there, this old rat-trap fence made of boards, the drive getting jammed in between 2 boards. The right-fielder went over and tried to wedge it out. But it was in tight, and Ugly trotted around the bases laughing, and even Dutch was laughing, and by then the Moorses and the people from Miami were laughing, and Bradley Lord, too, seeing all the rest, and about one minute later Lindon bounced one off the same fence that knocked the first ball through, and Mr. Left-Hander Number 6 went off to the shower. You really had to laugh. I mean, when a ball slams up against a fence your eye is back out on the field, looking for the rebounce, and then when it don't you think the whole world has went flooey or something, like when you drop a shoe you hear it clunk, and if no clunk comes you quick dial the madhouse. Every so often I begun to laugh, and Holly, too, and Old Man Moors turned around and give me a look, and me and Holly got up about then and yawned and stretched and bought a couple more peanuts and went home and waited for the phone to ring.

After supper it rung, and I sat beside it and left it ring 12 or 13 times until I picked it up and said in my most boring voice, "Fishing pier. Hook-worms for sale," only it wasn't Old Man Moors a-tall but Joe Jaros, and he said, "Author, how about a hand of Tegwar or 2?"

I already turned him down a number of times, not wishing to hang in the hotel and look anxious, but I was in the mood now, and I said, "We will be right down."

"Who do you mean by 'we'?" he said, and I said I meant me and Bruce. "Me and Bruce been play-ing quite a bit all winter," I said. "He is pretty good by now," though this was not true, for he was not.

"I will stay here," said Bruce, and that settled it, at least for now, and he stood with Holly. When I got there Joe had things set up in the lobby, a table for 3, one chair for me and one for him and one empty and waiting for the slaughter. He had a pocket full of change and little bills. Next to the empty chair he stood a lamp all lit and bright, and at the empty place a clean and shining ash tray. The empty chair stood just a little sideways so a cluck could slide in easy.

He shuffled, shuffling over and over again but never dealing, just waiting for the cluck to wander in sight. Joe knew. He can spot one a block away, or walk through a dining car and spot one, or pick one out in a crowd. He been at it 30 years, and I said, "Joe, when my wife goes home Bruce must play with us."

"Sure," he said, not thinking, but then it hit home, and he said, "Now, Author, Bruce is not the type. He is too damn dumb. Anyhow, the way Piney Woods been hitting Bruce might not last the year."

"You must promise me," I said, and he promised, for right about then he seen his party and would of promised you could hang him in the morning. He got all excited. "That looks like it," he said, and we begun to deal, and in through the lobby come a big chap wearing sun glasses, though he was indoors, and though it was night, his arms all red the way a fellow gets when he never sees the sun except a couple weeks on vacation, a big button in his coat in the shape of a fish saying FEARED IN THE DEEP that the local people hand out by the bushel to every cluck that don't actually faint dead away at the sight of the ocean. He bought a magazine and sat down in an easy chair and begun to read, soon wondering why he could not see, and then shoving his glasses up on his head, every so often peeking at us over the top of his magazine, me and Joe dealing fast and furious now, really working, too, because I will swear if you concentrate hard enough you can bring the

cluck up out of his chair and over, which we soon
done, for he closed his magazine and worked up his
energy and hauled himself up, his sun glasses falling back down over his eyes. Over he come, sticking his magazine in his coat and leaning his hands
down on the back of the empty chair and finally
saying, "Would you mind if I watch?"

We never spoke nor looked up. We played Casino, your 8 takes a 5 and a 3, your 10 takes a 6 and
a 4, like that, pictures taking pictures, and when
the hand was done Joe flipped his wrist around and
said, "A quarter of 8."

"No," said Mr. Feared In The Deep, "I said
would you mind if I watch."

"Oh," said Joe, "I thought you asked me if I had
a watch," not saying another word, only dealing
again, straight Casino again except with a little
switch here and there, maybe a 7 taking in a 5 and
a 9, or a deuce an ace and a 3, Casino, only doubled, so there was still some sort of a system to it,
though not too much system to the cash sliding
back and forth, the cluck watching and studying,
taking off his glasses and twirling them, 2 or 3
times starting to say something but then not saying
it, only saying once, "It looks like Casino," neither
me nor Joe answering him nor even hearing him
for all he knew until after the hand I said, "Did
you speak?"

"I only said it looks like Casino," he said.

"Casino?" said Joe.

"Like the card game called Casino," said Feared
In The Deep.

"You mean the game they play in boarding schools for girls?" said Joe.

"I did not know it was played there," said the cluck. "I personally played Casino myself from time to time."

"We only play men's games," said Joe.

We dealed again. "Would you mind if I sat down?" said the cluck. Nobody said "No," and he sat, and he slapped his pants where his money was and looked at his watch and sort of inched his chair around until he was finally forward over the table, his eye going from my hand to Joe's, the game becoming a little more complicated now, Joe calling once, "Goddam it, fence-board!" and slapping down his hand and showing how he fence-boarded, me laughing and gathering in the money, Joe saying, "I never fence-boarded before since one time against Babe Ruth in St. Pete," the cluck really quite confused about now and ready to go back and look at his magazine.

Right about then I was paged, and Joe went red. "Hang around," he said. "Never mind it. Hang around."

"It is the boss," I said.

"So you are Henry Wiggen," said the cluck. "I seen you was left-handed but did not know who. It is quite an honor."

"I must go, Joe," I said.

"Damn it, Author. Stick around." He was boiling inside, for Tegwar is serious business to him, the great laugh of his life. He will laugh for days after a good night of Tegwar. He will tell you Tegwar stories going back 30 years, of clucks on trains and clucks in hotels, and of great Tegwar partners he had, ballplayers now long since faded from the scene, remembering clubs not half so much by what they done but how they rode with the gag, how they gathered, like the boys even at that moment were gathering for a glimpse of the big fish on the line. It is the gathering of the boys that Joe loves, for without the watching of the crowd the laugh would be hollow. It would be like playing ball to empty stands, and the page come by, saying, "Mr. Wiggen, Mr. Wiggen," and Joe said, "Scram!" and the page scrammed.

But it was no good, and the boys knew it and Joe knew it and I knew it. It takes time. The cluck has got to lay his money on the table and leave it there awhile. He has got to think about it. It has got to be the cluck's own choice every minute of the way, and he has got to hang himself, not be hung by others. It must never be hurried. Yet with the page calling we could not play it slow, though we tried.

Then soon the boys all stepped aside, and Dutch come through and said, "I been trying for days to get some sleep and finally was just drifting off when I am told you are playing cards and too busy to talk contract. Do not push things too far, Author."

"It was my fault," said Joe. "I would not leave him go," and Dutch seen the cluck there and felt sorry for Joe, or as sorry as he can ever feel, and he said so. "What good is being sorry?" said Joe, and he slammed down the cards, and he swore, and Mr. Feared In The Deep begun backwatering as fast as he could, hearing both laughing and swearing but not understanding a word, and I went on up to the Moorses sweet, feeling sorry for Joe and yet also laughing.

Nobody else was laughing but me when I got there. I said, "Leave us not waste time talking contract unless you are willing to talk contract. I was taught in school where slavery went out when Lincoln was shot."

"I know," said Old Man Moors, "for you wrote it across the top of your contract."

"Not across *my* contract," I said. "Maybe across the contract of a turnstile turner."

"Author," said Patricia, "leave us all calm down." She was very beautiful that night, and I said so, and she thanked me. Her nose was quite sunburned. "You are looking over your weight," she said. "It will no doubt take you many weeks to get in shape."

"He looks 10 pounds over his weight at least," said Bradley Lord.

"*Mr.* Bradley Lord," said I, whipping out my loose cash. "I have $200 here which says I am no more than 2 and $\frac{3}{8}$ pounds over my weight if you would care to go and fetch the bathroom scale."

"What do you consider your absolute minimum figure?" said Mr. Moors.

"19,000," I said.

"In that case," said he, "we can simply never do business, and I suppose I must be put to the trouble of scouring up another left-hand pitcher."

"That should not be hard," and I, "for I seen

several promising boys out there this afternoon. Any one of them will win 4 or 5 games if God drops everything else."

"They are top-flight boys," said Mr. Moors. "Dutch thinks extremely high of at least 3 of them. I will tell you what I will do, Wiggen. I will jack up my absolute maximum figure to 13,500 and not a penny more, and if you have a good year we will make it back to you in 56."

"And when I have a good year in 56 you will make it back to me in 57," I said, "and I will go on being paid for the year before. This shorts me out of a year in the long run."

"We heard this one before," said Bradley Lord.

"Every time Bradley Lord opens his mouth I am raising my absolute minimum figure," I said.

"Bradley," said Patricia, "go get some drinks."

"You feel very confident about this year," said Mr. Moors, "and I will tell you what I will do." He turned my contract over and begun scratching down figures. "For the 20th victory you win this year I will pay you a bonus of 2,500, and for every game over 20 I will pay you 2,000 more, and then to show you where my heart is I will jack up my absolute maximum figure to 14,000."

"We are coming closer together," said Patricia.

"I believe we are just about there," said Old Man Moors.

Bradley come back with 3 cokes, giving one to Old Man Moors and one to Patricia and keeping one for himself.

"As a starter," said I, "I like the look of the

arrangement. But instead of 20 victories you must write in 15."

"If I write in 15 I must lower the amount," he said. "You are so damn-fire sure you are going to have such a top-flight year I would think you would jump at the arrangement."

"I am sure about the year I am going to have," said I, "but I am deep in the hole, owing money left and right and Holly pregnant and the high cost of Coca-cola. I am tired living like a sharecropper."

"Bradley," said Patricia, "go get Author a coke." Old Man Moors was sketching out the new bonus arrangement on the back of my contract, but he looked up now. "How much do you still owe the goddam Government?" he said.

"$421.89," I said.

He wrote this down on a separate sheet. "I will throw this in," he said, "plus pay you a bonus of $1,500 for the 15th victory you win this year, and 1,000 for every victory over 15. You are better off than you were under the first arrangement."

"Not if I win 25 games," I said.

"If you win 25 games I will round out Bonus Plan Number 2 to equal Number One," said he. "But you know you are not libel to win 25 games. I do not see why you are trying to heckle me. If you win 25 games I will be so goddam pleased I will pay you a flat 5,000 bonus if I do not drop dead from surprise."

"I won 26 in 52," said I.

"Yes," said he, "but never come near it since." He mentioned my Won-and-Lost for 53 and 54, which everybody knows, so no need to repeat. Bradley Lord come back with my coke, and Old Man Moors shoved him the separate sheet, saying, "Make out a check in this amount and send it to the United States Bureau of Internal Revenue in the name of Wiggen. Very well, Henry, your base pay will be 14,000 plus Bonus Plan Number 2. I think that is fair. I know that you are going to have a grand year," and he reached out his hand. He was calling me "Henry" now, all smiles, which he had a right to be, I guess, for I believe he was ready to go much higher on his absolute maximum. But I did not push him, for the main job was yet ahead, and I did not take his hand, saying, "Sir, there is one clause yet to go in my contract."

"Shoot," said he.

"There must be a clause," said I, "saying that me and Bruce Pearson will stay with the club together, or else go together. Whatever happens to one must happen to the other, traded or sold or whatever. We must be tied in a package on any deal under the sun."

"No deals are on the fire," said he.

"I never heard of such a thing," said Bradley Lord.

Patricia was powdering her nose out of a little compact. She snapped the lid shut, and it was the only sound, and she said, "It is not a matter of whether anybody ever heard of such a thing before or not, and it is not a matter whether any deals are on the fire or not. It is a thing we could never do for many reasons, the first reason being that Dutch would never hear of it, and all the rest of the reasons second."

"Boys and girls," said Old Man Moors, "leave us be calm. Wiggen, I will give you my verbal word instead of writing it in."

"It must be wrote in," said I.

"Bradley," said Patricia, "call Dutch."

"He is asleep," said Bradley.

"He been trying for days to get some sleep," said I.

"Call him," she said.

Bradley called him, and it rung a long time, and when you heard his voice you could hear it all over the room, like he was there, and Bradley held the phone away from his ear, and then he said, "Mr. Moors wishes to see you," and after awhile he come down in his slippers and robe, pajama pants but no top. "I been trying for days to get some sleep," he said, still not awake. "Go get me a coke."

"Tell him your clause," said Patricia.

He looked at me with his eyes shut. "So it is you with a special clause, Author? I will bet it is a dilly." His voice was low and full of sleep, and he kept scrounging in his eyes with his hands, trying to wake up. "Bradley, run get me a wet rag," he said. He took a swig of his coke. "Sterling must be shot for hay fever with a special shot. Vincent Carucci must have contact lenses. Gonzalez must have a buddy along to speak Spanish with, and Goldman must go home on Passover. What do you wish, Author, the Chinese New Year off or Dick Tracy's birthday?"

"I wish a clause," said I, "tying me in a package with Pearson."

"Does he owe you money?" said Old Man Moors.

Bradley brung him the rag, and Dutch squeezed it out on the floor. "Jesus, Bradley, you ain't got much strength in your hand," he said. "How do you mean tied in a package?"

"If he is sold I must be sold," I said. "Or if he is traded I must be traded the same place. Wherever he goes I must go."

His face was covered with the rag, and when he took it away the color was gone, drained away down in his chest. I will swear the hair of his chest was red, and then slowly it drained back up again, and he said, "This is telling me who I must keep and who not, which nobody ever told me before, Author, and nobody will ever tell me again as long as I am upright. If it is money talk money, and good luck. Talking money is one thing. But talking business is another, and I will as soon trade the whole club for a tin of beans as leave anybody tell me who stays and who gets cut loose."

"I am sorry to hear it," said I, "because without that clause there will be no contract."

"Then there will be no contract," said Dutch, "and I must suffer along the best I can."

"Several of those left-handers looked good to me," said Old Man Moors.

"Good for what?" said Dutch.

"Will you go sell insurance?" said Bradley Lord. "You do not know a soul on earth to sell insurance to outside of ballplayers. Will you sell insurance to other insurance agents? Where will you run up against people with money with the language you speak? I never seen you wear a necktie."

"Shut up," said Dutch.

"I am ignoring him," said I. "I am only laying it out straight, all my cards up. I do not wish to sell insurance. Insurance is for later. I rather play baseball than anything else. I do it best. I like the trains. I like the hotels. I like the boys. I like the hours and the money. I like the fame and the glory. I like to think of 50,000 people getting up in the morning and squashing themself to death in the subway to come and see me play ball."

"That is how I feel," said Dutch.

"I am dead serious," said I.

"What is up between you 2? A roomie is a roomie, Author, not a Siamese twin brother fastened at the hip. I do not understand this a-tall, and I will investigate it. I will run it down to the end of the earth. Are you a couple fairies, Author? That can not be. It been a long time since I run across fairies in baseball, not since Will Miller and another lad that I forget his name, a shortstop, that for Christ sake when they split they went and found another friend. This is all too much for me."

"You will understand it sometime," I said.

"When?"

"No telling," I said. "Maybe soon, maybe not for 15 years."

"I am 62," said Dutch. "I will certainly be hanging by my thumb until I hear. Christ Almighty, I seen you on days when you hated Pearson, when you ate him out as bad as I myself ever ate him out. I seen you about to kill him for his stupidity. I seen you once get up from the table and walk away."

"Because he laughed without knowing why," I said.

"Such a thing can be not only hate but also love," said Patricia.

"It is not love," said I.

"I do not mean fairy love," she said.

"He laughs because he wishes to be one of the boys all the time," said Dutch. "Must this clause go on forever?" He closed his eyes again, not sleeping but thinking. "I have 4 catchers," he said. "I have a catcher that is old and another that can not hit and another that is wild and crazy and another that is just plum dumb." He opened his eyes and begun checking them off on his fingers. "I would give both my eyes for Sam Mott of Cincinnati, but they want Author, and I cannot give Author, or if I give you I must have Scudder off Brooklyn which the son of a bitches will not give me except for all my right-hand power. I could spare my right-hand power if I could swing a deal with Pittsburgh, but Pittsburgh wants Author and I have already give you to Cincinnati on paper for Sam Mott. So I must play my old catcher on days when he feels young, and my catcher that can not hit on days the power is on, and my wild and crazy catcher on days he ever comes to his senses, which so far he has give me no sign of really having any. I will ship him back to QC and see if Mike can talk him off his motorcycle. We must never have another motorcycle in camp. I been trying for days to get some sleep. When you really stop and think about it I am libel to wind up using my catcher that is just plum dumb more and more." He finished off his coke and belched a loud belch and scratched the hair on his chest.

"Some day you will understand," I said.

"No," said he. "That is too much to ask. Forget it. I will agree to this clause. I never done such a thing before and would not do it now except there is a look in your eye that tells me that I must." He looked in my eye a long time. "Yes," he said, "there is a look which tells me that I must," and that was all he said but went back out and up to bed, and Bradley Lord drew up the contract and we all signed.

CHAPTER 6

We played 6 exhibitions down around St. Pete, but
I did not go. I wrote down the names of all the
doctors in St. Pete on the back of the papers the
doctors give me in Minnesota, and we checked
with Bruce morning and night. We talked very
careful because the operators listen in, saying only
"How are you?" and he was fine. In the hotel in
New York there's an operator name of Tootsie that
knows everything you know before you know it
yourself half the time.

Days I worked out with the QC Cowboys. I was
supposed to run it off, but what could be more of a
bore than only running, and what I mostly done I
stood around sweating in a rubber shirt. I sweated
myself down to 205 and felt good and started
throwing a little, though as soon as I started throwing I started eating again and ate myself back up to
208, which would of scared me silly except I noticed 2 things. I noticed that I was throwing
quicker, getting more speed out of less motion.
Also I felt tip-top, and it begun to seem to me that
if I felt tip-top there could be nothing wrong with

my weight. Holly said the same. "It is not half so much where your weight is but what your mind thinks about it," she said. You could feel 600 Dollars give a little kick every so often, and when he done so she said, "Patience, boy, you will soon enough be out and see it all."

The club got back on Tuesday night. Usually we always broke camp that night, but things been changed since I become Player Representative, and we do not leave until Wednesday any more. The boys get their full night sleep this way, and the day's gate we lose in Jacksonville is out of nobody's pocket but Old Man Moors.

Wednesday morning Bruce come down and helped us close the house, and we took the key to Tom Tootle, a hobbly old fellow, a great ballplayer with the Mammoths back around 1904–10. For $25.10 a year he watches your house for you and sends you a postcard every 2 months, which is what the 10¢ is for, saying "Your house is in good shape" and signing it with a little drawing of a steam engine, and out of the engine a little puff of smoke saying "Toot Toot," which is what everybody calls him, Toot Toot Tootle. You can take him off your tax. You can also take extra depreciation off your house down there on account of the salt air, which hardly anybody knows, though by now I told everybody along the beach. We also take extra depreciation off the car since it is parked $16\frac{2}{3}\%$ of the year in salt air.

We picked up Coker and Darlene Roguski in front of the Silver Palms and headed north for

Jacksonville. While loading Darlene's gear in front of the Silver Palms up walks Piney Woods. He was wearing these parachute shoes and airplane pants and a scarlet shirt and helmet and goggles, and he took a big watch out of his pocket and said to me, "It is 13 o'clock. I will give you a handicap of 45 minutes and beat you to Jacksonville." His clock shows 24 hours. The old-fashion 12 is not good enough for Piney. "So get going," he said, and he went back to his motorcycle piled high with gear, a catcher's mitt sitting on top. He pulled his goggles down and sat on his machine with his arms folded. I never give him another thought but got in and took off.

We sung, me and Holly and Coker and Darlene. Me and Coker sing in The Mammoth Quartet and pick up a little change now and then on the TV, and after we sung awhile Bruce begun, though I hardly ever heard him sing before except one thing and nothing more. Sometimes he sings—

> Yes, we have no bananas,
> We have no bananas today.

That is all he sings, never more. But now he sung—

> All that year the sun did shine
> Except it rained 'bout half the time.
> The well went dry, and so am I-I-I-I-I
> So pass the jug around.

* * *

He sung many songs, singing low and soft but also merry. In all the songs things started bad but turned out good, and they all took place in the dark, but with a moon, the kind of songs you pick up late at night on the road, especially down in the south, corn that you would switch to another station if there was another station on. But hearing somebody sing them they weren't so corn at that. There was one about a farmer boy in love with the girl down the road, but her old man said "Nix!" and built a fence between their house, and the boy clumb the fence, and every time he clumb it the farmer built it higher, and every time he built it higher Bruce sung higher, singing of the boy climbing over until he sung so high he could go no higher and said, "Holly, you take it from there," and she went up and up with the fence until *she* could go no higher and said, "Bruce, I am as high as I can go," and Bruce sung very low now of the boy digging under the fence, and the girl digging under from the other side until they met in the middle, and the girl's father come along and seen them and shot them and shoveled them over, and out of their heart grew these weeds, up through the ground and winding and winding around the fence forever, which I know sounds corny when you write it.

Soon Piney Woods come up behind us, probably going 75 or 80 and passing us, not looking at us but only sticking his arm out sideways at us and cutting in front with not more than a foot to spare so if I didn't come off the gas we would of clipped him, and Coker said, "You would think a young fellow like Piney would wish to live the summer through and see who wins the flag," and I cut him short, saying, "You been hitting good all spring, Coker, have you not?" but he kept right on, saying, "With all the ways of dying you would think a fellow would wait for them, not go out looking."

"My, Darlene," said Holly. "Is that a new dress? It must of set your husband back a pretty penny."

"What in the hell is the sense of dying young?" said Coker. "Why not live and see how life treats you?"

"Coker," said I, "I hear you are being sold." That stopped him, plus we come around a bend and seen Piney Woods by the side of the road whipping off his goggles and unstrapping his tools, and we pulled in, and we said, "What is the matter?"

He never looked up. "Nothing," he said, "I simply busted my master distributor. Do you have any spare parts?"

"Motorcycle parts?" I said.

Coker called back to the car. "Darlene, did we bring along our spare motorcycle parts this trip?"

"Tie her on the back," said I. "It is not far to Gainesville."

He still never looked up. "What would I do in Gainesville?" he said.

"Get a new part," said I, "or else you are libel to be out here in the middle of nowheres until 67 o'clock or half-past 41."

"I will beat you to Jacksonville," he said.

"OK," we said, and off we went, singing another 30 miles until up alongside comes Piney again, a little stream of brown and blue smoke trailing out behind, and past he went, sticking out his arm again, and we followed his trail for miles and miles, the smoke becoming more brown, and then pure blue, and then black, until soon we seen him at the side of the road again, wrapped in black smoke, all black himself now, sitting on the shoulder with his legs straight out, the parts of his machine all spread out in a circle around him, and we stopped again, and Bruce said, "You been smoking all the way."

"Tell me another," said Piney.

"You are libel to need a bath one of these days," said Coker.

"Get going," he said. "I will beat you to Jacksonville."

"He is going to carry her in on his back," said Coker, "juggling the parts in his other hand. Tell me, Piney, are you planning to go all the way back to QC on this motorcycle?"

"I am not going back to QC," he said.

"I will bet you $10," said Coker, "that you get shipped back to QC, and another 10 that you do not beat us to Jacksonville."

He finally looked up now. "It is a bet," he said, and up he got and counted out his money and give it to me to hold, never smiling, only spraddling down again and slamming his parts back in. "You better get going," he said.

He passed us about 5 miles out of town, smoking worse than ever but doing 80, a hanky tied around his mouth and tucked up under his goggles. He was waiting in front of the hotel when we got there. I give him back his 20.

We said "Goodby" to the girls. "Good luck, boys," said Holly. "I believe this is your year again," and she went around the car to the driver side.

"Take care of 600 Dollars," I said.

"He is always right here where I can keep a track of him," she said, and she kissed me and kissed Bruce, standing on her toes and kissing him solid on the mouth and then climbing back in under the wheel and taking off. She stood with Darlene 2 days in West Virginia, and then she went on home. I did not see her again until she come down for the doubleheader Memorial Day.

In the hotel in Jacksonville, and then again in all the hotels all summer, the first thing I done was flip open the book to the yellow page and wrote down the number of 6 doctors or so on the back of the pages the doctors give me in Rochester, Minnesota. He always seen me doing it, but he never said a word, only pulled a chair up to the window and kicked off his shoes and spit down once or twice, sort of trying it out, and then he sat back and stuck his feet on the ledge. He liked to watch people in windows across the way, and he liked to watch the signs flash off and on. He liked to watch the sun go down and up.

He begun thinking about baseball a lot, which

he never done before, always treating it before like it was football or golf, not a thing to think about but only play. He said to me, "Arthur, tell me, if you was on one club and me on another what kind of a book would you keep on me?"

"If I was to keep a book on you," said I, "I would say to myself, "No need to keep a book on Pearson, for Pearson keeps no book on me." Because if I was to strike you out on fast balls letter high you would not go back to the bench thinking, "That son of a bitch Wiggen struck me out on fast balls letter high, so I will be on the lookout for the same thing next time." No, you go back to the bench thinking, "I would like a frank," or "I see pretty legs in the stands," and by the time you face me again you have forgot all about the time before. You must remember. Or if you cannot remember you must write it down. The man you are facing is not a golf ball sitting there waiting for you to bash him. He is a human being, and he is thinking, trying to see through your system and trying to hide his own. This is not golf, goddam it, nor football, but human being against human being, and the son of a bitch that wears his thinking hat has got the advantage over the other."

"I will keep a book," he said.

"Either in your head," I said, "or better still on paper for awhile. You already have terrific power. But power plus brains is the difference between nobody and somebody."

"I must develop brains," he said.

"Plus confidence," said I. "Brains and power are nothing without confidence."

"I never had it much," he said. "You always had it, Arthur."

"No sir," said I, "but I always *looked* like I had it and *sounded* like I had it. Days when I am tired and days when my curve is not breaking it is confidence keeps me going. I hitch up my britches and spit. Crowd in and look fierce, and you will find it works wonders. Watch any of the boys when they hit. Watch Pasquale or Canada. They crowd in like they simply can not wait, though in their shoes they might know it is not their day. Half the pitchers you face are only country boys like yourself, and the other half are only country boys from the city. They are no smarter than you."

"I never been smart, Arthur."

"You been dumb on one count only. You left somebody tell you you were dumb. But you are not. You know which way the rivers run, which I myself do not know. Even Holly does not know, and I doubt that Red Traphagen himself can look at a river and tell you which way it runs without throwing a stick in it. All the way down from Minnesota I never knew."

"I thought you knew," he said.

"Because I bullshit you," I said. "You know what is planted in the fields and you know the make of cows. Who in hell on this whole club knows one cow from the other? I could be stranded in the desert with 412 cows and die of thirst and hunger for all I know about a cow. Did Hut Sut

Sutter know a cow or a river when he seen one? No, I guess not. And where did he wind up anyhow, this great brain you admire? A goddam professional football player! Would *you* like to be a football player in snow and ice up there in Wisconsin, up and down on the frozen ground? You have already proved yourself smarter than Sutter and smarter than 90,000 kids from coast to coast, every one of them dying to be in your shoes, a New York Mammoth riding the best trains and the best hotels. Why has not Dutch cut you loose if you are so dumb?"

"I do not know," he said.

"Simply because you are not," said I. "Dutch will be keeping you and shipping Piney Woods back to Mike. Is Dutch smart?"

"He certainly is," he said.

"Do you think he would stand for a dumb ballplayer?"

"No."

"Then if you were a dumb ballplayer would he be standing for you?"

"No," he said, "I guess not, Arthur, now that you mention it."

"Did you not buy an Arcturus policy? Did it not prove a smart move?"

"I guess so," he said.

"Can a dumb person do a smart thing?"

"No sir, Arthur, I guess not."

"Then wise up," I said.

"I will keep a book," he said. "I will have more confidence and brains. You are giving me the old confidence already. You are a smart fellow, Arthur."

"And tell me one more thing," I said. "Would a smart fellow like me room with a dumb one? How do people room with people around here? Do you room with your opposite type or do you room 2 by 2 like Jonah in the ark. *Take* Jonah. Who does he room with? He rooms with Perry, color with color, and Washburn rooms with Crane, color with color again, and George with this Spanish boy because language with language, and Pasquale and Vincent together because brother with brother, coaches with coaches, like with like. Goose Williams and Horse Byrd together, stinker with stinker. There is always a reason why 2 fellows are roomies. I never seen it fail yet. So I would not be libel to room with you if you were dumb because you yourself just said how smart I was. Did you not?"

"Yes I did," he said. "And I meant it," which he did, for he always thought high of me, thought I was just about the smartest individual going. He always asks me 1,000,000 things like who in hell is some cluck in the newsreel or why in hell did they ever take the 2-deckers off 5th Avenue or what kind of a salary does the President make, and I always told him, whether I knew or not, and he always believed me, dumb as he was.

He caught in about 8 games on the way north with Philly. It was cold. Also the railroad was out on strike, the Louisville & Nashville I think they call it, and twice we took planes. It was all a mess.

Standing around in the airport one day Bob Dietz of Philadelphia said to me, "Author, what in the hell was the name of your catcher last night? How come Dutch is using him all of a sudden? He is not a bad ballplayer, only hits too much in the same place all the time," which meant to me that they were keeping a book on him, which they never done before.

"I do not know," I said. I did not. I mean, I did not know why Dutch begun using him. I only know that by the time we hit home he went back to using only Jonah, deciding he had all the power he needed. We really had power all spring, Pasquale and Sid and Canada the big guns, especially against right-hand pitching. They hit 3 home runs in a row one night in Savannah, the kind of a thing that makes a pitcher lounge back on the bench with a smile on his face, which I myself done anyhow all spring no matter what, for I was hot, 9 pounds over my weight but faster than ever. The boys on Philly all said the same, saying, "Author, I never seen you so fast. I guess holding out agrees with you." I felt good in mind and body and said to hell with my weight and never stepped on a scale all spring. The Quartet sung in the shower, and we sung one TV date in Atlanta and picked up a little change. I remember we sung "Come Josephine In My Flying Machine" quite a bit.

I suppose he might of used him more if he wasn't such a bother, even with the power on, for Dutch can always use more power no matter how much he already got. But Bruce in the lineup was always a bother to Dutch. Dutch sits and shakes and says, "I wonder did the sign get through to Pearson," and everybody says, "Sure, Dutch," but maybe it did and maybe it didn't. The sign goes from the dugout to Perry or Coker and they then flash it home, but Bruce is not always sure where they are coming from, or when, and he often crouched there looking at Coker for his sign when it was coming from Perry, or the other way around, now one and then the other, or Perry might flash a phony sign, or Coker the same, to keep the opposition from swiping it, though what it sometimes amounts to is Bruce himself is the only person fooled. He is too ashamed to call time or come out for a conference, and he sometimes flashes the first sign he sees, and there is hell to pay afterwards, Dutch saying, "How come a curve ball to Williger? He *eats* curves."

"Pearson signed for a curve," says the pitcher.

"You signed for a curve?" says Dutch.

"Yes sir," says Bruce. "I must of missed my sign."

"I seen Roguski flashing it to you as plain as the nose on your face," says Dutch.

"I was looking at Simpson."

"Why?" says Dutch. "Is he more beautiful to look at? Was it not an odd-number inning?"

"Yes sir," says Bruce, "but I thought it was an even-number inning."

"What in hell do you think they build score-boards for?" says Dutch. "Count by odds."

"1, 3, 5, 7, 9," says Bruce.

It never happened when I was pitching, for I picked up the sign myself off the bench, or off Coker or Perry, and I talked some of the pitchers into doing the same. But you can not ask a pitcher to be looking 4 ways for their sign. They have got enough to think about without protecting their catcher. Dutch looked at me funny a couple times, staring at me, his face saying, "Author, what is the secret locked in your head?"

But then again Bruce had good days. In Atlanta he hit a home run one night off a right-hand pitcher name of Hrabak, now with Detroit, that probably went 475 feet in the air. It was a cold night, not much of a crowd, and you heard it go "Ping!" in the street beyond, and hit left-handers, too, which Jonah Brooks don't even hit as much as he hits right-handers, which is hardly any to begin with, and begun hitting the same boys over again, even though Philly kept a book on him now, leaning in more, his jaw working, saying over and over to himself, "This son of a bitch is only a country boy like me, or else a country boy from the city," looking fiercer, a big chew in his cheek and his bat gripped tight, though later Pasquale told him loosen up, and a smart thing, too.

One day in Knoxville against Philly he seen how they played him deep down the left side, and he bunted, probably the first time in his life he ever hit not only with his bat but also with his head, and he beat it out easy. Philly never played him too deep any more after that, and more than one hit he blasted through third that the third baseman might of handled if he been deeper but was afraid to play too deep for fear Bruce would bunt again. It did not need a genius to think this up, but for Bruce it was unusual, and maybe Dutch said to himself, "Is it possible that Pearson is waking up at last from his sleep of years?" I don't know. I mean I don't know if that is what Dutch said or not. All I know is this kind of a thing probably kept him from getting too goddam upset over keeping Bruce. He never jumped up in the air and kicked his heels, I suppose, nor ever said a good word to Bruce, nor ever spoke to him when he seen him around. But he carried him along. To him Bruce was a spare part rattling in the trunk that you hardly even remember is there between looks.

It was very cold up towards New York. We played one exhibition in Philly, though it was not on the schedule, and the boys all told me bring it up at the winter meetings, and I said I would, for an open date is supposed to be an open date, and I will, too, if I ever get to the winter meetings. But I must finish this cockeyed book first. I swore up and down to myself I would finish it or die trying, though to tell you the truth it is impossible to write around the house between the baby and the telephone ringing. It rings a lot these days, ringing all winter after a good year, and what I wind up doing is writing at night, and if the baby cries I snuggle her in bed with Holly, and she feeds her, and I go back and write some more, or sometimes write with one hand and the baby in the other until she dozes forward and I slide her back in the sack. Luckily I am a fast writer. Also, I do my *own* writing, though I been getting calls ever since October 7th from writers saying, "Author, why not go and relax somewheres and leave me polish off your book for you?" and sometimes the temptation gets me down. But they would louse it up, not meaning to but only pounding it out between the half of a football game or on the corner of a bar, and it must not be loused like that.

We hit Philly on a Friday morning, Good Friday, and pulled out that night. I pitched 7 innings, my last turn before the Opener. Canada played first base because Sid went home for the beginning of Passover, and Reed McGonigle took over in center field, joining us not 2 hours before game time, still in his army suit but officially sprung. Everybody was glad to see him, Dutch especially, for it meant we could carry 26, and he was in shape, for he played ball all spring, and Dutch started him, and Piney Woods was cut loose the same day, headed back to the QC Cowboys with his airplane ticket sticking up out of his pocket and stopping at my locker the last thing and saying, "Author, give Coker back the other 20," and I said I would, though actually Coker never give it to me, and I said, "Piney, I have a feeling you will be up in a year or 2 as soon as Mike learns you to keep your mind on business and not on motorcycles and such foolishness as that."

"I love motorcycles," he said.

"You are 19," I said. "You will get over it," and

he stood up and looked brave and said, "Well, maybe somebody will drop dead soon and open up a slot for me."

"Leave us hope so," I said, and he went out the door.

Jonah caught, and it was a pleasure pitching to him. Now and then I looked out towards the bullpen, and I seen Bruce there, and I thought how impossible it was, though sometimes I shook my mind off it, saying, "Well, Bruce now and all the rest of us later, so what the hell difference does it really make?" though I could never really convince myself any way you look at it. Dying old is in the cards, and you figure on it, and it happens to everybody, and you are willing to swallow it. But why should it happen young to Bruce?

It made me mad. I went my full 7 with never a hitch, and Dutch sat on the bench, leaning back on his hands and smiling. I sweated something awful, still weighing heavy, and this kid fanned me between innings, Diego Roberto or Roberto Diego, whatever his name was, the kid we carried for George. "Mister," he said, "you pitch tight baseball like hot stuff." He went back to Cuba when Red come back, for Red can speak Spanish with George. Diego could throw with both hands, though not too hard with either one, and he sometimes threw batting practice. I liked it when he did, for I could hit him.

We wound up the weekend and the spring with 2 with Philly at home, and Sunday night me and

Joe sat around about an hour dealing Tegwar without even a nibble. There was too much excitement in the air, the lobby full of 1,000,000 people saying, "Glad to see you back, boys," and saying they knew it was our year again, and slapping you on the back. Joe was awful put out. I told him forget it, there would be happy times ahead when things settled down, and he said he supposed so. Bruce went up to Katie's and come back and seen us there and said, "Why not 3-hand Tegwar just between ourself?" and Joe give him a look.

Monday we drilled light and left for Boston.

We were a strong club. We had the best left-hand pitcher in baseball, plus Van Gundy, Van Gundy a little thin boy you doubt can carry his hat, no speed but a lot of breaking stuff, and top control. We had strong right-hand pitching. We had good relief if Horse and Keith come through.

We had the best outfield in baseball, bar none, and the best double-play combination in Coker and Perry. We had good, solid right-hand hitting, and we had tremendous left-hand power if Sid and Pasquale both had a good year.

But we had weak catching and a weak bench, Goose old and fading, Bruce never reliable, and Jonah no hitter. The bench was young and not yet ripe.

I floated $250 on the Mammoths to win in a little pool run by a crook name of Suss Melner in the lobby, but he give it back to me when we come down again from Boston, saying, "No takers, Author."

On the following couple pages I am throwing in
the roster, which I done the same in "The Southpaw" and received many letters from fans saying
"Good idea," for it helped them follow whose who.
It seems crazy to me because I know the boys like
the back of my book, what their voice is like and
how they walk and talk and eat and comb their
hair, how they stand in at the plate, how they
throw, how they run, how they slide, where they
spend their pay, who they hang with, what their
wife and kids are like, or their girl. I know their
voice through a wall. I can see a waiter in a diner
with a tray full of food and pretty much know who
ordered it. I know how they bet at poker, and what
they smoke, those that do. I know whose rings are
which piled in Mick McKinney's box. Christ, if I
see somebody head down on Mick's table I know
them by the callous on their feet. More things I
know than this but probably better never mention
for fear of getting them in trouble with their wife
or their girl or the United States Bureau of Internal Revenue. Yet when you write a book you must
remember that everybody don't know what you
might know. Holly says the same.

Running down the roster I see where out of the
25 boys on the 52 club that won both the flag and
the Series only 16 are back. I also notice where I
was the youngest man on the 52 squad but am now
older than 9 others. Canada Smith is listed as an
outfielder but also fills in at first base.

OFFICIAL ROSTER

NEW YORK MAMMOTHS
BASEBALL CLUB, INC.

1955

LESTER T. MOORS, JR.
PATRICIA MOORS

MANAGER

SCHNELL, Herman H. "Dutch." Born February 23, 1893, St. Louis, Mo. Residence: St. Louis.

COACHES

BARNARD, Egbert. "Egg." Born October 2, 1896, Philadelphia, Pa. Residence: Philadelphia.

JAROS, Joseph Thomas. "Joe." Born March 31, 1895, Moline, Ill. Residence: Oak Park, Ill.

STRAP, Clinton Blakesley. "Clint." Born April 1, 1906, Mason City, Wash. Residence: Scranton, Pa. U. S. Army, World War II.

OUTFIELDERS

CARUCCI, Pasquale Joseph. Born August 10, 1923, Port Chester, N. Y. U. S. Army, World War II. 5'10½", 180 lbs. Bats L, throws R. Residence: San Francisco, Cal.

CARUCCI, Vincent Frank. Born July 17, 1925, San Francisco, Cal. U. S. Army, World War II. 5'10", 175 lbs. Bats L, throws R. Residence: San Francisco.

GLEE, Harry Justin. Born January 11, 1932, Chittenango, N. Y. U. S. Navy. 6', 190 lbs. Bats R, throws R. Residence: Chittenango.

LONGABUCCO, Frank Patrick. "Lawyer." Born September 18, 1931, Peekskill, N. Y. U. S. Army, Korea. 5'11½", 185 lbs. Bats R, throws R. Residence: Peekskill.

McGONIGLE, Reed. Born February 1, 1932, New Haven, Conn. U. S. Army. 6'1", 180 lbs. Bats L, throws L. Residence: New Haven.

SMITH, Earle Banning. "Canada." Born October 14, 1929, Winnipeg, Canada. 5'11", 185 lbs. Bats R, throws R. Residence: Winnipeg.

INFIELDERS

GOLDMAN, Sidney Jerome. "Sid." Born May 7, 1928, Bronx, N. Y. U. S. Army, World War II. 6'1½", 215 lbs. Bats L, throws L. Residence: Manhattan, N. Y.

GONZALEZ, George. Born February 11, 1926, Pinar

del Rio, Cuba. 5'9½", 175 lbs. Bats R, throws R. Residence: Havana, Cuba.

JONES, Robert Stanley. "Ugly." (Captain). Born September 6, 1921, Batesville, Ark. U. S. Marines, World War II. 5'11½", 185 lbs. Bats L, throws R. Residence: Little Rock, Ark.

ROGUSKI, John Llewellyn. "Coker." Born April 2, 1930, Fairmont, W. Va. 5'10", 180 lbs. Bats R-L, throws R. Residence: Fairmont.

SIMPSON, Perry Garvey. Born May 27, 1931, Savannah, Ga. 5'10½", 175 lbs. Bats R, throws R. Residence: Detroit, Mich.

TYLER, Willis James. Born April 16, 1933, Dade City, Fla. 6'2", 205 lbs. Bats R, throws R. Residence: Newark, N. J.

WASHBURN, Lysander. "Wash." Born May 17, 1932, Ellicott City, Md. U. S. Army. 5'10½", 175 lbs. Bats R-L, throws R. Residence: Ellicott City.

CATCHERS

BROOKS, Jonah Francis. Born October 9, 1932, New Iberia, La. U. S. Army, Korea. 6'4", 220 lbs. Bats L, throws R. Residence: New Orleans, La.

PEARSON, Bruce William, Jr. Born June 4, 1926, Bainbridge, Ga. U. S. Army, World War II. 5'11", 185 lbs. Bats R, throws R. Residence: Bainbridge.

WILLIAMS, Harold Hill. "Goose." Born August 26, 1920, Terre Haute, Ind. U. S. Marines, World War II. 6'1½", 200 lbs. Bats R, throws R. Residence: Chicago, Ill.

PITCHERS

BIGGS, Porter Leonard. "Blondie." Born June 7, 1932, Morristown, N. J. U. S. Army. 6'2", 200 lbs. Throws R, bats R. Residence: Morristown.

BURKE, Lindon Theodore. Born March 12, 1930, Lusk, Wyo. 5'11", 190 lbs. Throws R, bats R. Residence: Lusk.

BYRD, Paul Richard. "Horse." Born November 19, 1921, Culpeper, Va. U. S. Army, World War II. 6'1", 240 lbs. Throws R, bats R. Residence: Washington, D. C.

CASELLI, Franklin D. Roosevelt. "F. D. R." Born November 12, 1932, Oakland, Cal. U. S. Army, Korea. 5'10½", 190 lbs. Throws R, bats R-L. Residence: Mill Valley, Cal.

CRANE, Keith Robert. Born June 22, 1929, Wooster, Ohio. 6', 185 lbs. Throws L, bats R. Residence: Cleveland, Ohio.

MACY, Herbert. Born October 1, 1928, Athens, Ga. 6'1", 180 lbs. Throws R, bats R. Residence: Aqua Clara, Fla.

STERLING, John Adams. "Jack." Born March 16, 1925, East St. Louis, Ill. U. S. Navy, World War II. 5'9½", 170 lbs. Throws R, bats R. Residence: Newport News, Va.

VAN GUNDY, James Sweetser. Born January 2, 1932, Central City, Nebr. U. S. Army. 5'9", 155 lbs. Throws L, bats L. Residence: Central City.

WIGGEN, Henry Whittier. "Author." Born July 4,

1931, Perkinsville, N. Y. 6'3", 200 lbs. Throws L,
bats L. Residence: Perkinsville.

WILLOWBROOK, Gilbert Lillis. "Gil." Born May 15,
1929, Boston, Mass. 6', 190 lbs. Throws R, bats
R. Residence: Aqua Clara, Fla.

PHYSICIANS: Ernest I. Loftus, M.D., Hyman R.
Solomon, M.D.

TRAINER: Frank T. ("Mick") McKinney.

SUPPLEMENTARY

COACHES:

MULROONEY, Michael Conroy. "Mike." Born June
2, 1896, Coraopolis, Pa. Residence: Last Chance,
Colo.

TRAPHAGEN, Berwyn Phillips. "Red." Born De-
cember 9, 1919, Oakland, Cal. U. S. Medical
Experimentation Corps, World War II. Residence: San Francisco, Cal.

CATCHER:

WOODS, Thurston Printise. "Piney." Born September 18, 1935, Good Hope, Ga. U. S. Marines.
6'1", 195 lbs. Bats R, throws R. Residence: Good
Hope.

ROSTER COMPILED BY BRADLEY R. LORD, SECRETARY

CHAPTER 7

On the way up to Boston all was quiet, especially the new boys, for they were tight. Tomorrow was for the money. I was sitting reading a book Arcturus sent me name of "Widening Your Circle of Acquaintances." Every book they send you they send a card asking how you like it, and I send the card back, saying, "Good for laughs." I got more business than I can handle already and do not need to circle my acquaintances. Dutch come past and touched me on the shoulder, saying, "Author, come with me," and I went back to his room with him and sat down, not knowing what was up and wondering what I done wrong, and he said, "Are you ever planning to get down to your weight?" But he did not wait for an answer, saying instead, "Did you have your tooth fixed?" I had a hole in one of my cavities, and I started to say "No," which was true, for there was too much excitement over the weekend to go sit in the dentist. The club has this dentist name of Dr. D. K. G. Silverstein that opens nights and Sundays for Mammoths only, a Mammoth fan for years and years with a photo on the wall of each and every Mammoth he ever worked on. He has a big photo of Dutch that takes up half one wall that I personally do not consider the happiest thing to be staring you in the face at such a time. "How is the Mrs. coming along?" he said, which I did not even start to answer now, for I seen it was something else on his mind altogether.

"Author," he said, "Joe tells me you and Pearson been playing Tegwar over the winter."

"Sure," I said. "Why not?"

"When?" said Dutch.

"Just before camp begun," said I.

"Where?" said he.

"Down at Bruce's," said I.

"What were you doing down there?" he said.

"You mean besides playing Tegwar?" I said.

"Do not stall," he said. "Why did you go there?"

"He always wished me to meet his folks," said I.

"Was the Mrs. with you?"

"Sure," I said.

"You drove down by car?"

"Yes."

"Very well," said he. "We have got you and your wife by car in Bainbridge, Georgia. Leave us back up to whenever it was you spoke to Joe on the telephone in Chicago. When was that?"

"I never did," I said.

"You never did? Are you telling me Joe is a liar?"

"No," said I. "I never spoke to Joe. I suppose what he means is I spoke to his Mrs."

"Yes, you know very goddam well what he probably means. Do not stall, Author, for you are stalling the wrong man. When was it?"

"Probably around in January," I said.

"What were you doing in Chicago?"

"Besides calling Joe I was only changing planes," said I.

"For where?"

"For Minnesota."

"Where in Minnesota?"

"Minneapolis."

"What was up?"

"Insurance matters," I said.

"Name me somebody you planned seeing on insurance matters in Minneapolis."

"Aleck Olson," said I.

Dutch dug the Boston book out of his bag and looked up Aleck and threw the book on the bed. "Did you sell him?"

"I believe it is only a matter of time," I said.

"This is all a lie," he said.

"No, it is no lie," I said.

"I got a feeling that these little statements are true," he said, "but what they add up to is one big lie. Am I right?"

"About what?"

"About the feeling I got?" he said.

"I do not know what kind of a feeling you got," said I. "If you say you have got such a feeling I guess you do."

He laughed. "Get out," he said. "I sure wish you

could be wrapped in a sack and tossed in the river, all except your left arm."

The first thing I done at the park Tuesday was race over to the Boston clubhouse. The boys were all sitting around eating bananas. "Where did you get all the bananas?" I said.

"Off a tree," they said, and somebody threw me one.

"What in hell you doing in here?" said Alf Keller. "Get the hell out."

"I just come over to use your scale," I said. "What kind of a cheap management is it that got no scale in the visiting clubhouse?"

"What you need is a truck scale," said Alf.

"What you need is a ball club," said I. I stepped on the scale. "Alf, I know where you can pick up a couple girls off a softball club cheap." The scale said "211½" and I threw my banana away.

"What you need I already got," said he.

"Aleck," said I, "could I see you a minute?" and we stepped out in the alley, and before I said anything he said, "Dutch called me."

"What did he say?" I said.

"He asked me what you done in Minneapolis. I told him you bought a coat was all I remembered. He asked me if I bought insurance off you, and I said no, not yet. I think I will buy some."

"Never mind that now," I said. "What else did he say?"

"What is up, Author?" said Aleck. "I told him nothing if I could help it. If I knew what was up I could tell him the right thing. He asked me where you went. I said you got on the bus to see Pearson."

"Did you tell him where I was going to see Pearson?"

"I do not remember. I figured if you got on the Rochester bus you were going to Rochester."

"Ain't there places between Minneapolis and Rochester you might be going to see a man at?"

"Only Cannon Falls," he said.

"It happens that was where I seen Pearson," I said.

"OK, OK," he said. "Do not be mad at me. Only what in hell would anybody be seeing anybody in Cannon Falls for?"

"You might be going fishing," I said.

"In what?" he said. "In 9 feet of ice?"

"Hunting?"

"Yes," he said, "you might be going hunting at that, though you would be more libel to go up north hunting. That is where everybody goes. Have you boys got a girl in Minnesota?"

"That is just where I would not wish to go," I said, "where everybody else is, all packed in like sardines."

"Packed in in all them woods! You might go days without seeing a soul. Many a man froze to death up there before they found him."

"Thanks," I said.

"For what?" he said. "Listen, Author, I wish to talk to you about the annuity."

"Some other time," I said, and I went out and warmed.

It was the fourth straight Opener I worked. Sam Yale worked 14 in a row until I nudged him out of the spot in 52. I do not know why Dutch always likes left-handers against Boston, but he does. They used to be weak against left-handers, but not any more. Now they are weak, but not especially against left-handers, and if I been Dutch I would of saved me and Van Gundy more for somebody else and threw right-hand pitching at Boston. However, I am not Dutch.

The first ball I pitched Aleck Olson lined it in the seats in right, a solid blow though not a long one, and I said to myself, "This is a great way to start the year." Keith Crane got up off the bench and slung his jacket over his shoulder and started down to the bullpen, Bruce following along behind. Dutch stood up and took a bat out of the rack and begun tapping the handle on the step, like a drum, ba-da-dum, ba-da-dum, ba-da-dum-dum-dum, like the Lone Ranger's horse, Hiyo Silver, away. He breaks about 4 bats like that a year. Jonah come down the line with a new ball, squeezing it so little and white in those big hands, and the infield gathered around and gassed, and then they all went back to their spots except Jonah. He stood there a minute, rubbing the ball, not saying a word, only giving you the idea that nothing in the world happened worth talking about, then turning and hustling back up the line again. He never lets his worry show. He is steady, and he makes you steady. "Jonah knows," he says, and if you doubt him he knows that, too, reads your mind, and he sings, "Do not doubt Jonah. Last man that doubted Jonah wound up in the poorhouse," and you throw and do not doubt. He is the most under-rated man in baseball today, as me and the Mammoths know, and nobody else, and we got the son of a bitches out after that, 1-2-3.

Keith and Bruce put their jacket on again, for it was cold up there, and sat down in the bullpen. Dutch put the bat back in the rack. And Sid tied it up a minute later with a blow that sailed twice as far back in the stands as Aleck's ever done, and the ball game was new.

Then soon it was not new any more, neither, but ours, for the power was on, the boys all hitting solid and steady, though a couple times when we really got moving the tail end come up, Jonah first and me after, and this kept queering things, not only then but later in the summer, too. You are not libel to find 2 weaker hitters in a row anywheres. Jonah tries. I will say that. I myself pretty much give up even trying any more. We were ahead 6–2 in the eighth, which you might of still called a ball game until Perry and Pasquale both got on and Sid hit another, and it was 9–2 and everybody in the stands that didn't already freeze to death went home and probably never come back the rest of the year.

We won on Wednesday, too, which was colder yet, Van Gundy throwing these soft little hooks and sinkers all day that from anywheres in the park look like a sick child served them up underhand. I seen more articles all summer called WHY CAN NOBODY HIT VAN GUNDY? than any other kind except WILL SID GOLDMAN BE THE MAN TO BUST BABE RUTH'S RECORD? Sid hit another that day, which was 3, and we went back home on the evening train.

About an hour out a porter name of Marty told me Dutch wished to see me, and I went back to his room again, saying over and over to myself, "Cannon Falls, Cannon Falls." He was laying on the bed all naked with the sheet up over him, the Brooklyn book beside him, his hands back under his head and a cigarette in his mouth. The ashes kept falling down on his chest. "Ain't you afraid of burning a hole in your chest?" I said. He never answered, never even looked at me in the beginning, only stared up.

"I lay here reading the Brooklyn book," he said. "I keep trying to figure the son of a bitches out. But then do you know who I wind up thinking about? I wind up thinking about Wiggen and Pearson. Goddam it, Author, you told me you went back home from Minneapolis."

"So it is this again?" said I. "No sir, Dutch, I do not believe I told you that."

"You give me to believe it," he said. "And that is the same thing. Did you see Olson?"

"Did I see *Olson?*" I said. "The son of a bitch hit a home run off me."

"You know what I mean."

"Sure I seen Olson."

"What about?"

"Insurance matters. By the way, he mentioned you called him. Dutch, I would rather you did not push this thing too far."

"Why not?"

"Because it is a personal matter," said I. I got up and locked the door.

"Flip up the bowl," he said, and I flipped it up and he tossed his cigarette in and turned over on his side now. "How so?" he said.

"Well, Dutch," said I, "you will probably think I am a heel and all that, but there is this airline stewardess."

"What is her name?"

"Mary," I said.

"Mary what? Jones or Smith or Brown?"

"Mary Pistologlione," I said.

"So," he said. "Go on. I am trying hard to believe this. OK, so you fiddle along between Chicago and Minneapolis, and then you get on the bus in Minneapolis and go where?"

"Did not Olson tell you?"

"You tell me."

"Down to Cannon Falls," I said.

"What for?"

"To hunt."

"You never hunt. What kind of a gun do you shoot?"

"No kind," I said. "I only went because Pearson asked me to."

"What did you catch?"

"Nothing. We changed our mind and went back."

"Back where?"

"Home, him to Georgia and me to Perkinsville."

"I am sure you have drilled him up to the eyes," he said, "but I am going to hear how it sounds from him anyway. You sit right there." He rung for the porter. "How did he come up to Minnesota? Drive by car did he?"

"Yes sir."

The porter banged on the door. "Tell him go get Pearson," Dutch said. "I do not believe this cockeyed bull story about your friend Mary for a single minute, but if it is true you are making a mistake. Anybody with a wife like yours must count his blessings." Bruce walked in, and Dutch laid over on his back again and lit up another cigarette and reached under the bed and stuck the match in the spring. "How much money you owe Author, Pearson?"

"I owe him nothing," said Bruce. "Arthur, do I owe you any money?" He looked at me quite hurt.

"What train did you go up to Minnesota in?" said Dutch.

"No train sir. In my car."

"Is Cannon Falls a nice town?" said Dutch. "Tell me what is is like."

"It is pretty nice," said Bruce, "with a main drag and stores but very cold. We could not fish. The ice was 9 feet. We went hunting."

"What did you shoot?" said Dutch.

"Not so many niggers up there neither."

"I asked you what you shot."

"Nothing sir. We started hunting and changed my mind. I did not feel like killing anything any more."

"That knocks the hell out of hunting," said Dutch.

"Yes sir," said Bruce. "I guess it does."

"Then where did you go from Minnesota?" said Dutch.

"Back home."

"Alone?"

"Yes."

"You are sure?"

"Yes sir. Were we not, Arthur?"

"Were *who* not?" said Dutch, sitting up in bed all of a sudden.

"Me and Arthur," said Bruce.

"You 2 went down from Minnesota by car?"

"Yes sir."

"Flip up the bowl again," said Dutch, and I flipped it up and he tossed the butt in. "Now, Author, I believe we might be heading towards something at last, for 2 nights ago on this same identical train I said to you who drove your car down to Bainbridge, and you said you and your wife did, but now I hear something else again. Did you go down there and back home for your wife? Or did her and Mary Pistologlione maybe drive down together with Aleck Olson? Or in other words what in hell is going on here anyways, because you know as sure as your name that I am going to get to the bottom of this or kill myself doing it," and while he was talking my mind was whirling, and I let her whirl, and when he stopped I busted out laughing, saying, "Well, Dutch, the whole joke is on you."

"I am laughing my ass off," said he.

"Because if you will back the whole thing up," said I, "you will remember that I called you on the

telephone during this time and give you a little patter and told you I was up home when where we were we were right downtown in St. Louis. We would of went out and seen you but were not shaved and did not wish to see the Mrs. like that and finally made a gag out of it all. You can understand me not wishing to give away a gag that I might wish to try another time on somebody else."
I was laughing, but Dutch was not.

"This does not explain everything," he said. "It leaves me in the dark on a number of counts." He leaned back and laughed a little, though not hard, and he seen the Brooklyn book and picked it up and begun studying it. After awhile he said, "Get out."

When he really thought about it again he knew there was no Mary Pistologlione and never was nor ever could be. He always knew it was a phony story, but he never knew just where. The one big thing on my side was he thinks I am out of my mind to start with.

CHAPTER 8

Sid hit a home run in the tenth inning Thursday, Number 4, and we beat Brooklyn, and Friday was the last day of Passover and he was out of the lineup again. Dutch give us a lecture before the Friday game, saying we had all the power in the world and could whip along without Sid, but Goose caught, for power, and we lost, and Dutch swore there would be no more Passover clauses in anybody's contract. "Why in hell does it never rain on Passover?" he said. He was blowing his fume all over the place, the first time yet, and it made the new boys extremely nervous. I told them it happened every other day, 77 times a summer, and they said it must be quite a strain being on top of it all the time. "It wins flags," said Ugly.

"Mike Mulrooney wins flags," said Lawyer Longabucco, "and he hardly ever speaks above a whisper."

"You are in the big time now, son," said Ugly, "and you must get used to getting eat out in a big-time way."

"Yet it seems to me," said Lawyer, "that I have got no business getting eat out because Sid went

128

home for Passover."

"Do not always be a lawyer," said Ugly, which was how Lawyer Longabucco got his name.

Sid himself probably never heard a word from Dutch on the subject. He was back Saturday when Boston hit town, and Dutch forgets Friday when Saturday comes, new day, new ball game. Yesterday is in the books, dead and buried. He remembers old grudges from years and years, but he forgets yesterday and leaves you start each new day with a fresh slate and anyhow never eats Sid out much because Sid is not the type of a ballplayer eating out does any good to. He must be kept calm and not stirred up. Once in the park he is always after calmness. He will walk away from a discussion. He will never talk to writers nor fans nor even the boys much but only come up out of the alley and stand studying the bats one after the other, though then always grab the same bat, a Tommy Joyce Special. There are about 3 different types of Sid Goldman bats on the market, but I never seen him use one. Then he strolls up and stands by the cage and watches, and then he slowly steps in for his swipes. He takes a year or more to get his feet set. Then he tilts back a little, his knees bent, the bat resting on his shoulder until the pitcher pumps and you are ready to scream, "Christ Almighty, take the bat off your shoulder!" But he never does until the pitch starts through, and then the bat comes off, and eyes and wrists and power does the rest. He has the most amazing eye in baseball today. In Sid's language there is no such a thing as

"Almost" but only "Yes" or "No," where every pitch must be in there or else he will give it the go-by. A man must pitch to him or lose him, and when he sees what he likes he picks it out, and the wrists come around with the power behind it driving up from his toes the whole length of him. No matter if he only skies out, he skies high, but if he tags it square it is gone, and either way his face shows nothing, calm, never a smile nor a frown, and off the field the same, no monkeyplay but only quiet cards or the pinball machine or a magazine in the lobby. When he is hitting he rides the lobby watching the world go by, and when he is not he stays put in his room seeing nobody, only sitting in his shorts and looking in the mirror and wondering why. In New York he lives at home. In Pittsburgh he has a girl and in Chicago a brother or a cousin, and elsewhere he rooms with Lindon Burke. He dragged me and Lindon to a big blowout for some kind of a charitable outfit in Cleveland one night, and the women tore the joint down getting at him. He walked out of it, saying he could not stand it. It took his mind off. When the time come for the big speech the m.c. looked around for Sid, and he was gone, and I give it instead, saying we must all get behind and push, though never knowing what for nor how much they needed nor why nor when. He is a great drawing card and should have a better contract, but he does not think about it, only signs it and shoves it back in the box. He thinks about nothing, only his hitting. He walks in the clubhouse with the paper in his pocket and sits down and opens it and sees who the probable starter for the other club is and throws the paper away and sits and thinks about the probable starter and gets undressed and sits down in his jock again and thinks about it some more. Then he gets dressed and goes to the phone and calls the press-box and says, "Who is this?" and whoever answers Sid says, "I seen in your paper where So-and-so is the probable starter and wish to know is this the latest." Then he sticks his cap on his head and goes down the alley thinking about it.

I worked that Saturday with 3 days rest and my weight down to 210½, hooked up with Murtha, the same boy I beat Opening Day, in a ball game I will never soon forget. It was 2–2 moving along into the eighth when Dutch sent Bruce up to hit for me, the wind being right. I did not like being lifted, though what I like and do not like is a small thing to Dutch.

Bruce got hold of one he liked and slammed it in left, one base. I thought, "Good boy," and went back in the clubhouse and weighed myself and was down to 208 and went back out and seen Bruce standing on second dusting himself off. George was still at the plate, and I said, "Wild pitch?"

"No," said Coker. "He stole."

"He *stole*," I said.

"Without no sign," said Coker.

"Without no sign," said I.

"God save his skin," said Coker.

I looked at Dutch and he looked at me. Then he looked away. "Glee," he said, "go run for Pearson," and Harry Glee jumped up off the bench, his first big-time ball game, and Bruce come trotting in until when he was in front of the dugout he suddenly seen Dutch and changed his mind and circled around, down in the dugout at the far end, near the bubbler, and he kept right on trotting through the door and down the alley. The boys all laughed, and even Dutch laughed a little. George tried to punch one through the right side, but no go, and he was tossed out at first, but Glee went on to third and come home a couple pitches later when Perry lifted a long fly that Aleck Olson gathered in on the run and dug and spun and made the try on Glee but never had a chance. Keith Crane blanked Boston in the ninth and we took it, 3–2, our fourth win in 5 starts.

He was in the shower singing—

Yes, we have no bananas,
We have no bananas today.

"Bananas ain't all he is not libel to have pretty soon," said Perry. He begun to sing, Perry did, and we got the quartet going, and when we cleared out from the shower Bruce was still in there. Dutch come out of his office and stood on the scale and waited. Nobody could weigh theirself with him on the scale, though I guess nobody wished to. "Who is still in the shower?" said Dutch, and from the shower come Bruce's voice. "Nobody," it said, and he come out then, and everybody shoved over and left him a wide place to sit.

"Now boys," said Dutch, "every once in awhile there must be a certain amount of going back over things which people forgot in the meantime, such as the 2 things which are going to cost people money if they do not remember them and obey." He then listed them off. How many times in my life did I hear them! There are 2 things you will get eat out for. The eating out is worse than the money—

1. Missing your sign.
2. Not obeying orders.

Number One is mostly what you get eat out for, since if you do Number 2 you always claim Number One anyhow.

"Now Pearson," he said, "will you please tell me how come you missed your sign? What is the runner's sign for stealing?"

"Walloping your toe with the fat of the bat," said Bruce.

"Very good," said Dutch. "Did you see me walloping my toe?"

"No sir," said Bruce.

"Probably he thought he seen you," said I.

"No sir," said Bruce. "I just stole."

"Probably somebody else in along there on the bench was playing around with a bat was what Pearson thought he seen," said Sid.

"Probably I might of been playing around with a bat myself," said Vincent.

"No sir," said Bruce. "I only figured this murder was easy to steal off."

"Whatwhat?" said Dutch. "Whatwhat?"

"I was watching murder all Tuesday and seen how you might steal off him," said Bruce.

Dutch looked at me. "Author," he said, "can you make heads or tails out of this?"

"He means Murtha," said I.

"What about him?" said Dutch.

"I was watching him all Tuesday," said Bruce. "He looks at the runner. If the runner is leaning forward on his forward leg murder thinks you are bluffing him and pays you no mind. If the runner is leaning backwards on the other leg he holds you close."

"Is that so?" said Dutch. "Who told you this? It is the most thinking you figured out since Hector was a coon. Roberto, put it in Spanish for George."

"Yes sir, Mister," said Diego Roberto or Roberto Diego, whatever his name was, "George says pardon she for spoking but one stupid thing was never such hot-stuff baseball sending Pearson to stole a base."

"Tell George this is the same subject we are now discussing," said Dutch.

Roberto spoke in Spanish to George, and they laughed, and then George said it back to Roberto, and Roberto said it back in English to Dutch, which is how Dutch keeps a check on George. I actually believe George could speak English if he wished to by now, but I guess he does not.

Dutch was lost for words. I never heard a ballplayer tell him before that he done Number 2. Ugly says in more than 10 years under Dutch he never seen it neither. Dutch finally said, "It will cost you $100, Pearson," not loud nor mad but very mild like a fellow just trying to talk after somebody belted him in the stomach.

"Yes sir," said Bruce.

"I am sorry if it hurts," said Dutch, "but things that do you good have got to hurt."

"That is all right," said Bruce. "It does not hurt."

"Does not hurt?" said Dutch. "It is 5 trips to Katie's down a rat-hole. If it does not hurt I will make it 200."

"What he means," said I, "is it does not hurt *much*."

"What I will also do," said Dutch, "is kick you back 50 of it for the smart way you kept your eye on Murtha. I hope you will appreciate that. Do you appreciate that?"

"Yes sir," said I. "He does."

"I am not asking you," said Dutch. "I am asking him. Can he not speak for himself? Is that a lesson? If it is not a lesson my breath is wasted."

"No sir," said Bruce.

"It is not a lesson?" said Dutch.

"He means no you are not wasting your breath," said I, "but yes it is a lesson. I can tell you the 50 will hurt him plenty."

"I hope so," said Dutch, and he give Bruce one last look and turned and went back in his office, and in the end he kicked Bruce back the other 50, too, for we stole Boston blind when Murtha worked, though Bruce never missed the 50 when he lost it nor was glad to see it when it come back nor would not of cared if it been 100, nor 200. He did not think too damn much about money all year.

Sunday we split 2 with Boston. Sid busted up the first game with a home run, and Washington come to town on Monday after a happy week spent whaling Boston and Brooklyn, sitting on top of the league, which anybody could do easy enough if that was all that stood in their way. On paper Washington was no ball club and still isn't and never will as far as I can see, and Herb Macy beat them Monday and we moved up in a tie, and everybody now figured Washington had all the view they were libel to have all year of the top spot.

Around 10 the next morning the bellboy banged on the door with a note sealed in an envelope from Katie saying could she see me strictly alone in this certain restaurant, and I put on my pants and went. It was warming up, and the sun was hot in front of the hotel. The cabbie said, "Well, it sure looks good to see us up on top where we belong." I said it did. "Goldman sure been hitting," he said. "He is 4 ahead of Babe Ruth according to the paper." I said he was. "You pitching today?" he said. I said no. "Washington can not last," he said.

Nobody was there but Katie and the bartender and a colored fellow mopping the floor, the first time I seen her since 53 when me and Holly had this place on 66 Street, and she looked the same, and I said so. "You are looking extremely lovely as usual," I said. She was drinking a beer with one glove on and one off. On her meat hand she wore a wedding ring.

"Have a beer," she said.

"No thanks," I said, "but I think I could go for a bite of breakfast."

"Order up," she said, and I done so. "I was out the park Saturday," she said. "I thought I might see Goldman connect. I was glad to see Bruce in there for once. He done fine, did he not?"

"Yes he did," I said.

"How much did you finally sign for?"

"25,000," I said.

"How much does Bruce draw?" she said.

"15,425," I said.

"No," she said.

"Katie," I said, "state your business. What is up?"

The man brung me my breakfast and she whipped a 20 off the stack. We carried my dishes over to a table, for she thought the bartender was looking too curious. She does not trust anybody much. She spoke very low. "What is wrong with Bruce?" she said.

"Who says anything is?" I said.

"He says," she said.

"Well, what did he say?"

"He only said he was up in Minnesota, and then he clammed up. He says marry him and cash in on a big surprise."

"He is nutty," I said. "You get that way sitting on the bench too many years. He had pneumonia."

"What would you go all the way up to Minnesota with pneumonia for?" she said.

"Whatever it is it is not catching," I said, "so forget it. Do you think I would risk rooming with him if it was anything serious?"

"Rooming with him is one thing," she said.

"It is not catching," I said.

"*Is* not?" she said.

"*Was* not," said I.

"He sure thinks the world of you," she said. "He thinks you are the best friend a man could ever have. His idea of Heaven is me and you and him rooming together."

"That does not appeal to me," I said. "One of us has got to go."

"Why do you not ever drop up?" she said.

"I am a married man with ⅔ of a family on the way," said I. "Why not get married, Katie, and raise yourself some exemptions?"

"To who?" she said. "And for what? Why do you not play baseball for free, Author? Why should a girl go amateur when she has got the stuff to be professional? I do not see why you can not tell me what he had. You know, he is a nice boy, but a fool. I see myself in Bainbridge, Georgia, hanging up the wash and singing in the church, where maybe if I am a good girl he will leave me dig in the fields if the horse gives out and get up early and milk the cow."

"Fresh milk tastes good early in the morning," I said.

"Leave the milkman taste it," she said. "Can I drop you?"

"At the park," I said, and we hopped in a cab.

"To the Stadium," she said, and while we drove the cabbie looked at me a long time in the mirror until he finally told me who I was and started through the details of the present situation, Washington would fold and Goldman was 4 ahead of Babe Ruth and he was glad to see McGonigle back out of the army, and she said to me, "How many thousands of clucks do you think there are to the square mile?" I said I did not know. "If I was to marry," she said, "I would marry a man of over 80 in rocky health with a wad as thick as a mattress."

I begun singing "Mother," singing "M is for the million things you give me, O is for your only growing old," and she laughed. "But I am far from marrying," she said, "though the offers roll in every day. I have 100 men on the line that draw down a good bit more than a third-string catcher."

"I believe you," I said, which I had no reason not to. She is a professional, and good, or so I hear, and I hopped out, saying "Thanks for the lift," and she blew me a kiss and said "Good luck," and I said "See you around," which is what you say to people you hope you seen the last of.

We beat Washington that day, which was getaway day, Blondie Biggs going most of the distance but needing help from F.D.R. in the ninth, and we went down to Washington on the same train in first place, no strings attached.

A little ways out of New York Joe come up the isle and said to me, "Quick, Author, while Pearson is dozing off," and we went back a couple cars where Washington was. We begun dealing, straight Casino for maybe 15 minutes until along come this freckle-face boy name of Sampson Opper, an outfielder, his first year up from the farms, a good ballplayer. I believe he can get rid of the ball faster than anybody in the business except maybe Vincent Carucci, very young and very ashamed of it and very proud of being up. If he could of wore a sign saying I AM A BIGTIME BALLPLAYER NOW in 3 different colors he would of done so, and had it tattooed across his head. He stood behind Joe with his hands in his belt and watched and finally said, "Casino?"

Joe finished the hand and turned around and give Opper a quick look. "Hello son," he said. "You traveling all by yourself?"

Then we played another hand, and Opper moved down beside the table so Joe could see him better. But we never looked up, only played Casino again, and Opper said, "I do not suppose you would mind a third person."

"No," said Joe, "go see if one of the ballplayers wishes to sit in."

"I am a ballplayer," said Opper.

"Is that so?" said Joe, still never looking up. "Good luck to you, son. Do not drink nor smoke nor gamble for money and you will make the grade. Do not go professional before you are ready."

"I am Sampson Opper," said he, and he sat, but we did not deal him in. Instead we went into Tegwar now, no rules a-tall, and Opper was kind of glad he did not put his cash on the table. But we went back to Casino then, and he pulled his cash out of his pocket, and we played one hand of Casino and one of Tegwar, first one and then the other, and he kept tapping his fingers on his money, deciding if he should leave it on the table or put it back and get up and out, and the boys begun to gather, not only Washington but many of the Mammoths down from our own car, standing in a crowd behind us like a crowd around an accident, some of the boys standing on the seats to see until all of a sudden we dealt him in, and he was in if he liked it or not, and he said, "What in hell we playing?"

"More of the same," said Joe.

"I am not sure if I am clear on some of the new rules," said Opper.

"What new rules?" said Joe. "There ain't been a rule changed since the Black Sox scandal. Big League Tegwar is Big League Tegwar, known to every big-time ballplayer from Boston to Kansas City," and he went on and on, how it was first played among ballplayers in the days of the underhand pitch, and passed along from club to club and father to son until there was nobody did not know it, not the lowest punk on the lowest cellar club, and yet it was known to ballplayers, and ballplayers only, once they made the grade, and we kept dealing and saying, "That will be 14 cents to Joe and 12 cents to Author," and Opper kept shoving the money at us, and everybody was beginning to bust, yet silent, everybody there now, both clubs, and I would of begun busting myself except I seen Bruce amongst the crowd, and he said nothing to me, though yet he said, "That was a fine thing, Arthur, to run off and play Tegwar when I was dozing," and I said to Joe, "I think Bruce Pearson wishes to play."

"3 is enough," said Joe.

"Then leave him sit in for me," I said.

"No!" said Joe. "No! No! What are you 2 anyway? Are you Romeo and Juliet?"

"Then I must quit," said I, and I turned my cards over and rose up and pushed back through the crowd.

"I will make you sorry for this," said Joe, and he called me a couple dirty names again, and Romeo and Juliet, and he also later made me sorry.

But I do not know what else I could of done. I was sorry to quit but would of been sorrier still if I stood and played, one of those cockeyed deals where you are wrong if you do and wrong if you don't, like the old-time riddle where the fellow says, "Suppose you were up to your neck in a barrel of shit and a fellow was tossing baseballs at you. What do you do? Do you duck?"

CHAPTER 9

We beat Washington Wednesday night, our first night game, and Thursday afternoon, which meant we now beat them 4 times in 4 starts. We beat them 16 times in 22 starts all summer, leaving no doubt in my mind which was the best ball club. The reason they stood up there all year was they fatted up on the second division. They beat Boston 17 times and Brooklyn 18 and Chicago 20, though we had no idea in the very beginning but kept looking over our shoulder at Cleveland and Pittsburgh and even St. Louis and wondering who we had to beat, never figuring it would be Washington.

I beat Brooklyn Sunday, 6–4, not the best ball game I ever pitched if I do say so myself. Sid made me a gift of it with 2 home runs, 7 on his belt now, 4 up on Babe Ruth. He was pretty sick and tired hearing about Babe Ruth. "I am Sid Goldman and not Babe Ruth," he said, "and I would appreciate everybody keeping their trap shut in the matter," which we done, though of course the paper done no such a thing but hauled out the records every time Sid connected. Holly says there might be a few people do not know who Babe Ruth was. Babe Ruth hit 60 home runs in 1927, before I was even born, the most home runs anybody ever hit.

I seen in the paper where Dutch was worried about Jonah Brooks not getting a base hit since the seventh inning Tuesday, April 19, though if he was it did not show. Jonah caught all through April until the second game of a Sunday doubleheader with Pittsburgh, which Bruce caught, the first complete game he caught since Thursday, July 9, 1954, according to the paper.

He done well. I pitched and won. The sun was low, and the lower it gets the faster I look. He missed a couple signs but he banged out 2 hits, one a double, and was now batting 500 on the year, 6 for 3, his name at the top of the Sunday averages. It was the fourth game I won with the year nowheres even begun practically. I was beginning to get the sniff of that old bonus clause. However, Jonah was back in the lineup Tuesday night against Chicago, and then we wound up the home stand beating Washington 2 out of 3 over Friday and the week-end. Sid hit Number 9 and 10 and we went west 3½ games on top. He was still 4 up on Babe Ruth.

Why shouldn't Dutch of kept Jonah playing, though the paper kept crying "Weak stick, weak stick" and writing long articles about it if Sid didn't happen to hit a home run for them to quick drag out Babe Ruth all over again instead? The power was on and the pitching was steady and it would of made no sense benching Jonah.

Dutch kept tinkering all right, but not with Jonah. He kept juggling the order, and when that didn't work he kept juggling the bench, now yanking Canada and playing McGonigle, now yanking Vincent and playing Lawyer Longabucco, once even playing McGonigle in left though I know he would almost rather die than use a left-hander there, now yanking Coker and Perry and playing Ugly at short and Tyler or Wash Washburn at second, seeing what I seen and what the boys would of also seen if they cut out the horseshit long enough and what the paper would of seen if they ever stopped looking up Babe Ruth. It was not pulling like a club. It was 2½ and 3 and 3½ on top all through the west, but it should of been 4½ or 5 by now. It was firing along because me and Sid and Pasquale and Van Gundy and Herb Macy were turning in the work, but you cannot go all the way on a few bats or a few arms. The summer was still very young. The club was not a club, which I personally blame on Joe Jaros to begin with and Goose and Horse and the 4 colored boys and everybody else that couldn't get in the act quick enough, thinking they had the flag in their pocket in May and looking around for amusement, thinking it was amusement when what it was was horseshit pure and simple.

Every time he seen us he said, "Romeo and Juliet," and I laughed, and after he said it about 20,000 times I said, "Joe, I will leave you in on a little secret. After the first 20,000 times a joke stops being funny all of a sudden." But he kept on, and when he called me "Romeo" I called him "Grand-

father," which he is proud to be except if you say it
that certain way, and he stopped for a couple days
and then called me "Romeo" again, and I said,
"Romeo was a great lover, Joe. Are you jealous? If
you are so jealous, Joe, I believe you can buy these
little pills give you back your pep in bed you lost
when you were young like me," and he said, "You
mind your tongue, boy, and be careful how you rag
your elders."

"Do not pull your rank on me," I said. "Give is
give and take is take."

Ugly said the same. It must of been Ugly passed
the word along to Dutch because I know Ugly and
Joe didn't speak for awhile. Dutch put the squelch
on Joe. But he was mad and lonely. He walked
around with a deck of cards in his pocket and nobody to play Tegwar with.

Bruce never minded. He said, "They love to rag
us, Arthur," and I said they did, and I waited for
him to discover they weren't ragging me, only him.
It takes him longer than most to discover a thing
like that. Call *me* a name and I call you a worse
one back, and the laugh is on you in the end, but
call Bruce a name and he can never think of one to
call you back. It is easy pickings, like punching a
punching bag that can not punch back. Maybe it
would be a smart move some time to string up a
bag in the clubhouse and leave people punch it
when their gripe is on.

Horse and Goose picked it up, calling him "Juliet" and raking up all the oldest gags in the world,
saying, "How tall are you, Pearson?" and he said
"5'11"," and they said, "We never seen a pile of

shit so high before," or saying, "By the way, Bruce, what is your whole complete name?" and he said, "Bruce William Pearson, Jr.," and they said, "Well, up yours, Bruce William Pearson, Jr.," until quite a number of the boys told Goose and Horse why not cut out the horseshit and play baseball.

I said the same. I said, "One of these days we are going to start looking around behind us for Washington, but they will not be there because they will be up ahead of us," which was true, for we could not shake them off.

"It is a club of crying kids," said Horse. "It ain't the old Mammoths."

"If you rag them they run and tell Dutch," said Goose. "The game is gone to hell, and I am glad to be fading from the scene."

"Why not just fade quiet?" said Coker.

"Why not just shut your Polack mouth?" said Goose, "before I plaster it shut?"

"Why not try?" said Coker, and he stood up, and Goose stood up. But nothing come of it.

Goose hit 35 last summer. He was drinking quite a bit, borrowing 5 here and 5 there and going off alone and drinking it up and waking up with a head in the morning. One day he fell asleep on the bench in St. Louis, and Dutch seen him and begun to say something but then only turned around again. What would of been the use?

Holly says, "Henry, people will wonder how boys get such names as "Goose" and "Horse" and "Piss". You must tell them."

"It is all in "The Southpaw"," I said.

"Then tell them the pages," she said, and I said I would, and I spent about an hour flipping through the pages and could not find where I said it, though I know I did. I guess I ought to know.

"You find the pages," I said, "and write them down."

"That is all I have on my mind," she said. "I have washing and diapering the baby to do, and *your* mail to answer and *your* tax to be figuring out and *your* insurance racket and *your* food and *your* car to be running in and getting greased and *your* telephone to be answering all day, and now all I am supposed to do is start reading *your* book all over again."

"Do you wish me to finish this book before the winter meetings?" I said. "If so, find the goddam pages."

"I will not," she said, which she must of meant because she never did. "And do not swear around the baby."

"When she is old enough to understand I will stop," I said, and I will, or at least I hope I will, though I do not always do everything. All winter all I was going to do was lay around and play with the baby, and then I never done so. I will certainly do it next winter or die trying.

We come back from the first swing west by way of Washington, 3 games on top, and Dutch said in the Washington clubhouse, "Boys, tonight we start shaking the son of a bitches loose for good. You know," he said, "to me they are like a fly buzzing around your head, where you sit and watch it awhile without ever raising your hand against it." He jumped off the scale and pulled up a chair and sat down. "Like this," he said, sitting with his arms folded across his letters and his eyes looking at the ceiling, watching that fly go back and forth. "B-z-z-z," he said. "Go ahead, you old Washington fly. Buzz me one more time and I will snatch you out of the air, and you will buzz no more."

From over in George's corner comes the sound of a buzzing. It is Roberto Diego going, "B-z-z-z-z, B-z-z-z-z," putting it in Spanish for George. Red never does it like that. Dutch might talk for 5 minutes, and then Red boils it all own to 15 words, but not Diego. He must give it the full treatment, and when he was done George give it back to him, "B-z-z-z-z, B-z-z-z-z."

"Forget it," said Dutch to Diego. "This is not so much for George as for certain other persons to begin with. B-z-z-z-z goes the fly until you say to yourself, 'Enough is enough. I have give you over a month now to trail along $2\frac{1}{2}$ and 3 and $3\frac{1}{2}$ games behind, and now I think I will reach up and squash out your miserable life,' " and up he jumped, and up Diego Roberto jumped. Up on the scale went Dutch, and the weights all rattled on the stick. "Fly! You are done for! Whack!"

"Whack!" went Diego Roberto.

"But only one thing is wrong," said Dutch. "I look down in my hand and I have no fly, and I think to myself how could I of missed it when I already seen the circuit once around and know I am the only club in the league. How could I of missed?" He sat down in his chair again, and Diego Roberto sat down. "The fly is still going B-z-z-z-z, B-z-z-z-z."

"B-z-z-z-z, B-z-z-z-z," said Diego.

"Forget it," said Dutch. "I said forget it."

"Forget?" said Diego. "What is forget?" He whipped out his dictionary. "Mister, forget is not remember, but is too quick to not remember. She just now happen."

"Forget it means fuck it," said Dutch.

Roberto threw his dictionary away.

"Do you know why I missed the fly? Do you know why the fly is not dead? Do you wish to know why it was 2½ and 3 and 3½ and could never be shook, and maybe as time went by come up from behind and stole the flag right off New York? Do you wish to know? Tell me if you wish to know?"

"Yes sir," said the boys. "Yes sir, Dutch." "Sure, boss."

"Because he flew right through my fingers is why, if you must know, which he should of never done because on paper he was no club a-tall but only a couple dozen men and boys dressed up in Washington suits. And if you wish to know why he flew through my fingers I will tell you that, too. The reason was because my fingers did not work together. The first finger says to the second finger, "I do not like you because you will not play cards with me," and the third finger says to the fourth,

"I do not like you from way back," and the next finger goes back to the first and says, "You should hear what finger Number 2 been saying about you," and the third finger says to the fourth, "leave you and me cut finger Number 5 dead if we see him, and tell our goddam wife do the same, and bring up the kids likewise." Boys, this is suicide. I seen it happen on other clubs, and I was always glad. But it never happens on any club of mine if I can squash it, and by God I will. As a starter there will be 2 things. There will be no more cards and no more borrowing nor lending. If anybody owes you money write it down on a piece of paper and we will see if we can clear it through the front office. And tonight will be the beginning of the new way of things."

"Time, Dutch," said Egg, for Dutch forgets the clock when he gives you a lecture. "OK," said Dutch, "leave us go play real ball," and we all shot out, and when we got there it was raining, though we begun anyways, and Dutch did not like it and said, "Stall," and the boys stalled, and Frank Porter come over to the dugout and said, "Dutch, tell your boys stop stalling."

"It is raining," said Dutch. "Somebody will get hurt."

"It is I who decides if it is raining," said Porter. "I say it is not."

"Maybe not," said Dutch, "but water is coming down out of the sky, and moonbeams are dripping off your nose," and the boys went on stalling all the same, and Porter kept coming over and complaining. "I have no control over my boys," said Dutch.

"Then you are no use on the bench," said Porter. "Get out!"

"With pleasure," said Dutch. "May you die in boiled oil," and he went back in the clubhouse, the first time he been give the thumb all year, though not the last, and Joe took over and said, "Stall," and the boys stalled some more, and soon the rain come down hard, and Porter called it off.

And then not 30 minutes after the lecture, not 30 minutes, Perry and Keith and Jonah and Wash Washburn started singing "K-K-K-Katie, B-B-B-Beautiful Katie" in the shower again, only sticking these filthy and vulgar words to it.

"They are ragging us, Arthur," said Bruce.

"Yes," I said.

"You know," he said, "they are ragging me more than they are ragging you any more."

"You bastards," I shouted. "Did it all go in one ear and out the other?"

They pretended they did not hear me.

"Honey lamb," sung Perry, "tell me if I am the first."

And Keith sung out in this high, girly voice, "No, my sweetie pie, but there been only 4,000 before you."

"Sweet husband pie," sung Wash Washburn, "that will be $20."

"B-B-B-But I am your husband," sung Perry.

"It makes no difference," sung Wash, and Jonah laughed. The whole place shook when Jonah laughed, and you would of laughed yourself to hear him, laughing and hanging on the shower sprays to keep from falling, and finally falling down in a heap and rolling over and laughing, too weak to rise, and Dutch heard them, and he come out of his office and said, "Turn off the water," and they done so. "That will be $100, boys, to the 4 of you," and they quieted down fast then and begun figuring out if he meant 100 each or only 25. I never did know what he meant myself, and I never did know what they paid. In the end Dutch probably kicked it all back anyhow.

CHAPTER 10

"Arthur," said Bruce to me, "how do I change my beneficiary?"

"Who do you wish to change it to?" said I.

"To Katie," said he. "She is going to marry me at last."

"When?" said I. "When you change your beneficiary?"

"Arthur," said he, "you got no right to tell me who I can and who I can not change my beneficiary to."

"Why did she not marry you last year?" said I. "Or the year before?"

"She never loved me before."

"Before what?" said I.

"Before now," he said.

"How is now different?" said I.

"Will you change it for me," said he, "or not?"

"I will write away to Arcturus," I said.

"When?"

"Tuesday."

"Why not now?" said he.

"Because it is time to go to the park," I said.

"You have time," he said. "I seen you dash off many a letter in the cab or standing against the wall."

"This is a matter of $50,000," said I. "Such a large figure must be handled sitting down with plenty of time to wet your pencil."

"Very well," said he, "but do not forget and do it Tuesday."

Holly hit town that night, her belly button all punched out and 600 Dollars kicking up a fuss. "He is practicing slides," said I.

"This is nothing," she said. "You should feel him when he is swinging 3 bats before taking his swipes."

"He will be no hitter," said I.

"Sid sure been hitting," said she.

"He is neck and neck with Babe Ruth," said I.

"But something is wrong," said she, "for you should of long since shook Washington."

It was good having her there. It was good talking to somebody that knew the truth, for it was heavy carrying it around alone. We shoved the beds together, her in Bruce's bed, though the linen new. Bruce was up at Katie's all night. "I think Katie knows," I said, and I asked her did I have the right to swindle him out of a change of beneficiary, and she said I did, and she laid for a long time tapping her teeth with her finger like she does, and she said, "I am just now elected the new Change of Beneficiary Department of the Arcturus Company."

"That is a pretty damn smart idea," said I, "even if I do say so myself."

"I am thinking for 2," she said.

"I personally been doing the same for some months now," I said. "It is keeping me hopping. It is a strain."

"Where do you stow your official Arcturus paper?" she said.

"In the flat desk in the little bedroom," I said.

"It is no longer there," she said. "There is a crib there now."

"Where is the flat desk?" I said.

"In the play-room," said she.

"Whatwhat?" I said. "In the what?"

"In the play-room, which was formerly your ex-work-room," she said.

"Where is my work-room?" said I.

"In the kitchen," she said.

"Why not the living-room by the fire?" said I.

"It is too near the baby's room," she said. "You are libel to keep him awake swearing."

"I never swear," said I. "Or if I do I must of picked it up somewheres."

We seen the first game of the doubleheader Memorial Day from the Moorses box on the third-base side. There was a couple automobile people in it plus the Prince of Persia. I rather sit on the first-base side myself except I wished to watch Murtha work, a right-hander, the same boy Bruce stole off and told the boys how, which we would of done Memorial Day again except we hardly got anybody on base.

Down the right-field line, just shaded fair from the flagpole, the fans went mad when Sid come up, standing and hollering, "Here! Here!" upper and lower decks both and holding up these big signs with the number "16" painted red, meaning Sid should swat Number 16 in there. They probably had "17" and "18" and "19" along as well, but Sid swatted nothing off Murtha, and nobody else did neither. The power was off. We had a little rally going in the fourth, but Jonah popped out. We started moving again in the seventh, and Dutch yanked him altogether and sent Ugly up to hit, and Ugly drove in a run, the first and only run we scored off Murtha, and Bruce took over for Jonah. It was 2–1 at the time. I said "Goodby" to Holly, and she said "Good luck," and I went down and got dressed. It was 5–1 a minute later, for Kussuth homered off Van Gundy, the best hitter Boston ever owned since Casey Sharpe. He give me more trouble all year than all the rest of Boston lumped together. Dutch yanked Van Gundy.

I no sooner hit the clubhouse than he walked in, Van Gundy did, and I said, "What did he hit off you?" and he said, "I do not know any more. It makes no difference. You simply can not get the son of a bitch out. I think I rather face Goldman," and he tossed his glove down and kicked it across the floor, a drop-kick, like in football. Mick picked it up and dusted it off. Poor Mick! He must greet you alone in your worst minutes.

I got dressed and went out. The board showed Washington smearing Brooklyn all over the place, which cut our lead to 1½, the lowest it been all year. Bruce picked up a hit in the ninth, a hard single pumped down the line in left, and that made me feel better, though not much, and as soon as it was over I begun warming with Goose.

And that was really the big switch, when everything changed or at least begun changing.

I naturally had no idea. I walked over towards the warmup rubber with Goose, not talking, for we never talk, me and him. There was never anything to say. He had a couple balls in his hand, rolling one down his arm and giving it a little ride with the inside of his elbow, popping it back in the same hand again, a man I played ball 4 years with, rode trains with, and showered with, but never liked, nor him me, and I said, "I wonder what it is a good idea trying throwing that Kussuth," but I never got an answer, for the loudspeaker said, "Ladies and gentlemen, the national anthem of Persia," and we stood still a minute while they played it through, and the Prince of Persia took a bow, and Goose seen Holly in the box and said, "How is your wife, Author?" which for a minute never registered because he never asked me such a thing before, never cared about me, would not of thought much about it one way or the other if I dropped dead. "You know," he said, "I ain't took my wife out to the ball game in 11 years."

"Take her when we hit Chicago," I said.

"I actually first laid eyes on her in a ball park," he said. He was looking at me, I could see his eyes. They were halfway between brown and gold. His beard was 3 days old, and his breath stunk from these mints he ate to stink out the liquor he drunk. Sweat was hanging off the hair of his chin. He never even bothered wiping it off any more. It sparkled in the sun. "I probably looked like you," he said. "I shaved my face every day, and every new Kussuth that come along I went around asking everybody what to throw him. But there was Traphagen and all, and finally the only person that loved me I bashed her in the eye now and then to keep up my spirit. Yet I love her. Or at least I better start loving her again because I am all washed up and broke and will wind up in skid row without help."

"It is never too late for an annuity," said I.

"No, no, it is much too late. I am too old."

"With 7 or 8,000 Series money," said I, "I can fix you up with a plan as a starter. 7 or 8,000 will take up a lot of back slack."

"I was thinking of asking you," he said, "only a fellow hates to ask a punk of 23 for tips on things."

"What do you own?" I said.

"Own? You know what I own? I own a couple catcher's mitts and a baseball signed by each and every member of the 1944 Mammoths and a medal pinned on me by General Douglas McCarthy. Put them all together and you can get $5 in any hockshop in Chicago. What I own is debts."

"We will declare bankruptcy," I said.

"How?" he said.

"I will show you," I said. "But you must do me one favor. You must lay off Pearson."

"A man has got to have a little fun," he said.

"He is dying," I said.

The balls dropped out of his hand and he bent down and picked them up and then dropped them again and left them roll. "You mean dying? You mean where he is libel to blank out for good and ever? You mean soon? You mean any day?"

"They give him 6 months to 15 years," I said.

"Does Dutch know?"

"No," said I. "You must not tell him. You must not tell anybody, for Dutch would cut him loose in a minute."

"I can not believe it," he said.

"Only me and you know," I said.

"Only us will ever know," he said, and we shook hands, which must of looked peculiar out there, 2 fellows shaking hands. "We better start warming," he said.

I was blinding fast all day. In the beginning I could not think, and I was wobbly. "You fool!" said I to myself. "You fool, with your foot in your mouth for a change." I was sure I done wrong, and I wished I could take it back. I felt like going down the line and telling Goose it was only a gag. But it passed, and I become lost, thinking only of the hitter.

Goose was steady. The first couple innings I kept getting behind my hitter, and he kept pulling me out. He sung a little, singing, "No bopay ho, no bopay ho," meaning "No ballplayer here, no ballplayer here," until his wind give out along around the seventh. I could see how he was once a top-flight catcher, for he handles you nice, second fiddle all his life to Red Traphagen, but top-flight all the same, doing most of your worrying for you. He kept flashing 2 signs, and I flashed back the one I liked best, and he sung, "Lefflie, lefflie," "Leave her fly, leave her fly," playing mostly by memory now, no legs, no arm, but steady, and I give up only one hit in 8 innings.

It was o–o in the top of the ninth when a pinch-hitter name of Macklin slapped a single off me and was sacrificed along by Aleck Olson. Macklin was the first runner that reached second off me all afternoon. I was getting set to face Kussuth with 2 down and Macklin still on second when Dutch signed for the pick-off. What it is is the pitcher and the second baseman go into a count, counting "One cigarette, 2 cigarette, 3 cigarette, 4 cigarette, 5 cigarette," and after cigarette 5 the second baseman cuts for second and the pitcher whirls and throws. You must count exactly the same speed, the 2 of you, you and the second baseman. Many a time Dutch will say in the clubhouse, "Count by cigarette," and the pitchers and Perry and Tyler and Wash Washburn all stand and count together in their head, "One cigarette, 2 cigarette, 3 cigarette, 4 cigarette, 5 cigarette," and then all whirl and throw while Perry and Tyler and Wash all cut, all winding up their count on the same exact breath, and I signed, "OK, I got it," adjusting my cap with the glove hand, and Perry signed that he also had it, singing "This hitter is much of a phonus bolonus. This hitter is much of a phonus bolonus," Coker signing, Canada leaning in, ready to break and back in case the throw went wild, and on the second "bolonus" we begun counting, Coker drifting off towards third, Perry off down towards first, making Macklin feel comfortable with a big lead, me toing in and counting, Perry counting, "One cigarette, 2 cigarette, 3 cigarette, 4 cigarette, 5 cigarette," and then I whirled and threw, and Perry broke and dove across the bag and took the throw, and Macklin roared back in but seen he could not make it, and dug, backing and turning and heading for third, Perry up off his belly and running him down the line a little and firing to George, Macklin spinning again and George starting down the line after him, me backing George, and George fired to Coker, and Coker to me. Macklin reversing and reversing and reversing again, back and forth, me firing to Perry then, and Perry shouting "I got him," and starting after Macklin and catching him halfway and putting the tag on the son of a bitch.

Sid led off our ninth, and it looked like extra innings. There was a new Boston pitcher name of Debelak, and he took his final throws and said he was ready, and Sid stepped in and fixed his feet and wiped his hands and set his cap and finally looked down at the plate and told the ump dust it off. The fans were not shouting "Here! Here!" any more, and not waving Number 16 in the air neither. They were bushed. A ballplayer must never be bushed playing ball all year but a fan is in title to be bushed sitting on their ass keeping score. It is a cockeyed world. He stepped back in and got set all over again, his feet, his hands, his cap. Then he stepped out again and took a fresh chew of gum from his pocket and unwrapped it and stuck it in his mouth and put the old piece in the wrapper and wrapped it up and told the batboy come get it. Sid can't stand pieces of paper on the ground. Then he stepped back in again and fixed his feet and wiped his hands and set his cap, and Debelak threw, and Sid swung, and it rode on a line, like on a string, clearing the wall in right and probably punched a hole in somebody's Number 16.

That was Number 7 for me. I lost only 3 by then. I led both leagues in E. R. A. and was about tied with Rob McKenna in strikeouts. I smelled 20 and maybe even 25. My weight was down to 205½. I was still working every fourth day and feeling awful good.

Katie took us to dinner that night at a place called The Green Cow, $8 a plate, food extra. She looked at Holly's belly and said, "I trust it ain't catching," and the management tried to throw me out because I had no tie. Katie said, "Throw him out and you throw out me and all my trade with me," and the management said "Begging your pardon" in French. Bruce said he doubted that there was any such a thing as a green cow, and Katie said, "There must not be if my little old future husband says so." She called him her little old future husband about every 15 minutes, and they held hands when they walked. I would of puked if it been any less expensive. She dropped $56 down The Green Cow plus tips, and we went up to her place afterwards, the first time me and Holly been back to 66 Street in 2 years.

They all drunk a lot of wine except me. The telephone kept ringing, and I sat by it, answering it, saying, "Police Commissioner" and "Vice Squad" and "Dragnet! My name is Friday. My partner is Joe Smith. Dum da dum dum. Dum da dum dum" until after awhile it stopped.

I could see that she knew. But she was never sure if I knew she knew, and I give her nothing to go on, always saying to myself, pitching or anywheres else, "Half the fight is knowing, and the other half is not telling." She also played it close. There was 50,000 in a bundle, and she was hot after it.

She was extremely gorgeous, that night or any other. She drives you mad yet never gives you any kind of a come-on, never waggles her parts around like a girl in business might do, never speaks of bed but makes you think of it because you smell her when she comes near, and she touches you without ever touching you. Holly and Bruce got silly with the wine and wound up talking crosswise across Katie, foolish talk, talking about me mostly, each of them going the other one one better every time, telling things about me too wonderful for me to believe, and I talked across them at Katie, not wishing to talk but listen and maybe get a line on her, but then doing most of the talking myself, like

I was the one with the wine in my hand. I was hunting like mad for something to trade with in case the time come to talk trade, but I never knew much about her, then nor ever, where she come from nor why nor how long.

Me and Holly left around midnight. She kissed Bruce at the door, or tried to, but he drawed back, and Katie looked at us and smiled and said, "After all, what would a man's little old future wife think?" and they stood in the door holding hands.

CHAPTER 11

The following Thursday night he either had the attack or else only thought he did. I never stopped to worry which it was but flew out of bed and started waking up doctors. "Get back to bed and keep warm," said I, and finally a doctor answered, a fellow name of Charleston P. Chambers, M. D., and I give him our room and told him get over in a hurry.

"Wait now," said he. "Just what is the trouble?" and I told him, and he told me tell him get back in bed and keep warm, which I already knew from the sheet the doctors give me in Minnesota, and the doctor yawned a couple times and said he would be right over as soon as he was shaved and dressed and located his chauffeur, and he begun telling me he had this loony chauffeur that had a wife in 2 different places, one on the east side and one on the west, and he was never sure which wife he might be at.

"Never mind your chauffeur," I said. "I will have a fellow meet you in a cab," and I wrapped a towel around me and flew down the hall and pounded on Goose's door, and Horse opened it and said, "Come on in, Author," and I shoved past him and shook Goose awake and said, "I need help."

"What for?" he said.

"You know," said I.

"Oh," he said, and he was out of bed and in his pants in 15 seconds. "What do I do?" he said. "You can talk. Horse knows, for I told him."

"I thought you promised you would never tell a soul in the world," I said.

"Only my roomie," he said.

I give him the doctor's address and went back to Bruce. He looked OK, only breathing a little hard was all, and cold, and I piled blankets on him and stuck a hot water bottle in bed and sat down beside him. The sky was just beginning to light up a little, the quiet time when all the air is clean and you can hear birds, even in the middle of New York City, the time of day you never see except by accident, and you always tell yourself, "I must get up and appreciate this time of day once in awhile," and then you never do. Don't ask me why. "I am sorry to of woke you," he said.

"Make it back to me some other time," I said.

"I do not think there will be another time," he said. "Tomorrow is my birthday. I suppose my mother put a package in the mail. You can keep it when it comes, or cash it in if it is something you do not need. Give Katie a call."

"Lay still and save your energy," I said.

"I wish Katie was here," he said. "Probably Dutch will bring Piney Woods up. He is from

Georgia, and that is something, ain't it? You know, I will bet I am the first ballplayer ever died at the top of the Sunday averages." He was 12 for 7, 583. "Tell Sid I hope he beats Babe Ruth."

"All these things you will take care of yourself," said I, "if you will only lay still and save your energy."

"Is the doctor coming?"

"Yes," said I. "Goose went after him."

"Why Goose?" said he.

"Why not?" said I. "He was the first person I thought of. He has a heart of gold underneath."

"It just never really showed before," he said.

"People are pretty damn OK when they feel like it," I said.

"Probably you told him or something," he said.

"I never told a soul," said I.

"Probably everybody be nice to you if they knew you were dying," he said.

"Everybody knows everybody is dying," I said. "That is why people are nice. You all die soon enough, so why not be nice to each other?"

"Hold on to me," he said, and I took his shoulder and held it, and he reached up and took my hand, and I left him have it, though it felt crazy holding another man's hand. Yet after awhile it did not feel too crazy any more.

Soon the doctor walked in, all shaved and dressed, which really made me quite annoyed that he took so much time, and Goose and Horse with him. "Who is the sick ballplayer?" he said. "You do not look sick. Open your mouth." He whipped out a thermometer and stuck it in, and he took his pulse, looking up at Horse and saying, "Who are you?"

"Horse Byrd," said Horse.

"How did you ever get such a name?" said the doctor.

"I am a little large," said Horse.

"I would of never noticed," said the doctor, and he read the thermometer and shook it down, and he read the "Instructions for the physician" and went back and examined Bruce some more and asked him questions, and when he was done he sat down on the other bed and thought awhile. "I think it is something else," he said.

"You mean something else besides what they said in Minnesota?" I said. My heart jumped up.

"I could not say about that," he said. "I only mean I can see no danger as of this minute."

"It sure felt like it," said Bruce.

The doctor got up and walked back and forth, now and then stopping and looking at Bruce and asking one more question, then walking again. Finally he begun packing away his gear. "Boys," said he, "pardon me for asking a stupid question. But I actually thought Babe Ruth died some while ago."

"He actually did," I said.

"Yet I keep seeing Babe Ruth down there in the corner of the page every morning, plus this other boy."

"Goldman," I said.

"Which club is Goldman with?"

"Ours," I said.

"Pardon me for asking one more stupid question," he said. "No doubt I am no better than an Australian or somebody for not knowing a thing like this, but what club are *you* with?"

I told him. "Now you can do *me* one favor," I said. "You can send the bill to me in Perkinsville, New York, and also not leak anything to the paper."

"I am not in the habit of leaking my house calls to the paper," he said. "Tell Goldman I hope he strikes out Babe Ruth."

I lost to Chicago that night, though they are usually the softest touch in the world for me. But I never got back to sleep until noon, and when I did it was one of these hot, sweaty sleeps. Goose was tired, too. He been catching all week, Dutch benching Jonah and hoping Goose would power up the lower end of the order. He done so, too. We won 4 in a row between the game I won Memorial Day and the game I lost Friday night to Chicago which I would of never lost if I had any sleep under my belt. Dutch said he believed he would now rotate me every 5 days instead of every 4, which he done, rotating Van Gundy every 6 instead of 5, starting Lindon Burke and Blondie Biggs fairly regular now, and spot-pitching Piss against right-hand clubs if his hay fever wasn't acting up too bad. Around this time of year you wake up one morning short pitchers. In the beginning you look around you, and you say, "We are certainly loaded with pitching," and then all of a sudden doubleheaders start piling up and people give out or get hurt or just simply don't show quite the stuff they had in May.

We dropped back to the 1½ cushion over Washington, though we picked it up again Saturday, a real slaughter, beating Chicago 13–3, the most runs we scored all year so far. Sid hit 2 and was now 2 up on Babe Ruth, and Pasquale and Vincent and Canada and Goose hit one apiece.

The paper now took some notice of Goose. He wrote an article called "How I Hit the Comeback Trail at 35" which a writer name of Hubert W. Nash wrote and sold and give him $250 for and the magazine said it would print when his birthday rolled around in August, but it never did. I mean the magazine never printed it. I took 200 of the 250 and applied it against premiums and with 40 more he bought his wife a dress, saving out 10 for taxes which I told him to or else have the United States Bureau of Internal Revenue kicking down his door all winter. I did not like him hanging with the writers, for they will pump things out of you. He said he never said a word about it, and never would.

Saturday night after dinner there come a knock on the door, and in walks Goose and Horse with a birthday cake and 4 quarts of ice cream. I said to myself, "Buddy, now you seen everything." "Happy birthday," they said, and they laid the cake on the dresser and tore open the ice cream. There were 2 candles on the cake, one for the years and one to grow on. "Many happy returns of the day to you,

Bruce old pal," they said, and we said, "Same to you, boys," and we dug in. They also brung a carton of Days O Work, and Bruce said "Thanks" and picked out a chew and passed the box around, though nobody else took. "There looks like enough there to last you 15 or 20 years," said Goose.

"Do not lay it on too thick, boys," said I to myself, and I am glad to say they did not. They polished off the cake and cream and got up and took off.

Goose busted up both ends of the doubleheader Sunday with 2 doubles in the first game and a single with the bases loaded in the second, pinch-hitting for Jonah, which give us 3 out of 4 over Chicago, 7 wins in the last 8 starts.

Monday morning Bruce said to me, "You forgot to write away to Arcturus," and I snapped my finger and said, "So I did. As soon as I get back from drill I will." It was an open day, but Dutch calls drills on open days if things are going good, believing in keeping in stride. He also calls them when things are going poorly, believing that a drill on an open day will *break* your stride. I guess he knows because it works, or else he just misses being away from the park. Whatever it was we drilled, and all the way up and all the way back and all the while getting dressed Bruce said to me, "Do not forget and write that letter," and I told him I would if he ever stopped asking.

I was standing around shagging flies when Roberto Diego come running out. "Mister," he said, "Dutch is wishing you," and in I went.

"Author," said Dutch, "meet Mr. Rogers. Mr. Rogers, meet Henry Wiggen. Author, Mr. Rogers is a detective. Close the door and sit down. Mr. Rogers been down to Bainbridge and is now on the way up to Rochester, Minnesota, filling in some facts for me. However, you can save him a trip and the club some cash by filling in the rest of the story which Mr. Rogers begun."

"I will certainly try my darnest," I said.

"Tell him what you told me," said Dutch, and Mr. Rogers begun.

"I went and hung in Bainbridge a week," said he, "and I developed the following information." He had it all jotted down on little scraps of paper, and he kept looking at them. "I seen the following people," he said. "On May 19 I seen Mr. Randy Bourne at the crate and box plant, and on May 20 I seen Mr. Dow McAmis at the County Club, and on May 21 I seen a colored man name of Leandro."

"Never mind the facts," said Dutch. "Get down to the details."

"Well," said Rogers, "I was told that along about the end of October Mr. Pearson told these various people that he was not feeling so good and went to the hospital in Atlanta, and they told him why not try up in Rochester, Minnesota, and see what been ailing you. He drove up to Minnesota and returned in January with Mr. Wiggen, telling everybody he was cured of what he had. Him and Mr. Wiggen hung in Bainbridge a month and then drove off with a girl."

"My wife," I said. "Big exciting mystery."

"I developed the information that nobody knew what was ailing him," said Rogers. He folded his papers and laid them on Dutch's desk.

"Do you get paid for doing this?" I said. "Because you developed absolutely nothing that I could not of told you and saved you a hot trip down there this time of year, plus which you developed actually less than half the truth, which I will personally fill in now for Dutch and wind up the whole matter once and forever and get back out and drill where I ought to be keeping in stride."

"Do not stall," said Dutch.

"I actually developed a lot more than this but am only giving you the bare particulars," said Rogers.

"If you actually spoke to anybody worth the while," said I, "you would of learned that Bruce has this rotten habit of running off to Atlanta maybe once or twice a month. No doubt you developed this much."

"Well, yes, as a matter of fact I did," said Rogers, "but I did not think it worth mentioning."

"Because as a detective you are from hunger," said I. "No need telling you where he went in Atlanta. Everybody knows. And you know what you sometimes pick up in them places, which he did and which he rather not have them treat in Atlanta nor anywheres else near home for fear of it getting back and troubling his mother with her heart trouble. He was ashamed. You no doubt developed the information that when he went up to Minnesota he took along his fishing and hunting gear though when he got there found all the rivers

9 feet deep in ice. He checked in, got himself shot with a few miracle drugs, flirted with the nurses, checked out, met me in Cannon Falls, went hunting, changed his mind, and back down home again."

"Goddam it," said Dutch, and he flung open his door. "Diego Roberto! Run out and get Pearson in here." Then he picked up the phone and called Doc Loftus. "Come up here," he said, and the 2 of them wandered in about the same time. "Take down your pants," said Dutch. "Are you over the clap yet?"

"Yes sir," said Bruce. "Long ago."

"Check him over," said Dutch. "All I need is the clap running through my ball club."

"Do not forget to write that letter," said Bruce to me, standing there while Doc checked him over.

"What did you do for it?" said Doc.

"Got shot with miracle drugs," said Bruce.

"He looks fine to me," said Doc. He went over and washed his hands.

"Should I head out and develop this information further in Rochester, Minnesota?" said Rogers.

"Stay with it," said Dutch. "Some things have yet to be explained."

"While I am here I might as well write out a bill," said Rogers.

"If you charge more than $1.50 you are a swindler," I said, and I went out whistling.

That night I wrote the letter saying, "Dear Sir, please send me a change of beneficiary form for my insured, Mr. Bruce William Pearson, Jr.," and his policy number underneath, and I showed it to him and slid it in the envelope and told him I would mail it this instant before I forgot, and I done so, sending it up to Holly.

Cleveland moved in and we took 2 out of 3 and they moved out and St. Louis in, and we split 2 with them, Friday night washed out, and we went west 3 games to the good.

I pitched the first afternoon in Chicago and was really my top, which was a good thing, too, because the power was off. It is usually always off in Chicago because the wind in from right plays hell with Sid and Pasquale and Vincent. You might as well stay home some days as buck that wind with left-hand hitters. Sid only hit one home run in Chicago all year.

The second day Dutch moved Pasquale back to Number 6, moving Canada up to 3 and Coker to 5 and lifting Vincent altogether and playing Lawyer Longabucco in left, and then finally how we won it Bruce hit a home run in the eight, batting for F. D. R. who relieved, the first home run Bruce hit since Friday, July 25, 1952, according to the paper, and the first home run he *ever* hit in the pinch, a high and gliding type of a drive that started out too much towards left-center but then got hung in the wind and washed over towards left, and in. Gil Willowbrook mopped up in the ninth.

But Thursday you couldn't of bought a breeze, and we sat around in the clubhouse going through the old routine where the first fellow says, "I wish I was dead," and the second fellow says, "Why do you wish you were dead?" and the first fellow says again, "Because I will go to hell." Somebody is supposed to ask, "But why should you wish to go to hell?" I asked it myself one day in St. Louis my first year up, and I had to buy everybody a coke.

"I wish I was dead," said Gil.

"Why do you wish you were dead?" said Herb.

"Because I will go to hell," said Gil, and everybody waited, and now Wash Washburn said, "But why should you wish to go to hell?"

"Because hell will be cooler than Chicago," said Gil, "and that will be cokes all around," and Wash looked at Perry, and Perry said, "I guess it will, Wash," and it was, and Dutch come out and give the lineup, Goose catching, and Goose said, "Dutch, I am hot and tired." He was breathing, and he looked beat.

"Very well," said Dutch. "Brooks will catch," and he told Doc fork out some heat pills, and Doc brung them out and we passed them around and the boys swallowed them down with their coke, all except me and maybe 3 or 4 others. No doubt they are good pills, green for heat, white for weariness, blue and yellow for pain, depending where the pain is, for many of the boys been taking them for many years, and they sometimes help, and others been taking them rather than hurt Doc's feelings, but I believe they are all the same pill colored different. "Goose," said Dutch, "why not hang in town over the weekend and meet us in Pittsburgh Monday?" and Goose said he would. He took his wife and kids to the beach and was pretty much a new man by Monday.

I believe Dutch might of regretted it, but he never said a word. We lost to Chicago on getaway day, and then we lost 2 straight in Cleveland, the first time all year we lost 3 in a row, our cushion now skinned back to 1½ again, the power sometimes off and sometimes on and many people blaming Jonah, for even if it was on it was never on in the 8 spot, and Dutch benched Jonah and started Bruce, my day to work, warm but not hot, a perfect day for baseball and a great Sunday crowd.

I was hooked up with Rob McKenna, a left-hander. I beat Rob in a 16-inning ball game one night in July of 52, Chapter 28 in "The Southpaw" if you wish to read it again, one of the ball games of my life that I remember best, but he beat me after that more than I ever beat him, or anyhow beat the club, not me. We simply never hit him. He has an overhand fast ball that fogs through with a kind of a downspin, almost a sinker, and even if you hit it you hit it in the dirt. He fogged it through that afternoon like always, and we had holes in our bats, and it made me mad because I was working good and hate to see hard work end up in the lost column. Bruce said, "He sure burns them through."

"Damn it," I said. "Do not sit there admiring him. Think how to hit the son of a bitch."

"I am thinking," he said, and I believe he must of been. He had his chew up between his front teeth, where he keeps it when he is thinking, not chewing but only thinking, for he can not do both. "I been thinking I can never hit his fast ball but can whale his curve a mile."

"I rather see you whale it than talk about it," said I.

"I could whale it," said Bruce, "if I knew when it was coming, or else I am meeting it late."

"Then study him," said I, "and figure out when it will be coming."

"I am keeping a book," he said.

"What does it say?" said I.

"It says he will throw me a curve after 2 strikes and try and clip the corner, and if he misses he will throw me still another a little closer in."

But Bruce went on hitting in the dirt all afternoon, and the boys as well, all but Sid. Sid parked Number 20 in the stands in the fourth. He was now 2 behind Babe Ruth, and we went into the eighth trailing 2–1, Canada opening it with a single, Vincent Carucci trying to push him along but bunting foul twice and finally fanning, and Coker topping a fast ball and sending a slow roller towards short which if it been any faster would of been 2 for sure, but was slow, Coker beating the relay to first, and Dutch said, "Lawyer, if Pearson gets on you hit for Author." Bruce took the 2 strikes, and he leaned in and waited for the curve, and it come, and it was maybe an inch or 2 out, and Bowron called it a ball, Cleveland beefing hard, and the crowd as well, and I remember Dutch crying above the sound, "Good eye, Pearson," Bruce leaning on his bat and waiting for

Cleveland to calm, and then stepping back in, his
jaw working and saying, "Rob McKenna is only a
country boy like me, or else a country boy from the
city," Rob looking down at Coker on first, then
looking in, and kicking and pitching, Bruce counting on the curve, set for it, swinging, and when he
hit it you knew it was hit and never looked for it,
Coker tearing for second full speed and then slow-
ing and jogging on around and waiting at the plate
for Bruce, and shaking his hand. Longabucco sat
down, and I took my swipes, looking for the 2
strikes first, and then the curve, and swinging on
the curve, but fanning. The damn trouble is that
knowing what is coming is only half the trick. You
have still got to hit it. We took it, 3–2.

Goose caught the rest of the way through the
west, and things held up. We played 3 at night in
Pittsburgh, and 2 out of 3 at night in St. Louis, and
it was cooler. I knew Goose would not last the year,
and I am positive Dutch did, too, but Dutch was
now past worrying about the year. He was nursing
things along day by day, now 2, now 2½, pretty
much stuck with what he had. There was no use
hoping for miracles. Catchers do not drop out of
the sky. You have the people you have, and you
know what you are up against, and all you can
hope is your people will pull together, and if they
do you will also get a little help from wind and
weather and Mother Luck and the schedule and
the umps and charity bounces.

Goose brung his boy back to Pittsburgh with

him, halfway through High School with pimples all over his face name of Andy, the first time in his life he ever been out of Chicago. Doc give him pills for the pimples, and he stood with us until around July 4, a nice kid, but tough, always trying to talk out of the side of his mouth and swearing like 90 when Goose wasn't around. He drilled with us, all style but no results until Jonah told him one day, "Boy, catch the ball first and pose for your photo later." Goose left him strictly alone on the ball field.

St. Louis beat me 3–0. How can you win without runs? I had an 11–5 record when we started home from St. Louis Sunday night, but I actually never give it much of a thought nor stopped to think how close I was to the bonus clause. I know that nobody will ever believe me, so why I even bother to write it down is beyond me, but it is true. When your roomie is libel to die any day on you you do not think about bonus clauses, and that is the truth whether anybody happens to think so or not. Your mind is on *now* if you know what I mean. You might tell yourself 100 times a day, "Everybody dies sooner or later," and that might be true, too, which in fact it is now that I wrote it, but when it is happening sooner instead of later you keep worrying about what you say *now*, and how you act *now*. There is no time to say, "Well, I been a heel all week but I will be better to him beginning Monday" because Monday might never come.

CHAPTER 12

We got home from St. Louis very late Monday night. There was some kind of a wreck on the railroad, and Dutch yanked Van Gundy and Briggs off the train in Indianapolis and sent them home by air for the full night sleep. When we finally got there there was a letter from Holly, or I suppose you might say from the new Change of Beneficiary Department of the Arcturus Company saying the man in charge went out of town and wouldn't be back for a couple weeks, clearing up some business in Oregon. Every 3 or 4 days Bruce said, "That fellow must be back from Oregon by now," and I wrote another letter, and the reply come back saying he went from Oregon to Colorado, and things went on like that for quite a number of weeks. There was also a message in my box from Tootsie saying Katie called twice a day and she was getting tired hearing her voice, Tootsie was, and a note from a fellow name of Burton McC. du Croix offering The Mammoth Quartet a spot on a TV show the following Wednesday night, 100 apiece less his own 10%. I went up to Coker and Canada's, for I could of used $90 about then, and they said, "Sure, tell Perry," and I said, "You tell Perry because I am frankly not on very good speaking terms with him any more."

"Neither am I," said Coker.

"Why not?" said I.

"It is nobody's business but my own," said he.

"Then Canada must tell him," I said.

"Not me," said he.

"We will match coins," said I.

"Go ahead and match them," said Canada, and I done so, and he lost, but he refused all the same, saying Perry give him a pain in the ass and he stopped speaking to him, coins or not.

"It is all very sad," said I. "The 4 of us used to be as thick as flies not many years back. I remember the good old days on the Cowboys. The whole club gives me the creeps. I am libel to wake up some morning not speaking to myself."

"Everybody is nervous," said Coker.

"Why not cut Perry out and call it The Mammoth Trio?" said Canada.

"That is a good idea," I said, "but I got a better one yet. Why not cut Perry out and Bruce in?"

"He could not follow the music," said Coker.

"3 of us following the music is plenty," I said. But we got nowheres, and they said, "Leave us sleep on it," and I left and went down to Perry's myself and knocked on the door, and Jonah opened it an inch and peeked around and said, "Oh, hello, Author," and he left me in quick and shut the door. They were playing cards, the 4 of them, which Dutch said not to, and they said, "Pull up a chair, Author," fairly friendly, all but Perry, and I played a couple hands though my mind was not on it.

"Well," said Perry, "when is the big wedding?" They all laughed.

"Pretty soon," said I.

"No doubt he will invite us," said Perry. I said he would. "I just bet he will," said Perry, and they all laughed again.

"If you boys would give him a chance you would find out he is not such a bad fellow," said I. "In fact you would do me a great favor not ragging him."

"He deserves it," said Keith.

"Why?" said I.

He only shucked his shoulders and looked at Perry. They are good boys, never purposely nasty except they get kicked around a good deal where a white fellow might not. I knew that if they knew what I already knew and carried it around until everybody I met I felt like spilling it they would of buddied up to Bruce, or if not buddied up at least laid off, good ballplayers all of them, though Keith can not go the distance and will not learn from his betters, very effective for 3 innings at the most and then blows. Yet I did not spill it. Telling Goose was already too much. I kept expecting him or Horse to give it away any day, and I only said, "Why rag him about the wedding? It makes him feel good thinking about it. It keeps up his spirit."

"It keeps up our spirit ragging him," said Wash.

"What is wrong with your spirit?" said I. "You are a young fellow. What do you need your spirit kept up for so early in life?"

"Never mind the lecture, Author," said Perry.

"I will leave," said I.

"Nobody said leave," said Jonah.

"Leave him leave," said Perry. "He probably rather hang with his own anyway."

"With my own what?" said I. "I never expected I would hear such a remark from you."

"With Pearson," he said, "and Horse and Goose, the lowest type scum of the earth."

"You are wrong," said I. "Pearson has not got a nasty bone in his body, which if you ever give him a chance he would show you."

"He shown me plenty already. I seen going on 4 years of him, and enough is enough. I am not blind. Pearson would not give me the time of day if I was dying."

"He does not know it himself half the time," I said. "When he cuts you dead it is only because he got nothing to say, not because he does not like you. I hung down home with him over the winter, and more than once I seen him give a big hello to folks along the main drag, colored folks as well as white, the same big hello."

"And they probably said pardon me for living, Mr. Pearson, please allow me to kiss your wonderful white ass. Do not tell me what Georgia is like, Author, for I been there once too often and seen for myself."

"Can he help being from Georgia?" said I. "You was born there yourself."

"And I had the brains to pick up and leave," said he.

"Must he pick up and leave?" I said. "His folks and his home are there, and he hopes to die there when he dies."

"I hope he gets his wish," said Perry. "Somebody deal."

"Probably the sooner the better," said Wash.

"You are a fresh punk," said I. "What do you know about anything?"

"Anything I love is a nice friendly game of cards," said Jonah.

"Deal me out," said I. "I can not stand fresh punks talking about something they know nothing about. Do you think you are going to live forever? Is life so long you rather rag somebody than be nice to them?"

"Listen to me now," said Perry. "I said play cards or go somewheres else and preach. Nobody invited you in, so as long as you are here join in the fun or else disappear."

"I will disappear," I said, and I went back and called Croix, saying what everybody said was we needed new blood in The Mammoth Quartet. "How about dropping Simpson for Pearson?" I said.

"Who in hell is Pearson?" he said. "No, I would not drop Simpson if I was you. He is half the laugh. How about Goldman?"

"No," said I, "how about me and Pearson and

Goose Williams and Horse Byrd? Byrd weighs 240 pounds and would be good for quite a laugh."

"Leave me sleep on it," he said, "and call you back in the morning," and then he never called me but called Perry instead, and Wednesday night The Mammoth Quartet all of a sudden found their name changed to The Four Brown Mammoths, Perry and Jonah and Wash and Keith. They sung "Davy Crockett" and "Come Josephine In My Flying Machine," and they stunk.

If Washington wasn't always such a soft touch for the Mammoths they would of swept past us right there in that little stretch of 2 weeks between the time we got home from the west and the day of the All-Star Game. They kept smearing Boston and Brooklyn something awful up and down the east, slimming our cushion down to one game by the Fourth of July, which was my 24th birthday, 25% of the way along for me, for I believe I can live to 96 if I keep in shape and don't come down with a fatal disease and if the son of a bitches don't blow up the place with their cockeyed bomb. But we blew it back up to 3 on the Fourth, whipping them twice down there before a record crowd that grew quieter and quieter as the afternoon wore on and finally filed out the park without a peep.

Sid took fire once we hit home, and we played steady ball all week except we lost ground, Washington taking 4 straight from Brooklyn and 2 out of 3 from Boston. Sid hit Number 24 and 5 off Boston Thursday and 26 and 7 off Richie Erno

Friday night, which gives you some idea how hot he was. It was the first time he hit 2 home runs in one ball game off a left-hander since hitting 2 off Lowell Shrodes on Friday, April 24, 1953, according to the paper. He was even-up with Babe Ruth, which brung out a record crowd Saturday, Ladies Day, the whole park screaming their head off when he so much as spit. The only thing nobody noticed was we did not win on Friday, but lost, which chipped the lead to 1½. Beating paper records is fine and nice, but the game goes down in history as lost unless you keep the other fellow from scoring more runs, and the boys all said the same, and Sid as well, saying he rather break both legs and cop the flag than beat Babe Ruth and wind up second, and I believed him when he said it, for he is a friend of mine, though many of the boys did not. They never said anything to Sid himself, but they made these dirty remarks concerning Babe Ruth, saying they were tired hearing about him and tired seeing his name in the paper and tired following his record of 28 years ago when any day we were libel to go under if we did not start putting pitching and hitting together. "So what if Sid beats Babe Ruth?" said some of the boys. "Does it pay my bills? I will not be up here forever and must make cash while the sun shines."

"Right," said some of the boys.

"Right," said I. "Then why not pull together like a club? What is the sense blaming anything on Sid? He is doing exactly what he is supposed to be getting paid for. Why not everybody cut out the horseshit?"

"Author is right," they said, and for a couple minutes they all stood around saying, "Yes sir, Author is right," "Yes sir, Author hit it on the head," and then they no sooner said this than they started deciding just who was to blame in the first place and who was more horseshit than the next fellow until you were back where you begun.

Saturday we lost. Sid slammed one with George and Pasquale on in the first inning, and the crowd went mad, 5 home runs in 3 days, probably some sort of a record except I did not even look at the Sunday paper, and we jumped to a 3-0 lead but could not hold it. The power went off, dead, and we dropped it, 4-3. Goose tired, and Bruce caught the last 4 innings and cracked 2 doubles in 2 times at bat, the first time he hit for extra bases in 2 consecutive trips to the plate since September of 49, and we all dragged ourself back in the clubhouse with 2 new records racked up but one more game lost. We sat around listening to the last couple innings of Washington vs. Boston, which Boston finally won, and when it was over Lindon got up and switched it off, and Ugly said, "Lindon, you set a record switching off the radio."

Lindon looked at the radio. "I done what?" he said.

"You set a record," said Ugly. "Up to yesterday you probably only switched the radio off 15,738 times. Now you switched it off 15,739."

"Officially or unofficially?" said I.

"Every day you live you live one more day," said Lawyer Longabucco. "You beat your own record."

"Officially or unofficially?" said Blondie Biggs.

"I talked 3,112 official words today," said Jonah. "That puts me 3,112 official words up on yesterday."

"Today is the first time I ever officially hung this jock on this particular nail at 4:02 P.M. in the afternoon of July 9, 1955," said Perry.

"Today is the first day we ever lost to Brooklyn by a score of 4-3 after leading 3-0 in the first inning on Ladies Day I bet," said Harry Glee.

"Are the ladies official?" said Ugly.

"Some are and some ain't," said Harry.

"Today was the first time in my official and unofficial life I ever fouled out in the seventh inning with a count of 2-2 on me against a right-hand pitcher name of Fairbright," said Canada.

But nobody laughed. All the time we dressed we kept shouting out new records, how many times we now officially buckled our belt and tied our tie and laced our shoe or shaved or combed our hair, how many official miles the zip on your fly now went, how many times you zipped it with your left hand and how many times with your right, how many official times you looked in the mirror, how many official times you breathed, how many tons of water you showered in and how many times you stood at the clubhouse door and looked back and wondered what you officially forgot, shouting out your record but still not laughing, nobody feeling too much like laughing right about then.

Blondie Biggs started for us Sunday, a blond-hair bonus boy straight out of college with a side-arm delivery that the boys all say they rather see in a Mammoth shirt than on somebody else, though what they never told him in college was do not keep getting too behind your hitter. He improves as time goes on, but he still had a lot to learn that Sunday which Dutch probably figured could wait until some other time except when we were only 1½ games on top. July is no time to start learning, and he got jittery, Dutch did, and he said, "Author, go warm," and I went down to the bullpen with Diego.

"Mister," said Diego, "you only rest her up 3 days."

"You warm me and leave Dutch run the club," said I, and after I warmed awhile the crowd begun to boo. I looked around, but I could not tell what they were booing at. It was quite crazy. I telephoned back to the dugout and asked what was up, and nobody knew, and I kept on warming, and the crowd kept on booing. There was this one cluck hanging over the fence, and I said, "What you booing at?" and he threw his hands up in front of his face, afraid that I was going to paste him, though I was not. Finally he come out from behind his hands, still screaming, "Boo-oo-oo-oo, boo-oo-oo-oo, you bum, you phony, boo-oo-oo-oo," his face all red. He was a little bald up front, and the top of his head was also red, and he was mad and shaking his fist, and I said again, "Cluck! You! Cluck there! What you booing at?"

He was quite hoarse. He could hardly speak. "Ain't everybody?" he said.

"But why?" said I.

"I do not know," said he. "Boo-oo-oo-oo, bum, boo-oo-oo-oo," and the telephone rung, Ugly, and he said, "What did the cluck say?" and I said all he said was "Boo" but did not seem to know why, and I went on warming.

Horse and Bruce come down after awhile, and Horse warmed, and the booing started and stopped the whole time, turning to cheering when Sid come up, and silence when he did not hit a home run, and then they actually booed Sid himself in the seventh when he reached across the plate and dumped a single in left instead of waiting for the kind of a pitch he could homer on, the first and last time in my life I ever heard a local crowd boo a local ballplayer for collecting a base hit.

It was 2-2 in the top of the eighth when Blondie got himself in the kind of hot water he was not libel to pitch himself out of, and I went in and faced a left-hand hitter name of Stan Andersen that Brooklyn then lifted and sent up Hal Wilder instead, a right-hander, an old-timer that been on the roster of 6 or 7 clubs including the Mammoths of 42, a grandfather, I think the only grandfather on the active list, and Dutch come out to the hill and said he wondered if Horse might do better than me against Wilder. He stood thinking about it a long time.

"What in hell they booing at?" said I.

"Search me," said Dutch. "The press-box says they are booing me for working you before the All-

Star Game. I can not say that I am the slightest bit interested."

"They are simply out of their mind as usual," said Perry.

"Lay halfway deep on this son of a bitch," said Dutch. "He is fast for an old man, but not too deep."

The boys went back to their spots, and Jonah sung, singing, "Wing her through, Author, wing her through," and I threw only one pitch that inning, my best pitch, a half-speed curve that hooks away from a right-hand hitter and also sinks and slides, which some boys call my sinking screwball and others call a hooking slider, though I myself never bothered to give it a name. I threw it at his knees, and he went for it, thinking it was only straight but then seeing it hook. He tried to check his swing but couldn't, and he beat it down in the dirt towards second, and Perry come up with it and flipped to Coker, and Coker to Sid, and it was now my ball game to win or lose, which we did in the bottom of the ninth, Number 14 for me.

I still did not know what they were booing at, and the paper did not know, neither, some saying one thing and some another, but I now know it was none of the things they said. It was only a lot of disgusted people wondering how a club consisting of what the Mammoths consisted of in the way of power and brains on paper only managed to be 1½ games in front of the pack with time half run out. It was the same as saying, "Everything is at your fingertips. Yet you are libel to blow as high as the sky any day. Can you not get a move on?" I believe that for once in their life the clucks were right, and Holly says the same.

Me and Coker and Perry and Sid and George and Pasquale and Van Gundy left Monday for Milwaukee, 7 of us, more Mammoths than from any club in the league, which gives you some idea the kind of a club it was, rich with stars, and 3 of us were in the starting lineup Tuesday, me and Sid and Pasquale, and in the end it was George saved the ball game with a running catch over his shoulder in short left. He catches many like that, one a week, but Milwaukee never set eyes on him before, and it was all anybody talked about all night. I got credit for the win, my first All-Star win, the first All-Star Game I played in since 52, though I was on the squad in 53.

Back in the hotel Pop called and said, "Hank, I took Holly to the hospital."

"Is he born yet?" I said.

"Not yet," he said.

"Is something up?" said I.

"No," he said, "it is a first baby," which it was. "You looked good. Ain't you ever going to take the rest of your weight off?"

"Trade your set in on a smaller screen," said I. "I will look smaller then," and he got a great laugh out of that.

"I kind of looked for Sid to hit one today," he said. "It would of been a nice touch. How is Bruce?"

"The same," said I. "He is supposed to call me."

"I sure think about him night and day, Hank. You know, if you will pardon me for saying it, he sure been handed one shit deal."

"You are swearing," I said. You have got to make Pop awful mad to swear, and it give me a great charge inside. Here was somebody else besides myself carrying this mad around inside him. It really hit me, and I done a crazy thing. I got up and kicked the door shut, and it felt good, and I kicked the little telephone table there and sent it flying across the room, and the telephone come off the hook and the operator started screaming, "May I help you? May I help you?" over and over again, and I yanked a drawer out of the dresser and heaved it at her, and I remember I stood there bawling and breathing and looking for something to throw and finally seen the shower curtain, and I grabbed it and pulled it off the bar and tore it in 2 and kicked the toilet and stood with a glass in my hand and aimed it very carefully and slung it across the room at a painting on the wall of a girl carrying flowers and smashed the glass and the frame together and felt much better, and the house detectives busted in and put the phone back on the hook. "Where is the person you beat up in here?" they said.

"Person?" I said. "Person hell. There were 9 of them. Add up the damage and put it on the bill."

"Pay the damage in cash and no questions asked," the detectives said, and they added it up and I paid it, and they give me a receipt. We will put it on the tax on the long run, medical expenses, because somewheres along the line you have got to blow your fume little by little or else blow it all in one blow later.

I waited for Bruce to call, and he done so and was fine, and I went down and hung in the lobby. I seen a lot of old familiar faces, Sam Yale and Swanee Wilks and Hams Carroll from the 52 Mammoths. I thought Red might show, but he did not. He never does. Jocko Conrad took me around and introduced me to many old-time ballplayers, telling them, "Here is Henry Wiggen my very own discovery," which was about 2% true, but I said nothing. I used to correct people a lot when they lied, but I cut that out. They stood around lying and went in for dinner and lied some more, and they sat around all evening drinking and lying, telling me things I knew never quite happened that way, and I said, "Yes, I remember reading about that," or "Yes, I heard that game on the radio when I was a kid," or "Yes, my old man told me about that many a time," because why in hell snag old men on their lies? Who cares anyhow? Every year they die. You see an old fellow at the All-Star Game, or at the World Series, or in the South, or hanging at the winter meetings, and they lie to you, and the next thing you read in the paper where they are dead, old fellows not so many years before so slim and fast, with a quick eye and great power, and all of a sudden they are dead and you are glad you did not wreck their story for them with the straight facts.

In the middle of it all I called the hospital in Perkinsville. The operator would not leave me charge the call, saying, "Young men that smash up their room are not in title to telephone long distance," and I went down and paid cash and went back up and called, and the hospital said, "Nothing doing yet," and I flew home.

She was already born when I got there, laying on her belly in a little glass cart on wheels in Holly's room, practically bald, and I said to Holly, "How come no hair?" for I always had the idea you were born with a lot of hair.

"She is perfect in every way," said Holly, "and exactly at her weight, which is more than I can say for everybody," and we give her the name of Michele, for Mike Mulrooney, manager of the Queen City Cowboys.

"Flip it over," I said, "so I can have a look."

"You flip it over," said Holly. "And do not call her 'it' because she is a human person already."

I flipped her over, and then I picked her up and held her, Michele I mean, sitting on the bed with Holly, and the sun was first coming in the window like it was that morning when Bruce had the attack, or thought he did, and I was about ready to bawl again after just getting through bawling in Milwaukee, sitting there with this little bit of a human person in my hand.

"It was a good thing George made that catch," she said. "I could not of waited a minute longer. Then when I got here she did not wish to pop. You were a good boy to come. How is Bruce?"

"The same," said I. "He will be pleased. Not a day goes by but what he asks."

"Go grab some sleep," she said.

"I grabbed some on the plane," I said.

"I did not sleep," she said. "I just laid awake trying to cry."

"There is nothing to cry about," I said. "Why cry?"

"I do not know," she said. "Probably if I knew I could. I wonder if they made a mistake out there. It is hard to see how a fellow in such good shape as him could be in such bad shape. I am reading all the books on Hodgkin, and it is true."

"It is hard to believe they could make such a mistake," I said. "They have got such a wonderful reputation on paper."

"Go see your father," she said, and I stuck Michele back in the cart and kissed her and kissed Holly and went home in Neil Weiss's cab. Neil told me tell Dutch why not bench Vincent Carucci and play McGonigle in left, and why not buy a good catcher or else develop one in a hurry, and I said I would.

I called Pop. "Rise and shine, Grandpa," I said. "I will round you up some breakfast," and he come over and we ate, and he looked at me and said, "It gets more like looking in the mirror every day."

"I doubt that I will ever run as heavy as you," I said.

"Do not put money on it," he said. "That is a wonderful kid of yours, bright as she can be like her grandfather."

"Her hairline, too," said I. "She also gets that from her grandfather," and we laughed a good bit back and forth until Pop stopped laughing all of a sudden and said, "Write down Bruce's old man's address. I been writing him a letter in my head all summer and might put it down any day. You should of long since shook Washington in my opinion."

"In my opinion also," said I.

"Do the boys know?" said he.

"Only Goose and Horse," I said.

"That seems like a funny combination to tell it to. Piney Woods never showed the stuff. All spring it looked like he might. Well, life is life I guess, burn up the world in the spring and back to AA by summer." Pop talked and packed it away, both. I always love to watch him eat. It is almost as good as eating yourself. "I sure think a lot about the old man," he said. "Goddam it, you raise up a kid from 7 pounds to 205 and then some doctor comes along and tells you he has got a fatal disease. Nobody is supposed to die that young in these modern times, but I can not think what to write. Every time I put something down it looks like somebody else wrote it."

"Say it out loud first," I said, "and remember it and write it down, and then get up and walk around and say some more, and quick run and write that down, too. Write it like you speak it and then knock out the apostrophes."

"Why?" said he. "What have you got against apostrophes?"

"Nothing," said I. "They do it in the paper, so I do it."

"I guess you ought to know," he said, "being an Author and all."

I went to bed but I could not sleep. I started

writing in my head, the first time I done any since "The Southpaw" over the winter between 52 and 53, and I cou'd not sleep but got up and fished out the paper and started writing from the beginning, where the telephone call come, "Me and Holly were laying around in bed around 10 A.M. on a Blank morning," not remembering what morning because over the winter one day is about like the next. The summer you can follow in the paper. I hunted up the old telephone bills and saw when the collect call come from Rochester, Minnesota, and I checked it with my Arcturus calendar, and it was a Wednesday, and I filled it in, and then I wrote some more, and the more I wrote the better I felt, and I stopped and thought, "But if he does not die there is no book in it, and all my work is for nothing," and then I thought, "That will be good," and then I thought again, "Still, if he dies or not it might still be a book at that," and I went on writing until I simply could not keep my eyes open and went to bed and fell asleep pitching. If I give us 10 or 12 runs in the first inning I can make it the dullest game on earth and fall asleep easy.

We seen Holly and Michele in the afternoon, and Pop drove me to the train, and I brung cigars back for the boys and passed them around, and they all said "Congrats" and said they hoped she would not grow up and look like me, and I said I hoped so too.

The west moved in and put the stopper on Washington, and we picked up a game. It was not much, nothing like what we would of liked, but it was something.

Goose caught. The 3 days of rest over the All-Star Game done him a lot of good, and when he tired Jonah took over, for the power was on. Sid slammed Number 30 off Rob McKenna and was the talk of the town the way he was hitting left-handers, and Number 31 Sunday, which was the day I racked up Number 15, worth $1,500. It paid off the baby and a lot of little debts we been carry-ing on the books for quite some time. Sid was one up on Babe Ruth.

Bruce broke into the lineup on July 19. He caught the whole St. Louis series, the first time he caught 3 games in a row since Wednesday, Thurs-day, and Friday, August 15, 16, and 17, 1951, ac-cording to the paper, and he caught the first night against Pittsburgh, and done well, though we lost, my loss, a sloppy ball game, for it rained all day and the ground was soaked and should of never been played to begin with, and then when we got back to the hotel his father called and said his mother died, and Bruce spoke to him and hung up and looked at me and smiled and said, "She died," glad she died before she knew, and he called Katie, and she begun bawling on the phone and said she would be right down and help him pack, and she come, and we went to the airport with him, Katie crying all the way.

When he was in the air she said, "Leave us drink a drink together and drown our sorrow, Author, plus which I must discuss a little matter of business with you."

"I personally rather put away a good meal after a ball game and anyhow never drink," said I.

"No doubt such a meal has that extra zip to it when somebody else picks up the tab," she said.

"Very often such is the case," said I, and we went back in town to The Green Cow, same place we all ate Memorial Day night.

We ate in a private room, and after the food come she chased the waiters out and pulled the curtain. "Author," she said, "I have here 2 letters phonier than a rubber bat," and she shoved 2 or 3 of the Arcturus letters that Holly wrote under my eyes. "You may see but not touch," she said, "for any day I am libel to run these up to Boston and inform the Arcturus Company that one of their agents is trying to swindle one of their fully paid-up insurees out of the right to change their beneficiary, which will win you the heave from Arcturus and blackmail you out of the insurance racket forever and a day."

"They will laugh in your face," said I.

"I doubt it," she said, "because I doubt that they will like the looks of the signatures on these letters. I doubt that there are any such people working for them by these names because they are the names of very famous writers up in Boston quite some years back." She put them back in her purse.

"The day you open your yap to the Arcturus Company," said I, "I will stroll up to the police department on 66 Street and swear out a complaint against a certain whorehouse."

She laughed. "I am not anxious to go up to Arcturus," she said, "and I see no reason why me and you must have all this fuss and feathers between us. Who in hell are you protecting? His mother is dead and his father is a farmer. What does a farmer need with $50,000? The price of oats ain't gone up that much."

"It is the principle of the thing," said I. "I hate to see a man get took for a ride."

"What principle of what thing?" she said. "He been getting took for rides all his life. Everybody that ever laid eyes on him stole something off him. He is not only from the country but he is dumb from the country, and on top of that from the dumbest part of the country there is. He ain't even from Texas or Wyoming where the Lord knows they are dumb enough to begin with, but from Georgia. If he wound up in the black he would not feel natural, which he will not wind up in anyhow because if we do not take his money from him the doctors and the insurance company and the undertakers will get there before us and swindle the old man dizzy no sooner than the grave is dug."

"No doubt you are right," I said.

"There is nothing illegal in it," she said. "You are only doing what your customer asks you."

"He is more than only a customer," I said. "He is my friend."

"And what does your friend wish? He wishes to marry me. Do you wish to help him have his wish? Then get them goddam Change of Beneficiary forms down here from Boston. I will tell you another thing, Author, which I been saving for the dessert." The waiter brung the dessert and she told him close the curtain behind him again on the way out and disappear unless she rung, and she leaned forwards a little and she said, "Author, the day those forms are signed and sealed and sitting in the palm of my hand you are the lucky owner of a golden lifetime pass to 66 Street, summer and winter where the game is never called because of rain and where every day is a double-header for any young man with red blood. I got a girl 7 feet tall for you, Author, and another only half your size, never the same girl twice, girls just off the boat from Honolulu. Give a glance at a map of the world and tell me where you want a girl from and what language she should speak, girls that kings could not buy out there in them Arabian countries, girls that already turned Hollywood down, girls that will make you think you are being struck by lightning, and girls that will make you say, "Never mind Heaven because it can not match 66 Street," girls every color of the rainbow, you name it, brown girls, yellow girls, white girls, black girls, red girls, brown hair, black hair, blonde hair, red hair, girls that already forgot more tricks than they know, all ages from 16 to 60, all sizes and shapes, and never the same one twice."

"I already got a girl," I said.

"Buy your girl a tinkler for her arm," she said. "I noticed her arm was bare," and she went back in her purse again and pulled out a check for $2,500, made out to The Green Cow. "I will ring for the waiter," she said.

"Put it back," said I, and she put it back and pulled out another, $5,000, and rung the bell, and the waiter come.

"Cash," she said, and he took the check and went and brung back cash, 50 bills, 100 each, and she laid them on my plate, where my pie was but was no more, for I ate it, and I looked down at it, and I rung the bell, and the waiter come again.

"I rather have more pie," I said, and I handed him the plate, and he looked at me, admiring me, and he give Katie back the cash and went and brung another hunk of pie. She stuffed it in her purse and got up in a hurry. "You will be hearing from me," she said, and out she went.

CHAPTER 13

Talk about crazy coincidences, I was writing along in my book, still only the first chapter, and hit the part where I called Joe from the airport in Chicago when right that minute he shoved in opposite, and he said, "Should we not send flowers?"

I said I sent them, me and some of the boys.

"Like who?" he said.

"Me and Goose and Horse," I said, and I folded up my papers and stuck them in my pocket. "The club also sent some."

"You writing another book, Author?" said Joe, and he laughed. He hadn't spoke a nice word to me in weeks.

"No," I said.

"About you and Pearson?" he said.

"What makes you think so?" said I.

"Nothing," he said. He looked out the window. "Do not write another book until I read the first one. I can not keep up with you. I ain't even bought a copy yet. I am a little strapped this year."

"$3.50 is all it takes," said I, "or 35¢ in the quarter books. That ain't very steep, Joe."

"Who else sent flowers?" he said.

"Nobody else I know of," said I.

"That ain't enough," he said, and up he got and crossed the isle and collared Roberto Diego and told him tell George fork over $3. George give only one. Joe said, "3, George, I said 3," and he held up 3 fingers, and George dug back in and come up with the other 2, and then he spoke a lot of Spanish to Diego, probably swearing. I do not know more than 6 words in Spanish that I learned playing winter ball in Cuba, but I believe I know swearing when I hear it, and Joe moved on down the isle, and every seat he stopped at he held out his hand, and somebody put a dollar in it, and he looked at the dollar and said, "Is this all you can part with? I pity you. You can no doubt part with 4 for a silk necktie, or drop 5 at poker, or fill up your gas tank and think nothing of it, but ask a fellow for a few dollars for flowers for a fellow's mother and suddenly their pocket is locked and the key is in the river," and the boys all went back in their pocket again and brung out more, and Joe went down in the other car and cornered the boys at cards, and after awhile he come back and give me $60 about, and the next time the train stopped I sent the flowers. I did not know what type to send. I do not know too damn much about flowers. The telegraph girl said, "Never mind, I will send the right type. How do you wish to sign the card?" and I signed it "From the boys, with deepest regrets and sympathy," and I wrote down all their names, and she copied them off, all but "Piss." She got all red and said we could not send such a word on the wire, and we changed it to "Sterling."

"It would be easier just saying 'From all the boys,'" she said.

"No," said I, "send it like I wrote it," and that was how it went.

I kept the list. I have it yet. You start saving everything once you start writing a book, and every little thing brings back memories all their own, like in the song.

I don't know how Joe knew. I never asked. Goose or Horse must of told him, and I was quite mad at them for a minute, and then it passed. Who told Goose after all but me? And then when he knew he could only carry it around so long until he had to tell somebody else, like carrying heavy bags that you have either got to change them around from hand to hand or stop and sit on them awhile or else finally break down and pay a redskin to help you, or if you don't tell somebody you might start writing it down and get it off your chest that way, telling paper.

Wednesday they hit Chicago, Bruce and his father between the doubleheader, and they walked in the clubhouse and the boys all stood up, for the old man if not Bruce, and Bruce said "Howdy boys" and started getting dressed.

"Do you feel like playing ball right away?" said Dutch.

"Yes, sir," said he. "I do."

"Good," said Dutch. "Boys, we lost 2———ball

games to a club we should fat up on every time if Mr. Pearson will pardon the expression. I do not generally use such an expression except under unusual circumstances."

"That is all right," said Mr. Pearson. "I heard them once or twice down home." He took off his coat and sat down on a pile of towels. His suspenders kept drooping down over his shoulder.

"I guess you did at that," said Dutch. "I am suppose to be responsible for the character of these young men and do not wish you to think I ever forget it for a minute. But you come at a bad time, sir, these son of a bitches with their nose up my rear when they should of been shook by June. Leave me introduce you around," and he introduced Mr. Pearson to the coaches and the boys, and he went up and down the line and shook their hand. Every time he shook it his suspender flopped down again, and he snapped it back up, shake, flop, snap, shake, flop, snap. Him and Dutch moved down towards the colored boys, and I held my breath a little, not knowing if he would shake their hand or not, but he done so, and then he went back and sat on the towels. "I am going to bat right-hand power and see if we can not beat this wind," said Dutch. "What a place to build a park! You might as well build it uphill. Hanging is too good for the——built this ball park. Longabucco will play in left and hit for Vincent Carucci. Pasquale, you hit 8 and Goldman 7, Smith hit in the 4 spot and Roguski 3. Who does that leave open?"

"That leave Pearson in the 5 spot if that is the

way you wish it," said Egg. "Probably you made a mistake in your thinking."

"I guess I know what I wish," said Dutch.

"He batted in the 5 spot in the Alabama State Amateur Baseball League down there," said Mr. Pearson, "and also when he was with the Cowboys. He will live up to your faith, for one thing that keeps him sitting on top of the world is your faith in him."

Clint and Egg shook their head "No."

"I hope he has got a better grip on the top of the world than we have got on the goddam pennant race," said Dutch. "I am probably out of my mind batting him 5, but a man must take a desperate gamble when God himself is against you, blowing a wind in like that against your left-hand power. No! I will bat him 6 and move Longabucco up to 5. How does that look?"

Clint and Egg shook their head "No" some more. "Why not shove Goldman in there in the 6 spot?" said Egg.

"And follow Pasquale right after," said Clint.

"A catcher works hard," said Joe. "You should not bat him too high in the order."

"He is fast," said Mr. Pearson, "and young, and great in his faith in you."

"Fast as a dear," said Dutch, "and that is a fact, and my faith in him is greater than ever. I believe this might be his year at last, but the truth of it is I must trust in the word of my staff, and I will move him back to the 8 spot after all. There is nothing personal in that."

"That will keep you from having too many right-hand hitters in a row anyhow," said Joe. "It will prove your faith in him."

"Yes it will," said Dutch.

"I guess it will at that," said Mr. Pearson, though I suppose he might of wondered how. I myself wondered but said nothing, never speaking unless spoke to after pitching a bad ball game, which I just got done doing in the first game, though actually not too bad of a job now that I look back at the clips but one Coker and Perry threw away behind me, messing up a double play at a poor time, plus some better umpiring might of helped, plus also the wind. Perry said if I stopped thinking so damn much about the bonus clause I might of been more effective, which was a lie and I said so, and Goose said if I threw anything stupid a-tall it was Jonah's fault, and Jonah said one more remark like that out of Goose he would start separating somebody's head from their shoulder if it wasn't against the law to murder old men, and there would of been some really nasty things said except it was right about then Mr. Pearson walked in.

Bruce caught the second game, and we won, which I was glad for, his father sitting up behind the dugout watching. He only seen Bruce play for the Mammoths once before, coming north for the 52 Series when Bruce pinch-run for Swanee Wilks in the fourth game, Swanee now managing the Mammoth farm in Appalachia in the Ind-O-Kent League, Class C, where Bruce broke into the organization. We won with the power off but the right-hand hitting putting singles together, Blondie Biggs going good for 7 innings until needing relief, Horse finishing up, Horse very effective all during that swing which if he hadn't of been would of meant "Curtains."

That night we sight-seen around town, me and Bruce and his father and Horse and Goose and Joe in Joe's car, Michigan Boulevard and the stockyards and Soldier's Field where General McCarthy pinned the medal on Goose, and State and Madison, the busiest corner in the world, and we circled around the other ball park, where I myself never played. They say the wind is better there. We drove through the South Side, blocks and blocks of colored houses, everybody hanging out the window for a breath of air. Mr. Pearson was very impressed with the whole town and said he wished his wife ever seen it, and Horse said, "Well, you will tell her about it when you see her again, for we all must die."

"I will," he said. "I been keeping a track of things to tell her."

"No sense keeping a track," said Joe. "You will have millions of years to think back, all the time in the world up there out of the hustle and the bustle and the heat. It will be a better place than Chicago."

"Lay it on thin, boys," said I to myself, and we went to Joe's and drunk beer, or at least they did, for I do not drink, and Joe's Mrs. waited hand and mouth on Bruce, running back and forth like a madman every time he needed a refill or even only looked like he needed one, and I knew she knew but never give it a thought, though in the end she was the one left the cat out of the barn and blew the roof off things.

Me and Bruce and his father and Horse went back to the hotel, and we gassed a long time, the 4 of us, and the old man slept in the room with Bruce, and I spent the night with Horse. The last thing Horse done before bed he fished out this little pencil about an inch long and a hunk of hotel paper, and he sat writing in his shorts, probably a half an hour or more, and I said, "I hope you are not writing a book, for a club has got room for only one Author at a time."

"No," said he, "I am writing a letter home, but I am a slow writer," which he certainly was because in a half an hour he only done 9 lines or less. "To tell you the truth," said he, "I am out of practice and anyhow can never think of a thing to say. What in hell is there to say? All my life I double-timed her, and all I can say is I will try and see if I can stop for once. She will not even believe me." He licked the flap closed and stuck it in the door of the medicine chest.

"She might," I said, "if you sound sincere enough."

"Sincere?" he said. "Goddam it, that is a good word," and he went and got the envelope again and ripped it open and squeezed another sentence in and wrote a new envelope and licked it and stuck it back in the medicine chest and turned out the light and got in bed, and we talked some, and first time in 4 years up that I ever really talked to the fellow, and he is not a bad fellow a-tall when he tries.

Bruce caught again Thursday, and we won and took a split on 4. Washington split 2 that day in Pittsburgh, and we left for Cleveland 2 games to the good. The old man could not decide if he wished to go on to Cleveland with us or go out to Seattle and stay with his daughter awhile, and finally he decided on Seattle, saying "Goodby" in the clubhouse and shaking hands all around again, and some of the boys said, "Do not leave us, for we won 2 in a row since you come."

"I believe you will start shaking Washington for good pretty soon without me," he said.

"Besides," said I, "if he stays and we lose everybody will start blaming it on him."

Everybody laughed. "I will be back and luck you through the Series," he said, and we said we hoped so, which we certainly did.

Bruce caught the west through, every day, which the paper never noticed, all the writers probably thinking tomorrow or the next day Dutch would throw Jonah back in as long as the power was on, or Goose if it was cool, and then when they noticed it they noticed it all at once and busted out in a rash of articles called CAN THE MAMMOTHS WEATHER THE STRETCH WITHOUT A CATCHER? There was a drawing of Dutch one day called GETTING TO SLEEP ON HOT NIGHTS, showing Dutch in bed counting catchers jumping over a fence, and every catcher was Red Traphagen. Bruce read them and never give them a thought, or if he did never mentioned them but only went on playing ball, and we kept floating, never gaining but at least never dropping back, 2, 2½, 2 again, 1½, back up to 2, all through the west, staying alive with pitching some days and power the others, never putting the 2 together like we should of been doing on paper, Sid blowing hot and cold, hitting 4 in 3 nights in St. Louis after not hitting one for a week, and then not hitting another until back east again, neck and neck with Babe Ruth but not libel to last, for the Babe hit 17 in September of 27, according to the paper. We knew Sid would never make it. We only hoped nobody else got as hot as Babe Ruth in September, Washington or even Pittsburgh or Cleveland, because if anybody *really* got hot it was their chips to rake in October.

He only went on playing ball, Bruce did, hitting pretty good, keeping a book on pitchers and never much getting fooled twice in a row any more. Dutch moved him up to the 7 spot and shoved Coker back to 8, Coker in a terrible slump, finally yanking Coker altogether and playing Ugly and hoping Ugly's legs would hold up until Coker got back his eye or his timing or whatever it was made him slump. He never really knew, and in the end what I believe it was it was his nerves give out. Doc Solomon said the same and put him on sleeping pills. I do not mean Bruce busted down fences left and right, but he hit solid and he hit steady, 265 or

270, a little one way and a little the other, talking to himself up there and looking fierce and crowding in, getting dusted more than once, pitchers trying to talk him back and keep him from tagging the curve, which he done more and more now, picking it up when it broke. He begun wearing a protective helmet. Yet every time they dusted him he come back off the ground and crowded in again, same as before, hitting right-hand pitching as good as left and sometimes better, and pushing a good many drives into the opposite field.

Pasquale dropped in one night and said, "Me and my brother been thinking. Why not loosen up your grip more?" and Bruce thought about it and said, "I will try it," and he done so, getting more wrist in his swing and driving a longer ball and saying a few nights later, "I believe I must go and thank them for the tip," and going and never coming back until I begun getting worried and went after him and found him playing Tegwar in the lobby with Joe and a flour salesman. He played every day between Chicago when he got back from the funeral and Labor Day, baseball I mean, not Tegwar.

But he was no catcher, and many a time I wondered if maybe the one mistake Mike Mulrooney ever made was making a catcher out of him instead of an outfielder. He would of never been a top-flight outfielder neither, but not being an outfielder is not so dangerous as not being a catcher, and there were days when I was sure Dutch was about to say, "To hell with the power," and send Jonah back in.

To Bruce a pitcher is only a fellow throwing the ball, and a catcher is only there to stop it and keep the game from dragging, which is not what a pitcher is and not what a catcher is except maybe in the Alabama State Amateur Baseball League, which is why it is the Alabama State Amateur Baseball League and not New York. A pitcher is a fellow with a baseball in his hand facing a son of a bitch with a stick of wood in his hand, trying to keep the man with the wood from hitting the base-ball solid because if he hits it too many times the pitcher becomes a man without a job, and he is throwing with his arm and his brain and his memory and his bluff for the sake of his pocket and his family, and he needs help. His catcher must help him, must also be brain and memory and bluff, not only just stop the ball in case the hitter don't. A man's catcher must be eyes and ears, watching runners, watching wind, watching the lay of the land behind the box, watching the board, watching signs, picking up everything the pitcher might miss, which Bruce never was, this year nor any other in all his life, for he never loved catching that much. He loves hitting. He wishes you could hit and not be bothered with catching, loving to do only the one thing he does best, which in many a sport you can get away with. You can be a block of cement and do only the one thing a block of ce-ment can do and call it "Football," or you can be 7 feet tall and stand around dropping balls in a basket and call it "Basketball," or you can whack a little ball and walk after it and whack it again and walk some more and call it "Golf." But these are not baseball.

Catching he was never thinking, only going through the motion, only picking up his gear from the floor and strapping it on and pulling his mask down over his face and grabbing his mitt and reaching up on top of the dugout for his sponge, always putting it there to dry out between innings, and going out and taking a couple warm-up throws and firing to second and crouching down and looking for his sign, then stopping the pitch in case it got past the hitter and firing it back out, firing high or low or however the mood hit him, not saving his pitcher, only keeping the game moving, and crouching down again and spitting through his mask and picking up his sign again if he could figure out where it was coming from, half the time not knowing who the hitter was, not knowing the umpire behind the plate, only crouching there until the pitch started coming, sometimes leaning on his arms, his mitt flat in the dust, his arms hanging like these monkeys in the zoo, until when he took the pitch his mitt sent up a little puff. And when the side was down he put his sponge back on top of the dugout and sat down in his gear and wiped the juice off the chin of his mask and threw the mask on the floor. "Who swipes?" he said, and if it was his, or his soon, he jumped up and dropped the rest of his gear and grabbed a bat, loving to hit but not loving to catch, like Jonah

Brooks loves catching but not hitting. What Dutch finally decided was he needed his hitting catcher the most, and shut his ears and stopped reading the paper and played Bruce on the gamble all the way home through the third swing west, and it worked, for we stood above water.

The boys mostly laid off him. If they ragged him they had not only me to answer to but Goose and Horse, and later Joe. They begun ragging Diego Roberto, believing he was bad luck. Diego believed the same, saying Josh Klang put the double whammy on him, Josh the Boston coach and a great kidder. Diego and George started scrapping but could not tell me what about. I think George thought Diego was giving away certain confidential matters behind his back in English, which he was, but whether they were the same things George thought they were or not I never found out. Diego said they were not, but George's side of the argument I got through Diego, which probably loaded the stack against George, and in the end they never settled it, or if they did they did it without any help from me. I can say "Which way to the ball park?" in Spanish, for they told me how to say it when I went to Cuba, "Ah dondey estar el estadio bazeball?" which folks on the street understood all right, especially if I also carried my glove. I lugged my damn glove all over Cuba.

It was my turn to work Thursday night in Brooklyn, but Washington got beat by Boston in the afternoon and Dutch felt he could gamble, sav-

ing me to shoot at Washington Friday night, which
I never thought a thing about until Friday morning Winston Waters called, the saloon writer, and
he said, "I do believe Dutch is skipping your turn
on orders from the club to keep you from cashing
in too much on your bonus clause."

"No comment," I said.

"Is it not possible?" he said.

"No comment," I said. "It is possible the morning dew will wash away the park."

He hung up, and he wrote in his column that I
said such a thing was "possible," and Dutch got
booed for it.

I beat Washington Friday night, probably the
best job I turned in since the 2-hitter Memorial
Day. I give up 4 hits, and Sid hit 39 and 40. I was
now 17-8 on the year. It was the largest Friday
night crowd in August since Friday night, August
12, 1949, according to the paper. Van Gundy beat
them Saturday, another great crowd, but we lost
Sunday. It was the largest 3-day crowd for weekend
singletons in August since August 17, 18, and 19,
1945, and the cushion was now 3 full games. Everybody breathed a little easier than they breathed in
a long time.

After the Sunday ball game we sat around drying
off and not feeling too sorry for ourself, quiet, not
ragging anybody and not scrapping, which I rather
hear quiet than horseshit, although too much quiet
puts me in the gloom after awhile, and Ugly said,
"Exactly when in hell will it all be over?"

Lindon had a schedule taped on his locker, and
he looked at it and said, "The 25th."

"That gives me 6 weeks," said Sid, "to hit 21 home runs in 42 days and beat Babe Ruth."

Everybody laughed.

"Probably we can hang on for 6 weeks all right at that," said Coker.

"I wish it was tomorrow," said Canada.

"I wish it was yesterday," said Lawyer Longabucco.

Bruce spoke to me in a quiet voice. "Tell them they are wishing their life away," he said. He never speaks up in front of everybody but says it to me first saying, "Tell somebody this or that," never lifting his voice unless asked.

"You are wishing your life away," I said.

"I am only wishing 6 weeks away," said Canada. "Not my life."

"I wish I could go to sleep tonight and wake up on the 25th and be done with it one way or the other," said Lindon. "We should of been on Easy Street by now."

"We should of shook the son of a bitches by July," said Pasquale. "Who have they got? What keeps them on the up?"

"That Revak is not a bad ballplayer," said Vincent, "nor that Opper nor that kid that pitched Friday night."

"That is 3," said Pasquale. "You would not wish to sweat blood until you can name another."

"It could go on," said Bruce, speaking up now. "I even do not mind catching too goddam much any more."

"Nobody ever accused you of catching," said Jonah.

"You shut your fat black mouth," said Goose.

"Shut up, boys," said Ugly.

"It was only a little joke," said Jonah.

"Little jokes wind up in big bloody messes," said Goose.

"I said *shut up*," said Ugly.

"I like sweating," said Bruce. "I like hitting. Sometimes I even like popping out, looking up there and seeing how high you drove it."

"I do not like popping out," said Sid. "Even high."

"Still and all I do not mind," said Bruce.

"He is in love," said Herb.

"With a pure bride," said Perry.

"I love stinking," said Bruce, "and coming in and ripping off your clothes and getting under the shower and thinking about eating," and he sat thinking over what he said, and the more he thought about it the better it sounded, and he went and showered, and the boys all done the same.

CHAPTER 14

Monday was open, and we drilled. Dutch was not at the drill. Somebody said his Mrs. hit town, and Clint run the drill.

Afterwards we went and sung on Charles Marschand's TV Supper Club, 60 apiece, peanuts, me and Bruce and Horse and Goose, calling ourself The Mammoth Quartet. A lawyer called me up a couple days later and said he was suing me on behalf of Coker and Canada for stealing the name unless I wished to settle out of court, and I said, "Go ahead and sue me, pal," and I hung up the phone and never give it another thought until just this minute. It all comes back. On the same show they had these Three Harmonettes, pretty little blondes that swang their ass while they sang, and Bruce got all hotted up and went up to Katie's, and I went back the hotel and done some writing, whipping through Aleck Olson in Minneapolis and down to where I was eating away in that kosher restaurant in Rochester, Minnesota, actually the last meal I ever ate before I knew about Bruce when you stop and think about it, and the telephone rung, and it was Red from San Francisco, California.

"Author," said he, "what is up? I got 2 wires and 2 telephone messages saying call Dutch, and I wish to be filled in before I do. The first wire says he wishes me to come and coach the summer through for some exceptional wages which I will not mention on the telephone, and the second wire doubles it. I hate leaving here in the middle of things, although to tell you the truth this ain't a very fancy paying racket as far as the money goes."

"How much do you get per annum?" said I.

"I am ashamed to say," said he. "It is not enough to live on, and we are in the poorhouse. I believe I might get used to it in a few years."

"At least you do not split fingers," I said.

"That is true," said he.

"It is a job where when your legs give out you can sit down and still hold it," said I. "A lot of boys wish they had such a fix to look forward to."

"But you do miss the noise and the excitement," he said. "You never pass a ball field without lumping up a little in your throat. Goddam it anyhow, by the time you are old enough to have more sense than power you realize you already pissed away the most exciting days of your life."

"Do they leave you swear like that out there?" I said.

"Everybody swears everywhere," said he. "Shakespeare and all the rest, all up and down the years they swore at life. Plain old mother talk ain't nowheres near strong enough to describe such a terrible mixup as life, Author."

"Life is good," I said. "How would you like to die tomorrow?"

"I would not," he said, "because I am under contract to fill out the year here, and because I keep laughing every minute, and because I wish to finish up a book I am writing, and because I would like to see if you boys can cop the flag which you should of copped by now. You should of shook them son of a bitches long ago."

"I am also writing a book," I said.

"What about?" said he.

"Oh, a little bit about everything," I said.

"That is too goddam big," he said, "though a genius like you will handle it easy."

"Leave me read you a few pages," I said.

"Not coast to coast on my telephone bill," he said. "I wish you would tell me what is up."

"I will nose around and call you back," I said. "Collect."

"Sure," he said, "and be quick," and give me his number and I wrote it down on top of one of my pages and stuck them in my pocket and went and pushed the elevator. I give a couple elevators the go-by until finally Peter come, and I told him ride me up and down empty once or twice. "What is new?" said I.

"Dutch's Mrs. is here," said he. We rode up the top and got out and he took a couple puffs on his cigar. He leaves a cigar burning on top of the fire-box up there. He laid it back on top of the box and we got back in and started down again. "Patricia is also here," he said. "Tootsie can tell you more. The long distance been flying far and fast all over creation." I got out on the lobby and bought some cigars and took them back and give them to Peter, and I strolled over and said to Tootsie, "Tootsie, I never seen you looking quite so gorgeous before."

"It sure was good to hear Red," she said. "And he was right, every word he said. You should of shook them long and long ago. It is not your fault, Author, for you are 17 and 8 on the year and been pitching your heart out, but something is wrong beyond understanding. I could use 2 grandstands any day or night the week you get back from Washington."

"Sold," I said.

"Old Man Moors is flying down from Detroit and Mike Mulrooney is flying in from QC with Piney Woods. Swanee Wilks is flying out from Appalachia to manage QC for Mike. Doc Loftus and Doc Solomon been on the wire all day with Rochester, Minnesota. I only catch a little bit now and again but I do not believe they are getting any satisfaction."

"Concerning Pearson?" I said.

"Certainly," she said. "Who else?"

"What is wrong with Pearson?" said I.

"I do not know. They are talking this medical double-talk. I believe he has a leak in his blood somewheres. For 2 more grandstands on the following day I heard something else."

"Sold," said I.

"You are in the doghouse because of the bonus clause in your contract."

"The bonus clause?" said I.

"Certainly," said Tootsie. "What else?"

"How did they find out?" said I. "I mean how did they find out about Pearson?"

"Dutch's Mrs.," said Tootsie. "She heard it off Mrs. Joe Jaros who heard it off Joe who heard it off you who heard it off Goose Williams, for Goose was in Rochester, Minnesota, all winter with Pearson. They got some kind of a big hospital out there. Third-base side, Author, lower deck, not too far back and not behind no pillars nor posts."

I called Red from a pay phone, and I told him what was up, the whole truth, and he said he would call Dutch and try and jack the pay up a little and fly on in, and I went up to Dutch's sweet and knocked, and they said "Come in."

Everybody was there, Dutch and his Mrs. and Patricia and the coaches and Ugly and Doc Loftus and Doc Solomon and 2 lawyers, one a man and the other a lady. "Good evening to all," I said.

"So!" said Dutch. "I knew that I would get to the bottom of it."

"Good evening to you," they said. They all sat around not talking. My contract was on the table in front of the lawyers, and every once in awhile they picked it up and looked at it and threw it down again. I waited for somebody to say something, and finally Patricia spoke up. "I never heard of anything quite so terribly horrible," she said. "I can not understand why I am not crying."

"Keep your hanky handie, dearie," said Dutch's Mrs., "for it first must penetrate your skull. I myself thought nothing of it when she told me but only went about my business shucking my shoulders until all of a sudden it knocked me down."

"You keep thinking it could be your own," said Joe. "I started dreaming these dreams."

"Do you not think," said Dutch, "that we already discussed it enough as far as how very terribly horrible it is? Can we not stick to the subject? Tomorrow is a baseball game as usual and we are no nearer knowing than before." He looked at me now. "Author," he said, "you got us into this, so now get us out."

"What is the problem?" said I.

"The problem is what to do," said he. "If you will back out of your clause like a man we can release him and bring in some protection, which I doubt that you will have the kindness and decency to do but would rather go on knifing us in the back. I admire you for it, believe me. I knew something was up when I left you put the clause in but had no sleep in several nights due to that goddam motorcycle driver, which the idea of putting up with the rest of the summer makes my belly crawl."

The telephone rung, Red, and Dutch clapped his hand over it and said, "How much can I offer?"

"The sky is the limit," said Patricia, "but use good taste."

"Hello there, old pal," said Dutch.

"Hello there yourself," said Red. I could hear his voice but I could not hear the words. "It would all sound find to me," said Red, "except I can not leave here. They can not find another man on such short notice."

"To do what?" said Dutch. "They can find 40,-000 men in a minute."

"I am making money hand over fist out here," said Red.

"Horsefeathers," said Dutch. "Nobody makes money in such a racket but the football coach. I will up it 33⅓% and not one penny more."

"I can not stand the noise and the excitement," said Red. "I quit it for good and never miss it and am glad to be done with it. Keep it and best of luck."

"Very well," said Dutch, "I am sorry to troubled you."

"Goodby," said Red.

"Goodby," said Dutch.

"Goodby," said Red.

"I will up it 16⅔% more," said Dutch. "That is twice the first wire plus 33⅓% plus 16⅔%. I am under strict orders to go no higher."

"Tell him I said hello," said Ugly.

"Ugly says hello," said Dutch.

"Tell him I also said hello," I said.

"Author also says hello," said Dutch.

"Sold," said Red, and Dutch hung up. "Somebody remember and can Diego Roberto when Red hits town," he said. "Every cloud got its silver lining."

The lawyers looked at the contract again, and Dutch looked at me, and then away. "I still believe we are in title to some help from the Commissioner," he said. "Cleveland was helped when Mays killed Chapman if memory fails me. Why Cleveland and not New York?"

"You can not get help from the Commissioner and keep it in this room both at the same time," said Joe.

"Then we must let it out," said Dutch, "except she says it would not be human. Yet is it human to lose the flag? What have you thought up yet, Doc?"

"Nothing else," said Doc Solomon. "We been thinking."

"You are a slow thinker," said Dutch.

"You must be calm," said his Mrs. "You must think of the boy."

"I am thinking of the boy. I been thinking of nobody but the boy all afternoon and all night and am not libel to stop. It is more thinking than I done about him in my life before. He was $1,000,-000 worth of promise worth 2¢ on delivery. It is Mike Mulrooney's fault, goddam his Irish soul if you will pardon the expression." He looked at the lady lawyer.

"I am not Irish," said she.

"I thought you were," he said. "Goddam his Irish soul then, a great and wonderful man but a soft-hearted bastard. Now I must put up with him and Red and that motorcycle driver. What in hell was his name? Do you mean to tell me he is libel to die without any warning? Why in hell do they call it that?"

"Piney Woods," said Ugly.

"That was it," said Dutch. "My good hope from Good Hope, Georgia."

"It is named for Hodgkin, the man that discovered it," said Doc Loftus.

"Maybe he knows something about it," said Dutch. "Is he alive himself? Maybe he thought up a cure by now which those jugheads out in Rochester, Minnesota, ain't heard about yet. What kind of a place is that to have a goddam hospital, anyhow, out there in the wilds of nowhere? Does a man not freeze his ass off by the time they get him in bed?"

"It is pretty built up," I said.

"They have got some of the best-paid amateur leagues in the country out there," said Ugly.

"You ought to know," said Dutch to me. "You were there. You sneaked out there in the middle of the winter, and all the rest was hokus, Mary Pistologlione and hunting on the ice and gags by telephone and miracle drugs for the clap. Then I hired a goddam detective. What was his name, Author, anyhow?"

"Rogers," I said. "Mr. Rogers."

"Fine name," said Dutch. "He could not detect cow-flop in a barnyard."

"Leave us go sleep on it," said Patricia. "We will decide something," and we went. But I don't think they ever decided anything, or if they did they never left me in on it. Red come in and coached catchers, and Mike come in and kept Bruce's spirit high, and Piney with him, just in case. Tuesday was baseball again as usual, like Dutch said it would be. We lost to Brooklyn, Washington beating Boston and chipping the cushion to 2.

CHAPTER 15

The first the boys knew anything was up, Piny Woods walked in the clubhouse in Brooklyn Tuesday night wearing cowboy clothes, pants and shirt and a 10-gallon hat and high-heel boots and a rope and a gun on his belt and carrying a guitar. "Howdy, partners," he said.

"Howdy there, Piney partner," the boys all said.

"Did you come in by horseback from QC?" said Gil.

"No, partner," said Piney, "we flew."

"Did you stop and camp along the way and cook up your grub by the fire?" said Herb.

"No," said Piney, "we ate on the plane."

"Who is we?" said Sid.

"Me and Mike," he said, and the boys all begun wondering how come Mike come. "How come Mike?" they said.

"I do not know," he said. "All I know is you been needing catching protection."

"We been needing no such a thing," said Goose. "Pearson been doing a man-sized job."

"Probably they shipped you along to water the

coyotes," said Horse, "and keep the rustlers out of Brooklyn."

"I guess I could," said Piney, taking his gun off his belt. He put it up on the shelf, and it fell off, and everybody jumped. It broke open, and the bullets spilled on the floor and rolled here and there and everywhere, and he crawled around after them and put them back in.

By Wednesday morning the whole of New York knew something was up. Red hit town in the morning. The paper just got through wondering all over the place why Mike was there, and now Red give them new food for their fire. They begun calling everybody up and rapping on the door.

The only individual in town it made no impression on was Bruce. "It sure is good to see Mike," he said, and that was all, except when Red come he said it sure was good to see Red, and he looked in the paper and told me who said what, saying, "Tex O'Malley says in his column Dutch is on the outs with the Moorses and being canned," and saying "Winston Waters says in his column Dutch is splitting with his wife," and saying "Krazy Kress says in his column Piney Woods is a sure bet for 56," and I kept waiting for the paper to stop hitting around it and learn the truth, which I doubted O'Malley or Winston Waters would ever do, though Krazy might of, for he is quite a writer about 2 shots in 5, and then when he closed the paper Red come busting in, and I got out of bed and never went back.

He was looking very white. "I live in a foggy part of the town," he said, and he sat down and we talked, the first time we seen him in over 2 years, and Mike come in soon after and also sat down, and Goose and Horse, and I sent for coffee for all, though by the time it come Ugly and Joe drifted in, and I sent the boy back for more, and then Patricia come and I got back in bed on account of these pajamas I hang out in. Somebody should invent pajamas with zippers, though to tell you the truth she is far from the blushing type.

And writers come, and they said, "Tell us what is up, boys," and dragged chairs in and sat down and looked around and drunk coffee. "I can not figure it," said Krazy. "All of you here that I doubt I ever seen in one room before, people that never hung together in their life off the ball field," which was true when you thought about it, for Red has no use for Patricia, and Patricia none for Ugly, and Mike none for Red, and Goose and Horse no use for anybody but themself. But nobody told the writers what was up, and after awhile they stopped asking, and they left, and the boy kept bringing coffee, and then food, and all of a sudden it was quite a large party for such a small room. Dutch wandered in, the first time in my life Dutch ever come to my room since the morning of Opening Day in 52, page 198 in "The Southpaw," 202 in the quarter book. "It looks like Pearson and Author are the most popular fellows on this ball club," said he.

"That is all right," said Bruce. "Have a chair," and he got up and give his chair to Dutch and sat on the window, and every so often he turned around and spit down and told what he spit, in-curve or outcurve.

"It is too bad a fellow can not pitch spit," said Dutch.

"I would sure have a lot of breaking stuff all right," said Bruce, and everybody laughed very hard, too hard in my opinion, and I said to myself, "Lay it on thin, boys."

"I got the Mrs. off my back and on the train," said Dutch.

"I guess that is a day's work," said Joe.

"I do not mind seeing her too much," said Dutch. "She keeps me human. Probably many a boy gets the idea I am not human. Did you ever get such an idea, Author?"

"Not personally," I said. "People sometimes tell me you are not human, but I say you are. It simply never shows." Everybody got a great laugh out of that.

"Probably you sometimes thought I was not human," said he to Bruce.

"No sir," said Bruce.

"Probably I ate you out now and then. But I never ate you out without reason."

"No sir," said Bruce. "You ate me out for doing dumb things."

"I ate you out for the good of the club," said Dutch, "and for the good of your own pocket, never for anything personal because you know as well as I do that personally I never had only the greatest respect for you as a human being."

"Yes sir," said Bruce. "That was how I always felt."

"I guess I have my human side all right," said Dutch. "Maybe not in the summer, but certainly in the winter."

"Yes," said Mike, "you are no doubt very human in the winter."

"Or anyhow in the very coldest part," said Red. "Leave us get over to Brooklyn," which we done.

Red put on his old number again, and Mike the same, Mike after 10 years in QC, and Dutch locked the clubhouse against the writers. It was a very large crowd for a Wednesday night. Thousands were over from New York for a sight of Red again, plus it was me vs. Scudder, always a great ball game usually. Red warmed me. Me and him come up out of the dugout together, and there was this tremendous ovation, cheering from the Mammoth fans and booing from Brooklyn, for they always hated Red in Brooklyn, and I said, "I will bet you get nothing like this out there in San Francisco, California."

"No," said he, "they pray that I do not show for the class, and if I am 10 minutes past the hour they run out laughing for a beer," and he touched his cap, and Mammoth fans begun singing "Happy Days Are Here Again," and the Brooklyn band tried drowning them out, playing "California, Back I Come," and the bulbs popped, and he laughed and yet cried a little. "It is a mad country, Author, and bound to go down."

"I do not think so," I said. "I been in 4 countries, Mexico, Cuba, Canada, and Japan, and we got them all beat."

"Beat at baseball maybe," he said. "These clucks been educated to read a scorecard. They are like the seals in the zoo, which if you feed them and give them a roof they will jump on a box and bark. Throw me a few easy until I sharp my eye a little."

I threw a few down easy, and little by little he lowered himself to the crouch. "Now I am down," he said, "but I am not sure I will ever get back up." I threw more. What a man he is to throw to! He knows what you are doing before you do it, knows how you feel before you say. "You are tired tonight," he said.

"Yes," said I, "a little."

His ear forgot nothing. He knew what was being hit where by the sound, hearing all the sounds behind him, and seeing all that went on in front, stopping and turning and watching Jonah in the cage, then crouching back down again and thinking about Jonah, telling Jonah take over and warm me awhile, and standing and watching Jonah, studying, studying, like you read in the paper where a fellow knew somebody died far away and sure enough he done so though nobody told him, eyes in the back of his head, eyes in front, eyes to the side of him, all eyes and ears, picking up everything eyes and ears pick up plus a few things eyes and ears miss but some part of him picks up, his 6 sense. "You are warm," he said, "go wash your face and run your wrist in cold water and tell Doc give you a green pill and a lemon-color pill."

"Them phoney pills?" I said.

"Wash down the green pill with a coke and the lemon-color pill with black coffee. They will wake you up."

"They are phoney pills," I said.

"OK," said he, "fall asleep on your feet then." We stood in the dugout a minute. He watched Bruce hit with one eye and Scudder warming with the other, and then we went back in and I told Doc give me a green pill and a lemon-color pill, and I washed them down with coke and black coffee, and I woke up on the spot. Mick give Red a rub and the boys come drifting in.

There was no lecture that night. Dutch stood on the scale, and I thought there would be, but there was not. He only said, "Piney Woods, where is your gun?"

"In my belt," said Piney.

"Hand it here," said Dutch, and Piney fished it off the shelf and handed it to him, the barrel end first, and Dutch turned it around quick and held it facing the floor. "I am not in the mood to see somebody laid up with a bullet wound."

"I am very careful," said Piney.

"That is what everybody says," said Dutch, "yet the hospitals are full of babies. McGonigle, did you shoot a gun in the war?"

"No sir," he said. "I played baseball."

"Great fucking war," said Dutch. "Goose, you was in the war. Take and empty this gun."

"Where?" said Goose.

"At Bill Scudder," said Sid, and everybody laughed, and Goose took the bullets out of the gun and give the works to Dutch, and Dutch put the bullets in his pocket and threw the gun back at Piney. George spoke in Spanish to Red, and Red said, "George says you should go fire it at Bill Scudder."

But George opened the ball game with a single, and Sid right away hit Number 41 with 2 gone, the first home run he hit off Scudder in 2 years, and we picked up another in the second, Bruce leading off with a single, Dutch batting him in the 6 spot now, and going to third on another by Vincent Carucci, and coming home on a long fly by Coker, Coker still not out of the slump but Dutch using him against left-handers all the same. I remember Bruce scoring from third that time, standing on third with his back to the plate, waiting for the catch and then pushing off backwards from the bag and spinning and charging down the line towards home, the lights on his face, not running hard or anyhow not looking like he was running hard, though he was, no feeling in his eyes of hurry nor strain, looking at me for his sign, and I signed "Stand up," for the throw was cut off in the infield, and he crossed home and run right on past me but circled a little and come back and stood in front of me. "What?" I said. He said nothing, only stood there a minute like he ought to said something, not go flying past a fellow without talking. "What?" I said. "Nothing," he said, and he went on in.

I was glad whenever Sid hit one, then and after. Every time he connected the paper left off nosing around for the truth and rushed through a new

article called WILL SEPTEMBER BE SID GOLDMAN'S
MONTH OF DESTINY? or SUPERHUMAN TASK FACES
GOLDMAN. Dutch moved him up to the 3 spot to-
wards the very end to give him extra swipes.

After a couple innings Red said to Bruce, "After
every pitch I wish you to lay the ball in your glove
and stand up straight with your meat hand down at
your side. Then bring it up slow and take careful
aim and fire it back at Author's chin," and Bruce
done so. I do not know why I never thought of it.
It slowed things up, and it rested me, for it kept me
from reaching now down and now up, now left and
now right, which Bruce makes you do, thinking all
he need do is fling the ball back at his pitcher,
never mind how. After every inning he sat by Red,
and Red talked to him, and whatever Red told
him he done, and it helped. "That is right, Red,"
he said. "Tell me what you see, for I know I got
faults and always did."

"Yes," said Red, "as long as I am in town anyway
I will pass along what I see."

"What else do you see?" said Bruce. "Tell me
more."

"Well," said Red, "squat even on both legs. Do
not lean towards the curve. You are helping the
enemy read your pitcher."

"Squat even on both legs," said Bruce. "What
else?"

"That is enough for one night," said Red.

I blanked them for 6 innings. They picked up
one in the seventh, and they threatened in the
eighth, and Horse come in and pitched out of it

and went on and saved my game. He was the greatest reliefer in baseball down the stretch, fat old Horse, a rock of strength all September. Red said he must of give up beer and found the Fountain of Youth instead.

Old Man Moors hit town that night, though I never seen him. He was gone by morning, back to Detroit, and Patricia went back up to Maine or Vermont or wherever. She acts in shows. Red says she owns the theater. He never did like her.

By the time we left for Washington Friday morning everybody was used to seeing Red and Mike around and stopped thinking too much about it. The paper cooled off on it. Everybody in the know was mum and I believed the truth had got about as far as it was going.

But I was wrong. Thursday night Red said to me, "Drop up and bring your book," and I said I would, and when I got there he was reading and George was looking at the TV, not listening but only looking, for Red can't stand the noise and George don't particularly miss it. "How much you wrote by now?" he said.

"I am finished 2 chapters," I said.

He took it and ruffled it through and laid it on the dresser, and I said, "I believe George can read and wish you would not leave it laying out."

"He already knows," said Red, "for I told him. I could not keep it in." George spoke in Spanish. "George says it is some shit deal Pearson been handed," said Red.

"Si, senior," said I.

"I wonder if they made a mistake," said Red. "These doctors can be as wrong as hell when they try."

"We are all hoping so," I said.

"Who all knows?" he said.

"Me and his father and minister and Holly and some people Holly told up home."

"I mean on the club."

"Me and the brass and Horse and Goose and Ugly and now George," I said.

"He does not seem sad," said Red. "He keeps thinking about what he is doing and trying to improve himself. He is quick to learn, and he is certainly hitting splendid. I must tell him either chew or not chew when he hits. There is a system to his chewing, and the enemy will read him."

"He stops chewing when he tenses," I said.

"I believe so," said Red. "But he is a much better ballplayer than when I last seen him."

"He is gaining the old confidence," I said. "He has more friends. He never had any before." A little breeze blew in the window and begun sliding my pages along the top of the dresser, and I got up and sat a glass on top. "It will all be in the book," I said.

He took the glass off the pages and started reading, and when he read 6 pages he said, "I read 6 pages and it is not yet so much about him as you. Should it not be all about him and nothing about you?"

"Read more," I said. "Pretty soon I drop out of the picture," and I went and sat by George and watched the TV, picture but no noise, a yarn about a girl and 2 men, one of the men with a black mustache pasted on. I looked for the cops to come and haul off the fellow with the mustache because it was 5 minutes before the hour, and they done so, and the girl and the shaved fellow kissed and melted out in the pitch. George never took his eye off it. He reached for a cigarette, but his eye never left the screen, and Red stood with my book. "I will come back," I said.

"No," said Red, "stay. I have read enough to see that this book will never be about Pearson but about you and airline stewardesses and Goose's wife and Aleck Olson of Boston and kosher restaurants and Holly and riding in automobiles through South Cedar Rocks, Iowa, and who the hell knows what all else by the time you are done. But it must be more about Pearson being doomeded, which is what we all are, ain't we, me and you and George. Ain't we, George?" he said, and he kicked the TV and spoke in Spanish, saying in Spanish, "We are all doomeded, ain't we, George?" and George got up and pushed the TV back in the middle of the table and said we were in Spanish, if Red said so. "He says so too," said Red, "but you are facing terrible odds, for George will never read your book, being trained to read a scorecard only and live like a seal. And even the people that read it will think it is about baseball or some such stupidity as that, for baseball is stupid, Author, and I hope you put it in your book, a game rigged by rich idiots to keep poor idiots from wising up to how poor they are."

"I would never put any such a thing as that in

my book," I said. "It is not true, besides, which it is my bread and butter. It is a game loved by millions in 4 countries, Mexico, Canada, Cuba, and Japan."

"Stick to Pearson!" he said. "Stick to Pearson, Pearson. You must write about dying, saying 'Keep death in your mind.' "

"Who would wish to read such a gloomy book?" I said. "Everybody knows they are dying."

"They do not act like they know it," he said. "Stick to death and Pearson."

"I will try," I said, and I done so. I wrote Chapter 3 and then again 4 mostly about Bruce, like Red said to, writing right there in the room with Bruce not 8 feet away. He never asked what I was writing, and never cared, and will never read the book itself when it is done, which might be any day now with luck and quiet.

Lindon Burke worked and lost Friday night in Washington, a good job, complete, but the power was off. I felt sorry for Lindon. Sid did not pick up a base hit since his home run off Scudder the first inning Wednesday night and felt a slump coming on, which it soon did and would of meant "Curtains" only Bruce was on fire, and also Ugly. Dutch moved Bruce up to the 5 spot and Ugly 6 and later benched Sid altogether. The writers now forgot Babe Ruth and begun wondering if Sid would even equal himself as of 53, when he hit 51 home runs. WHA HOPPEN TO GOLDMAN? they wrote, SAD SLUMP SINKS SID'S SPIRIT, and they give him a good deal of advice on how to pull out of it.

If we had of lost Saturday we would of dropped back in a tie. This brought all Washington out hours early, and I remember the traffic was jammed and the cabbie finally turned his motor off and sat with his arms folded and said back over his shoulder, "You gents from out of town?"

"From good old South Turtle Landing, Arkansas," I said. "We run the dancing school down there but flew up in a hurry thinking we might see this whizzard Henry Wiggen pitch." Bruce started jabbing Mike in the ribs with his elbow and whispering, "This is a gag." Mike laughed on the inside, his whole stomach shaking, but his face straight, winking and nodding at Bruce, same as saying, "I am glad you told me or I would not of knew," though God knows Mike knows a gag when he sees one after 59 years. "If you ever pass through South Turtle Landing, Arkansas," I said, "drop in and waltz around with us one time."

"I ain't been out of town since 1921," he said. "I hope this goddam Wiggen does not pitch. We ain't beat him more than once or twice all summer."

"You ain't beat him *a-tall* all summer," said I. "Do not think you can pass out phoney information just because we are clucks from the country. We get the paper down there, and many of us can read."

"Nothing personal meant," said the cabbie, and he turned back around and started up his motor, and Red put it in Spanish for George, Red never laughing, though George did, Red only smiling out of one side of his mouth. The cabbie drove on, saying nothing until when we got out he said, "Nothing personal meant again, but if I heard on the radio where Wiggen dropped dead tomorrow I would not shed a tear."

There was an overflow, the first time in many years down there. They roped it in the right-field corner, maybe 3,500 people. I personally thought nothing about it, figuring our left-hand power was the equal of theirs, and Dutch said the same, saying "Anyhow, is it human to fight over such a small thing?"

"I do not know if it is human or not," said Clint, "but I believe an overflow in Washington must be roped in left. It is libel to cost us the ball game otherwise," and they sat around trying to remember the last time there was an overflow, Dutch and Joe and Egg and Clint and Mike and Red and Goose and Horse and Ugly, but none of them could, and Dutch called Krazy Kress in the press-box, saying, "Krazy, do you remember where they roped the overflow the last time they ever had one down here?" for anything Krazy can't remember probably never happened, and Krazy said, "Yes, Dutch old pal, I remember, only the clubhouse door is locked in my face these days."

"It will be locked in your face forever and a day," said Dutch, "unless you tell me."

"In left," said Krazy, and the brass all sat down with the Washington book and figured out which way was libel to hurt us less, and they figured left, and Dutch went and collared the umps and told them move the overflow in left, where it belonged

according to the regulations, and Washington said
"No!" though knowing they were wrong. But they
finally done so, the field crew unroping the ropes
and hustling the fans across the grass into left. The
spot the crowd was hustled out of was covered with
bottles and wrappers off franks and such, and by
the time the field crew swept it up the game was 20
minutes late getting under way.

Washington yanked all its left-hand power and
threw in right-hand power, not much, and Dutch
done the same, dropping Sid to the 7 spot and Pasquale Carucci 8 and yanking Vincent Carucci altogether, batting right-hand power 1-2-3-4-5-6,
George and Perry and Canada and Bruce and Lawyer Longabucco and Coker, the first and only time
in his life Bruce ever batted as high as 4. It looked
mighty peculiar, but it worked, and it was a wild
and crazy ball game, your left-fielder laying in it
looked like practically just behind short, and
everybody aiming all afternoon for the overflow,
popping them in there amongst the fans, 2 bases.
We set all kinds of records, the most doubles in a
ball game for 2 teams, the most doubles for one
team, us, the most doubles in one inning, the most
consecutive doubles, the most doubles after 2 out,
the most doubles for one ballplayer in a 9-inning
ball game, Bruce, the most consecutive doubles for
one player in a 9-inning ball game, also Bruce, the
most doubles with bases loaded and the most doubles with bases loaded in consecutive innings. We
used 5 pitchers and Washington 7, all right-hand-

ers, and it run 4 hours, and we took it, 16-11, and the cushion was 2 again.

Sunday there was no overflow. It rained, and we were late getting started again, and we sat in the clubhouse and Piney played his guitar and sung, taking off his cap and putting on his 10-gallon hat instead, and wrapping his belt with his gun around his middle, half Mammoth and half cowboy. You could hear the crowd shuffling around above, trying to jam in under the roof and out of the rain. Piney sung pretty good, singing—

As I was a-walking the streets of Laredo,
As I walked out in Laredo one day,
I spied a young cowboy all wrapped in white linen,
All wrapped in white linen and cold as the clay.

"Now the cowboy speaks," said Piney.

"Try a different song," said Mike. "That is all I heard all summer."

"No," said Piney, "it is the best of them all," and he sung on—

I seen by his outfit that he was a cowboy,
And as I walked near him these words he did sigh,
"Come sit down beside me and hear my sad story,
"I am shot in the breast and I know I must die."

"I believe it is letting up," said Ugly.

"It is corn," I said.

"No," said many of the boys. "Leave him sing. It sounds good."

"Then the cowboy tells him his sad story," said Piney, and he sung on again—

"It was once in the saddle I used to go dashing,
"Once in the saddle I used to go gay,
"First down to Rosie's and then to the card house,
"Shot in the breast and am dying today.
"Get 16 gamblers to carry my coffin,
"6 purty maidens to sing me a song,
"Take me to the valley and lay the sod o'er me,
"I am a young cowboy and know I done wrong."

"Come on boys," said Piney. "Why do you not all join in a little? The boys in QC sing all the time." But nobody did, and he thumbed a bit, and then he sung it through—

"O bang the drum slowly and play the fife lowly,
"Play the dead march as they carry me on,
"Put bunches of roses all over my coffin,
"Roses to deaden the clods as they fall."

It made me feel very sad. Yet I knew that some of the boys felt the same, and knowing it made me feel better. Not being alone with it any more was a great help, knowing that other boys knew, even if only a few, and you felt warm towards them, and you looked at them, and them at you, and you were both alive, and you might as well said, "Ain't it something? Being alive I mean! Ain't it really quite a great thing at that?" and if they would of been a girl you would of kissed them, though you never said such a thing out loud but only went on about your business.

Van Gundy worked when the rain stopped, and he was rocky. It is no good cooling after warming. Washington kept getting hold of little pieces of him, waiting for the curve when it did not break quite right, which it begun to do more and more until Dutch lifted him in the fifth, and Keith relieved, and I went down and warmed, and the crowd booed me on the way down, and I raised my arm at them and waved and smiled, like I thought booing was a compliment, and they stopped booing and laughed, and I warmed with Jonah and went in in the bottom of the eighth. The score was 5-5. I was hot and quick.

We went ahead in the tenth on a single by Bruce which drove Pasquale home, Bruce batting without his chew and using Perry Simpson's bat, for Red told him, "A strong boy like you need only meet the ball, not murder it, so use a lighter stick," and he used Perry's, waiting up there for the one he was looking for, and splitting Perry's bat on the drive, a hard smash punched through third and close to the line, and the crowd groaned but then cheered, seeing Sampson Opper coming over very fast and taking it backhand on the bounce in foul territory, the same boy we played Tegwar with on the train that time, and digging and stopping and firing it home, a perfect throw, a great young ballplayer that I know Dutch will dicker for at the winter meetings but probably never get, and Pasquale slid in under the throw, safe, and the one was more than plenty for me. Dutch played Canada at first in the tenth, and McGonigle in center, and he sent Coker in at short for Ugly, and Jonah caught, the best defense he could field, though it was not needed, for I was still hot and quick and could of went another 5, even with only the 3 days rest.

Perry eat out Bruce for splitting his bat, and the boys all laughed, saying "Go soak your head, Simpson," and we went back home with the cushion at 3, the most lead we ever had all summer since May.

CHAPTER 16

I beat Cleveland Friday night, Number 20, August 26, 1955, a date which I am not libel to forget very soon and probably never, going afterwards to The Green Cow. Katie had a girl with her, never mind her name. If I name her I am libel to be sued. I was almost sued by Old Man Moors for saying in "The Southpaw" that Patricia and Ugly had illegal relations on page 152, 155 in the quarter book, though I actually never said such a thing. It may of been between the lines, but certainly I can not help what relations go on between the lines. She introduced me to this girl and said, "Does her name sound familiar to you?"

"Yes," said I, "I seen her on the TV and movies."

"Plus which," said Katie, "she was voted Miss Industrial Progress not long ago."

"I believe I recall the event," I said.

Katie pulled the curtain. "Get up and walk back and forth a couple times," she said, and Miss Industrial Progress done so, and I watched her. It would of been difficult not to unless I was awful sick. She carried her knife and fork with her. "Thank you," said Katie, and Miss Industrial Progress sat down again and went back to her food. "Tell Author what your present business address is," said Katie.

"66 Street," said the girl, not looking up, only eating.

"Where you got a golden lifetime pass to," said Katie, "as soon as I clap my hand over the Change of Beneficiary form we discussed not so long ago if you remember."

"I remember," I said.

"What you been doing about it?" she said.

"What am I eating?" I said.

"Do not stall," she said. She told me what I was eating in French. "In English it means the cow's ass," she said.

"It is awfully tasty," I said.

"Stop stalling."

"Well," I said, "the next time we are in Boston I will drop in on Arcturus and shoot it all through."

"When?"

"I do not know. I carry no schedule with me. All I do is follow the boys on the train."

"Very well," she said. "I will give you until you get back from Boston before I personally go up there myself and raise holy hell and pull the skids out from under you good and proper."

"Stop worrying," I said, "before you get ulcers. I won Number 20 tonight."

"So I heard," said Katie. "Miss Industrial Progress is a baseball fan from way back, ain't you, honey?"

"I sure am," said she.

"It was worth $1,000 to me," I said. "So far I picked up $6,500 in bonus money with the summer still a month from over. Do you think I am too worried about losing my insurance license?"

"You will not be playing ball forever," she said. "You have a short life."

"So do you," I said. "So does everybody."

"Then why not live it up a little?" she said. "Why worry so much about Pearson's old man?"

"I do not know," I said, and that was true, for I did not. Do not ask me why you do not live it up all the time when dying is just around the corner, but you don't. You would think you would, but you don't. "I do not know why," I said.

On the way past the desk Tootsie said, "Must be quite a celebration."

"You said it," I said. I didn't know what in hell she was talking about, some kind of a celebration somewhere, always something going on that you never heard about or else forgot, like some days the flags are half-mast, somebody died, some high official, some brass, and you ask, "Who died?" and nobody knows, and you think you might see it in the paper tonight, and then you forget to look.

In the elevator Peter said, "What are they celebrating?"

"The fassa walla dogda, naturally," I said, and Peter said, "Oh, I must of forgot," and I got off and started down the hall and turned the corner and heard it, and it was my room, and I pushed open the door except somebody was sitting against it and it did not push all the way, and I squeezed through, and it was full, maybe 15 boys in there and others coming and going all night.

"Hats off to Arthur," said Bruce. "Come right in and join the celebration."

"I guess I will," I said. "I live here. What in hell is going on?"

"We are celebrating," said Bruce.

"So I see," said I.

"Bottoms up in honor of Author," said Perry Simpson.

"My bottom is up," said Wash Washburn, and he flipped over and done a handstand on a chair, and everybody watched, and then he climbed up the rungs of the back, hand over hand until he was standing on his hands on the top of the chair, and the chair swayed a little, backwards and forwards but never falling, and everybody clapped, and then he climbed down again and jumped on the floor and begun walking across the floor, and Jonah stuck a cigarette in his mouth, in Wash's mouth I mean, and Wash started out the room, still on his hands, and down the hall, and the first door he come to he knocked with his feet and a chap answered, a fellow in a bathrobe. I don't know who. He is always in the lobby reading racing magazines. "Pardon me, sir," said Wash, "but I need a match," and the fellow went and got a match, and Wash reached up and took it and brung it down ever so careful and lit it, standing there on one arm, and he blew a puff and said "Thank you, sir" and give the chap his matches back. "No trouble a-tall," said the fellow, and Wash walked back in the room on his hands and kicked the door shut behind him, and we all clapped, or maybe all but me. I don't remember. I was still pretty confused and all.

Holly telephoned and said "Congrats." I could hardly hear her. I took the telephone in the bathroom. "What in the world is going on down there?" she said. "Who is singing that music?"

"Piney Woods," said I. "We are celebrating."

"He is quite a horrible singer," she said. "Celebrating what? Number 20?"

"I do not know," I said. "I believe they are in on the truth."

"Since when?" she said.

"Since sometime in the last couple hours," I said.

"Wait," said she, "Michele is crying," and she run and brung her to the phone, and I flung open the door and said, "Boys! Listen!" and they all quietened down and Michele cried for them awhile.

"Leave us sing her a lullaby," said Jonah. "Piney old boy, sing her an old-fashion Georgia lullaby."

"I do not know none," said Piney, "and I do not think you can play a lullaby on a guitar, but I know a song. Listen to this, honey. You just shut up now and listen, for it is a tale told by a cowboy," and he sung—

My pal was a straight young cow-puncher,
Honest and upright and square
But he turned to a gambler and gun man,
And a woman sent him there.

If she been the pal she should of
He might of been raising a son,
Instead of out there on the prairie
Killed by a ranger's gun.

When he was done the boys all clapped, and Michele started crying again, and the boys all laughed, and Holly, too, though I could tell it was laughing and crying, both.

"I will sing her another," said Piney.

"Not on my bill," I said.

"It is night rates," he said. "You just picked up another $1,000 anyhow."

"Bottoms up to Author's bonus clause," said Coker.

"Author, dear Author," called Keith Crane in this high, girly voice, "come here and make love to me and tell your wife go feed the child."

"Who is that?" said she.

"Keith," I said.

"He is right anyhow," said she. "I better feed her. She ain't gained an ounce since Tuesday and I am worried sick."

"Holy Moses," said I. "Mike, what if she ain't gained an ounce since Tuesday?" Mike has 8 children, one of them signed by the Mammoths only just a couple weeks ago and libel to wind up playing for his old man at QC some fine day.

"Lace her milk with a slug of whiskey," said Mike.

"The baby's?" said I.

"No," said he. "Holly's. It will relax her mind."

"Mike says forget it," I said.

"That is what the doctor says," she said.

"She is named for me," said Mike. "What do you boys think about that?"

"And many another baby looks like you," said Horse, "but does not bear your name."

"That is a lie," said Mike.

"35 years ago today I was born," said Goose.

"Bottoms up to Goose," said Canada.

"We are celebrating," said Bruce. "Hats off!"

"He said hats off," said Ugly, "so take off your hat, Piney," and Piney took off his 10-gallon hat, saying "Whatever Bruce says I will do, for in my opinion there is no greater catcher in baseball today."

"Lay it on easy, boys," said I to myself, and they sung—

> Happy birthday to you,
> Happy birthday to you,
> Happy birthday, dear Goose,
> Happy birthday to you.

"Speech!" they cried. "Speech! Speech!" and Goose stood up with a beer and said, "I will now deliver you boys my farewell speech, for when a man turns 35 he must play out the string and be gone. I believe Red was wise to quit when he did, though he had a thing to go back to while I have nothing. I was never as smart as him and never the great catcher, though I believe on any other club I would of played regular."

"It is in the past," said Red.

"Some people are born luckier than others," said Goose. "I wish I was being born again and dropped in at a movie and seen my whole life ahead. I would of done it over better."

"We will all be born again," said Mike. "We are only passing through to a better deal than this."

"Maybe so," said Red, "though I am leery of magic."

"There is no maybe nor magic to it," said Mike. "There is time to do over again what you done wrong, even at 35."

"You have probably got to hustle," said Goose. "I have got too many goddam black marks against me. Nobody knows what a son of a bitch I am except her, and I do not think I can hustle that fast, plus which if she gets there first she will put the finger on me."

"She will forgive you," said Mike.

"Put an ad in the paper," said Jonah.

"Do what?" said Goose.

"Put an ad in the paper. Down home you put an ad in the 'Picayune.' You tell the saints you done wrong and will do better and he shoots the word up." Red laughed and put it in Spanish for George, but George did not laugh. "Black and white all the same," said Jonah. "I put an ad in the 'Picayune' saying to my saint please do not leave me sign on with any organization but the New York Mammoths."

"What did Washington do?" I said.

"They won," said Horse. "The son of a bitches."

Piney put his hat back on and begun thumbing his guitar.

"Hats off," said Ugly.

Piney whipped it off. "What to?"

"Hats off to you," said Ugly. "You rounded up them corrals down there under the lonesome star and lassooed your horse and headed them off at the pass."

"I got no horse," said Piney. "I am going to buy one in the winter and name her Good Hope 2." His motorcycle is Good Hope One.

"Hats off to motorcycles," said Coker, and Piney reached for his hat, except it was already off.

"Breed your motorcycle to your horse and come up with a horse on wheels," said Herb.

"Or a 4-legged motorcycle," said Gil.

Then they kicked that around awhile and come up with some rather unusual combinations.

"Hats off to hats off," said Coker. "Bottoms up to hats off," and they all drunk, all but me, and they kicked *that* around awhile, bottoms up to bottoms up and hats off to hats off, swigging a little swig with every toast, beer only until they sent down for some whiskey to wash out the dirty old beer cans with. I begun getting undressed, for I was tired, and every once in awhile somebody said, "Leave us go elsewhere, for Author is turning in," and they talked about it but never went, and I scrubbed my teeth and sat in the bath awhile, soaking out a little Charley horse I had and reading a book Arcturus sent me name of "Widening Your Circle of Acquaintances." The boys kept floating in and out the bathroom, some of them getting rather tanked up by now. I got out and dried off and crawled in bed, and the boys all said, "Leave us go elsewhere, for Author is turning in."

"You do not bother me," I said, and I pulled the cover up over my head and laid there listening, dozing off and on a little, hearing little snatches of things that now come back to me more and more while I write. I remember they talked about Sid's slump, and I remember Mike told some stories of the old days, stories I heard in QC but forgot, and somebody read out loud from the book, "Widening Your Circle of Acquaintances," and Bruce said he would be marrying Katie any day, and Goose shouted over to me, saying, "Author, where do you keep your bullets?"

"In my top drawer with my gold nuggets and extra socks," I said, and he went and put a bullet in Piney's gun, or said he did. Piney said he didn't. "Very well," said Goose, "I will dare you to point this gun at your head and pull the trigger," but Piney wouldn't do it, knowing there was no bullet in it, yet not so sure.

Goose said, "I will go and get a *real* bullet," and I heard him leave. That was the last I heard for awhile.

Yet I could hear them even while sleeping, and I kept saying to myself in my sleep, "It is all a dream. I am only dreaming. I will wake up in the morning and they will be slinging horseshit at each other again on schedule," and I kept waking myself up every hour or so and looking around, and it was not a dream. It was real. They were sitting there, and Bruce amongst them, and it was a club, and I sat up and said, "How about turning off the light and turning on some lamps?"

"I will shoot out the light," said Goose, "like they do in the west," and he aimed at the light with Piney's gun.

"Why do you think a cowboy is a hero?" said Red to Piney. "Cowboys no doubt think ballplayers are heroes."

"There is no bullet in it," said Piney.

"There is no such a thing as a hero," said Red. "The only hero is a man without heroes."

"Will you bet $100?" said Goose.

"Done," said Piney, and Goose aimed and fired, POOM!, and people started running up and down the halls and knocking on doors and screaming "Bloody murder," and the boys all laughed in the dark.

"You will have to go west in the winter and brand up a great many stampedes to make that 100 back," said Ugly to Piney.

"Open up in there," shouted the house detective, and somebody opened up and he walked in and flipped the light on, but it did not light. "Who is in the bed?" he said. "Turn on the light," and I reached up and turned on the bed-light. "So it is you, Author. Did you hear that shot?"

"How could I of possibly heard it," I said. "It come from clear over the other side of the room."

"Give me that gun," said the detective.

Piney took it out of his belt. "I do not know how it got there," he said.

"It must of jumped in," said Perry. "And then the belt just jumped around his waist and the hat just jumped on his head."

"Frame-up," said Piney. "I been frame-upped."

"Is not the switch on the wall a satisfactory way enough of turning out the light?" said the detective. "You will pay for the light and the hole in the ceiling and give me that gun besides," and Piney give him the gun. "Come with me," said the detective, and off they went, and I dropped back to sleep again.

They were still there when I woke up. It was just coming light, and they were drinking coffee and talking quiet, and I laid looking up at the busted light, 100 times between August 26 and the end I flipped the switch but got nothing, for the hotel never fixed it, though it was paid for, and every time I done so I remembered the night. "This night cost you a rodeo or 2," said I to Piney, "the $100 to Goose plus damages."

"That ain't what rodeo is," he said.

"We all kittied in on the damages," said Bruce. He brung me a cup of coffee. "And Goose give him back the $100."

"It is a great bunch of boys," said Piney.

"They always was," said Bruce.

But it was a sad lot of Mammoths faced Cleveland Saturday, and we lost, and no wonder, and the lead was chipped back down to 2 again, Washington beating Chicago. You can not play baseball hung over. It is not like most businesses I ever seen, insurance business, TV business, the writers, where everybody you meet is hung over or boiled, one day one and the next day the next, boiled, hung, boiled, hung. The only one not hung over was Sid, for he lives up home on Riverside Drive when we are in New York.

After the ball game Dutch said, "Very well, boys, you had your little celebration, and we will now not have another until the day we clinch it," and the boys all said "Yes siree, boss" and "You said it, Dutch," and such as that.

"What celebration?" said Sid. "What was being celebrated?" and he sat drying off and looking up and down the line. "Is my memory gone, too," he said, "as well as my eye? I heard of nothing worth celebrating," and he stood up and grabbed his shaver, getting ready to shave. He always shaves after a bad day. If he has a good day he leaves it grow. "Somebody name me something worth celebrating," he said, but nobody answered, and he took and flung his shaver against the wall and it fell apart in 100 pieces, screws and bolts all over the place, probably a $25 shaver or more, and he looked at it but said nothing, saying only, "Celebrating," and walking down the line then and looking in everybody's locker, which nobody ever does, and taking a razor off Gil's shelf and walking on, and taking a tube of cream off Vincent Carucci's shelf and walking on some more, and taking a pack of blades off Horse's shelf. "Celebrating," he said. He lathered up his face with Vincent's tube and threw the tube on the floor and looked at Vince, same as saying, "I dare you to say something," but Vincent said nothing, only picked up the tube and put it back, and he took a blade out of the pack and threw the pack at Horse's feet, and Horse picked it up and said nothing, and he stood looking in the mirror and shaving. "Celebrating," he said. "I have picked up 5 hits in 43 times at bat and we are about to be dumped on our ass. Yet we are celebrating," and his hand shook and he cut himself in about 4 or 5 places, and when he was done he never even washed the razor off but only shouted "Gil!" and flung it more or less towards Gil, and Herb caught it and washed it off and handed it to Gil. He was bleeding around the chin, and it dripped on his shirt when he dressed, and Harry Glee said, "You are dripping blood on your shirt, Sid."

"Leave it drip," said Sid.

"It is a new shirt," said Harry.

"Leave it drip all out of me until I am dead. It is my shirt and my blood and you mind your own goddam business to begin with," and out he went and slammed the door behind, and we sung in the shower, the quartet, the old quartet, the good quartet, me and Coker and Canada and Perry, singing Piney's song, only not slow, like Piney sings it, but quick and gay.

We sung it that afternoon and all through the west, and we sung it on TV later in September when all of a sudden everybody in New York that stood around biting their nails all summer started falling all over themself handing you the town on a silver spoon, 200 apiece for a TV spot and more spots than you could of possibly took and kept your mind on baseball at the same time, which made Mr. Burton McC. du Croix quite mad, our TV agent.

CHAPTER 17

Cleveland moved out and Chicago moved in, which everybody was glad to see because if there is one club we always walk all over at home it is Chicago. We beat them both days, Sunday and Monday. Sid went 5 for o Sunday and Dutch benched him, and Canada played first and Harry Glee in center. Dutch's real problem is getting a hold of one more dependable outfielder, which is nothing against Harry nor Lawyer nor McGonigle, good boys all and good ballplayers, but never the absolute tops. Mike worked with them a lot in September, and they might look better in the spring. Mike said he might as well make himself useful. He was brung in from QC to kind of keep Bruce's spirit high, though in the end it was Bruce kept Mike's, for Mike can not stand being so far from his family and ranch in Last Chance, Colorado. He telephoned them every night and spoke to them, one after the other, his wife and 6 of the kids, running up a fairly large bill and moaning about it. I told him call it deductible. "Do you not ask how the cows are?" I said. "Is it not a necessary expense to keep an eye on the cows?" but he said he had a foreman kept an eye on the cows and was already deducted as far as he could go anyhow, 6 kids still home.

He sat down at the end of the bench, Sid I mean, looking like the end of the world, scowling and blowing out his lips and squinting at everything, testing his eyes. For a couple days he thought he was going blind, and then when he got over thinking he was going blind he was sure he was losing the strength in his hands, and he kept studying his hands, flipping them over one way and then the other and gripping things hard, seeing how his grip was. He was really quite nasty to everybody. He said to me, "I suppose you are quite happy the way your friend Smith been playing first base these days," calling him "Smith" like he was a stranger.

"Well, Goldman," said I, "I am naturally happy to see him doing good down there because our regular first baseman is in a slump."

"Yes," said he. "I read about it in the paper."

Chicago moved out and Pittsburgh moved in and we beat them Tuesday night, plenty of power, Sid or no Sid. He kept roaming up and back along the bench and calling people by their first name again. "Maybe I will catch what you boys got," he said, and we all laughed. We now won 4 in a row and should of beat them again the following day, Wednesday, only we didn't, my loss. It shouldn't of been. I shouldn't of even pitched. I had this Charley horse which Dutch said maybe I rather rest it one more day, but the boys all said, "Go ahead and pitch, Author, and pick up another $1,000 for we will get you 17 runs to work on," and I give in and worked, like a fool, thinking it would please the boys, and I got slapped around pretty bad for 3 innings before Dutch lifted me, which he should of done the first inning and not waited 3. It was just one of those days nobody got out of bed with any sense to start with. I went back in and listened to it on the radio with Mick, and in the end we lost it, and the cushion was only 2½ instead of 3½ like it should of been, and Mick run and snapped the radio off before the announcer could come through with the final summary, "Losing pitcher, Wiggen," like they do, though who in hell cares who the losing pitcher is beats me.

We bounced right back on Thursday. Cleveland moved in for a singleton, and we beat them, and the lead held steady, and we went on up to Boston.

Me and Bruce and Mike just sat down in the diner on the way up when Sid come in and looked around and seen us and shoved in. He was looking very pale, and he said, "Howdy there, boys," in this very enthusiastic voice and rubbed his hands and looked down the menu, saying, "Well, what is good? Yes sir, what is good? What is good, Bruce?"

"So far the water is pretty good," said Bruce, and Sid said, "That is a hot one" and laughed and laughed awhile, about the same kind of a laugh you hear when the Regional Supervisor tells a joke to a bunch of salesmen around the Arcturus Company in Boston, which I listen to but never laugh, even if it is funny, which it usually never is, only standing there with the straight face pretending I am waiting for the kicker, laughing on the inside only. But now I laughed to help Sid out, and Mike laughed, too, because somebody just told Sid the truth. I don't know who, and it makes no difference. I don't know who spilled it the first night, either, between the time I ate dinner with Katie and Miss Industrial Progress and the time I got back to the hotel. I asked around, but everybody said they already heard it from so many different boys there was really no way of tracking it down even if you wanted to, and anyhow what difference would it make, for it was out and you could not call it back.

We took 3 out of 4, last times in Boston, Friday, a doubleheader Saturday, and a singleton Sunday, playing to an empty park. I do not think 10,000 people showed up in the 3 days, though I don't know why. Boston was a better club than that. But they weren't winning, and what folks want is a winner, "Never mind good baseball, give us a winner," not loving the game but only loving winning, all these towns screaming for big-league ball that don't know good from bad to begin with. All they know is names. They rather sit home and stare at some big-league catcher's big-name ass on TV and the umpire's ass behind, thinking this is the same thing as *seeing* a ball game, which it is not. It all sounded hollow up there in the empty park, all echoes, and you waited for noise on a good play,

but all you heard was somebody clapping here and
somebody else clapping about 19,000 miles away,
and then 2 more people another 19,000. It was
hard to keep remembering that these were ball
games we needed, hard to keep hustling, hard to
keep remembering we were still in the middle of
the race with an awful lot of money riding on a
day's work.

It was gloomy up there. I keep thinking it driz-
zled or at least was cloudy, but I see by the clips
that it was not so. It was only a feeling you got in
the quiet park, like everybody in the whole of Boston went out of town for the weekend or else died
for all you could tell. All the same, we hustled,
maybe even hustled more than usual, or else it only
sounded that way because you could hear everybody clearer in the quiet, hear the boys calling to
themself, hear the singing, almost hear them thinking, see Perry and Coker talking behind their hand
across second, see Vincent looking across from left
at his brother and doing what his brother said, see
Lawyer Longabucco between, also looking at Pasquale, and Pasquale doing their thinking, waving
them now in, now back, now left, now right, hear
Red calling to George in Spanish, hear Clint and
Joe in the coaching boxes, hear them even hustling
in the bullpen, see them all picking up their sign
and hitting or taking or running or playing it safe,
hustling, hustling, so if you seen a movie of it with
the date blacked out you would of said it was sometime in April or May, never guessing September.

We went back home Sunday night with the cushion at 3½.

In the morning he did not feel too good, Monday, Labor Day. "I will call Doc," I said.

"No," he said.

"Does it feel like the attack?" I said.

"Yes and no," he said. "I feel dipsy. Maybe I will feel better opening the window," and he went and opened it and sat by it and breathed it in and went and put a chew of Days O Work in his mouth and went back and spit down a couple times.

"Maybe it will rain," I said.

"Not soon," he said. "Maybe by night," leaning out and looking both ways and up. He knew if it would rain or not, which I myself do not know without looking at the paper and even then do not know because I forget to look. In the end I never know if it will rain until it begins. But he knew by the way the clouds blew, and he said he felt better now, and he shut the window and called Katie, saying he felt dipsy today, and he said in the phone, "No, I do not think he did" and clapped his hand over the phone and begun to say something to me, and I said, "No. Tell her no. Tell her I forgot," and she eat him out, and he said, "But Katie," and then again, "But, Katie, but," until she hung up, and I did not look, and he went on talking, like he was still talking to her, and finally he said, "Well, OK, Katie, and I love you, too" and hung up, all smiles, and we went out to the park and he still did not feel too good, and he told

Dutch, and Dutch said, "Well, we can not do without you, but we will try. Will we not try, boys, and make the best of a bad blow?" and the boys all said "Yes siree bob" and "You said it, boss" and "Sure enough" and all, and they hustled out, and me and Bruce laid on the table and listened with Mick.

There was plenty of scrap left in Washington yet. They did not know they were beat. You probably could of even found a little Washington money in town if you looked hard enough, not much, but some, for the town did not know what the Mammoths knew, not knowing the truth, not knowing Washington was beat on August 26, which I personally knew laying in bed and listening to the boys, and knew for sure when Goose shot the light out, knowing what it done to a fellow when he knew, how it made them cut out the horseshit and stick to the job. Washington hustled, jumping Van Gundy for a run in the second and another in the fourth, and we laid there, not moving, only listening, Mick folding towels but not hurrying like he hurries when he is nervous, only sitting there folding one after the other and setting it on the pile and creasing it out and reaching over slowly for the next, the 3 of us as calm as we could be like we were looking at the front end of a movie we already seen the back end of, and you knew who done it, who killed who, and we thought, "Washington, you are dead and do not know it."

George opened our fifth with a single, and they played Perry for the bunt, which he crossed them up and slammed through first and into the opposite field, and it was Pasquale that bunted instead and caught all Washington flat-footed, George scoring and Perry going clear to third and Pasquale winding up at second, for George dumped Eric Bushell in the play at the plate, and they passed Sid to get at Canada, and then they passed *Canada,* not meaning to, and Bruce said he felt better now, and we went down and warmed.

We warmed close to the wall. I remember every now and then he stuck out his hand and leaned against it, and I said, "Still feeling dipsy?" and he said, "No, only a little," and he crouched down again, first sitting on his heels and then flatting out his feet behind him and resting on his knees and looking back over his shoulder to see where Dutch was looking, for Dutch will fine a catcher for catching on his knees. "Maybe it will rain," I said, and he looked up and said "I hope so."

"I am warm," I said, though I was not, and we sat on the bench in the bullpen.

"It is a big crowd," he said. "It is Labor Day, that is what it is," and he took out a chew and broke it in half and give me half a chunk, saying, "Chew a chew, Arthur," which he always asked me and I always turned down except I took it then and chewed it and did not like it much, having no use for tobacco nor liquor, and every time I spit it dribbled down my chin. "Keep your teeth tight shut when you spit," he said.

It run long, for we begun hitting quite a bit, and he said, "You must be getting cold by now," and I said no. "It is getting cold," he said, and he reached around behind him for his jacket except it was not there, and I jiggled the phone, saying, "Send up a jacket for Bruce," and 3 boys sprung up off the bench and raced down the line, Wash and Piney and Herb Macy, and the crowd all begun yelling and pointing, never seeing such a thing before as 3 men all racing for the bullpen like that, and Krazy Kress sent down a note saying, "Author, what the hell??????" and I looked up at the press-box and give Krazy flat palms, same as saying, "What the hell what?"

We started fast in the second game. It was raining a little. Sid hit a home run in the first with Pasquale aboard, Number 42, the first home run he hit since August 17, according to the paper, and Bruce shook his hand at the plate, and Sid stopped and told Bruce, "Wipe off your bat," and Bruce looked at his bat and at Sid, not understanding, not feeling the rain, and Sid took the bat and wiped it off, and Bruce whistled a single in left, the last base hit he ever hit, and made his turn and went back and stood with one foot on the bag and said something to Clint, and Clint yelled for Dutch, and Dutch went out, and they talked. I do not know what about. Dutch only said to me, "Pick up your sign off the bench," and he sent for Doc, and Doc sat in the alley behind the dugout and waited, and the boys sometimes strolled back and sat beside him, asking him questions, "What does he have?" and such as that. They smoked back there, which Dutch does not like you to, saying, "Smoking ain't learning. Sitting on the bench and watching is learning," but he said nothing that day. You knew he wouldn't.

Washington begun stalling like mad in the third, hoping for heavy rain before it become official, claiming it was raining, though the umps ruled it was not. Sy Sibley was umping behind the plate. They stepped out between pitches and wiped off their bat and tied their shoe and blew their nose and gouged around in their eye, saying, "Something is in my eye," and Sy said, "Sure, your eyeball," and they stepped back in. As soon as they stepped back in again I pitched.

He never knew what was coming, curve ball or what. "Just keep your meat hand out of the way," I said, and he said he would but did not. It did not register. He was catching by habit and memory, only knowing that when the pitcher threw it you were supposed to stop it and throw it back, and if a fellow hit a foul ball you were supposed to whip off your mask and collar it, and if a man was on base you were supposed to keep him from going on to the next one. You play ball all your life until a day comes when you do not know what you are doing, but you do it anyhow, working through a fog, not remembering anything but only knowing who people were by how they moved, this fellow the hitter, this the pitcher, and if you hit the ball you run to the right, and then when you got there you asked Clint Strap were you safe or out because you do not know yourself. There was a fog settling down over him.

I do not know how he got through it. I do not
even know how yours truly got through it. I do not
remember much. It was 3-0 after 4½, official now,
and now we begun stalling, claiming it was raining, claiming the ball was wet and we were libel to
be beaned, which Washington said would make no
difference to fellows with heads as hard as us. Eric
Bushell said it to me in the fifth when I com-
plained the ball was wet, and I stepped out and
started laughing, "Ha ha ha ho ho ho ha ha ha,"
doubling over and laughing, and Sy Sibley said,
"Quit stalling," and I said I could not help it if
Bushell was going to say such humorous things to
me and make me laugh. "Tell him to stop," I said.
"Ha ha ha ho ho ho ha ha ha."

"What did he say?" said Sy, and I told him, telling him very slow, telling him who Eric Bushell
was and who I was, the crowd thinking it was an
argument and booing Sy. "Forget it," said he. "Get
back in and hit."

"You mean bat," said Bushell. "He never hits,"
and I begun laughing again, stepping out and saying how could a man bat with this fellow behind
me that if the TV people knew how funny he was
they would make him an offer.

"Hit!" said Sy. "Bat! Do not stall."

"Who is stalling?" said I, and I stepped back in,
the rain coming a little heavier now.

I threw one pitch in the top of the seventh, a
ball, wide, to Billy Linenthal. I guess I remember.
Bruce took it backhand and stood up and slowly
raised his hand and took the ball out of his mitt

and started to toss it back, aiming very careful at my chin, like Red told him to, and then everybody begun running, for the rain come in for sure now, and he seen everybody running, but he did not run, only stood there. I started off towards the dugout, maybe as far as the baseline, thinking he was following, and then I seen that he was not. I seen him standing looking for somebody to throw to, the last pitch he ever caught, and I went back for him, and Mike and Red were there when I got there, and Mike said, "It is over, son," and he said "Sure" and trotted on in.

In the hospital me and Mike and Red waited in the waiting room for word, telling them 1,000 times, "Keep us posted," which they never done and you had to run down the hall and ask, and then when you asked they never *knew* anything, and for all you could tell they were never *doing* anything neither, only looking at his chart, standing outside his door and looking at his chart and maybe whistling or kidding the nurses until I really got quite annoyed.

He was unconscious. Around midnight he woke up, and they said one of us could see him, the calmest, and I went, and he only said "Howdy," but very weak, not saying it, really, only his lips moving. He looked at me a long time and worked up his strength and said again, "Howdy, Arthur," and the doctor said, "He does not know you," and I said he did, for he always called me "Arthur." Then he drifted off again.

They told me take his clothes away, and I took them, his uniform and cap and socks and shoes, and I rolled them up with his belt around them and carried them back out. Red and Mike went pale when they seen me. They went pale every little while all night, every time a phone rung or a doctor passed through. "Relax," said I. "He is not dying."

"You never seen anybody die," said Red.

"I seen them in the movies," I said.

"It ain't the same," he said.

"He will not die," said Mike. "He will only pass on."

We went out and got something to eat. It was still raining, and we walked a long ways before we found a place open. It was very quiet in the streets. We ate in one of these smoky little places, everything fried. The paper said MAMMOTHS COP 2, GOLDMAN SWATS 42nd, and there was a picture of Sid crossing the plate and Bruce shaking his hand. "Then he hit," I said.

"And then he did not know what happened without going back and asking Clint," said Red.

"It is sad," said Mike. "It makes you wish to cry."

"It is sad," said Red. "It makes you wish to laugh."

We went back in the waiting room and stretched on the couches and slept. While we were asleep somebody threw a blanket over me, and over Red and Mike as well. I don't know who. When we woke up the sun was shining, and I went down the

279

hall and asked, and they looked at his chart and said he was fine, and I heard him singing then, singing, "As I was a-walking the streets of Laredo, as I walked out in Laredo one day, I spied a young cowboy all wrapped in white linen, all wrapped in white linen and cold as the clay," and I run back for Red and Mike, and they heard me come running and went all pale again, and I said, "Come with me," and we went back down the hall again. You could hear him even further down now, for he sung louder, "It was once in the saddle I used to go dashing, once in the saddle I used to go gay, first down to Rosie's and then to the card house, shot in the breast and am dying today." We stood and listened and then run in, and he stopped singing and tried sitting up, but he was too weak, and we said, "Get on up out of there now and back to work," and "This sure is a lazy man's way of drawing pay for no work," and he said, "Did anybody bring my chews?"

"I will go get them," said Mike, and he went back to the hotel and brung them, and clothes as well, saying, "I hope I brung the right combination," and Bruce said "Yes." He never cares about the combination anyhow, only grabs the nearest. If I did not shuffle his suits around he would wear the same one every day.

We hung in the hospital. Dutch called from St. Louis around supper, glad to hear that all was well again, and he told Red why not come out now, as long as the worst was over. "Business before pleasure," said Red, and he went.

He was so weak he even got tired chewing, shoving it over in his cheek and leaving it there, and his hands shook. He could not hold the newspaper nor his knife and fork but would eat a little and lay back again, saying, "No doubt I will pep up and be back in action again in no time," and we said he would, me and Mike and the doctors and nurses as well, though we knew he would not. Maybe I never seen a man die and wouldn't know if I did, but I knew when a man was not libel to be back in action very soon.

I picked up the club in Pittsburgh on Friday, and I pitched on Saturday and won, Number 22, which give us a sweep of the 2 in Pittsburgh, 6 wins in 7 starts, according to the paper, 9 in the last 11, and 14 in the last 17, counting back to August 26, Goose's birthday, the night the boys all knew the truth. The cushion was 6½, and it was now only a matter of time. We needed 3 to clinch.

Him and his father and Mike were in the clubhouse when we hit Chicago, and the boys all went wild to see him, not phoney wild, neither, but the real thing, admiring him, and he stood up and said, "Howdy, boys," and they pumped his hand and told him how they missed him, and he got dressed, and he was white and thin, and he was cold, always cold, and he sat on the bench all wrapped in jackets, getting up off the bench every so often and going back and laying down awhile, and then coming back out.

We whipped Chicago twice. Nothing in the

world could stop us now. Winning makes winning like money makes money, and we had power and pitching and speed, so much of it that if anybody done anything wrong nobody ever noticed. There was too much we were doing right. It was a club, like it should of been all year but never was but all of a sudden become, and we clinched it the first night in Cleveland, Blondie Biggs working, and we voted the shares, 30 full shares and a lot of tiny ones, $1,500 to Mike and the same to Red, and $1,250 to Piney for playing the guitar, and $1,000 to Diego Roberto for talking Spanish to George, and little slices to batboys, big hands and big hearts like you have when you win, not stopping rolling then but rolling still and winning though we did not need to win but could of relaxed and played out the string, yet hating to relax either because we were playing ball at last like it was meant to be played.

He went with us all the way. He dressed every day, and then he sat, no stronger than ever, thin and white and his cheeks all hollow, but his spirit high. Sometimes he picked up a bat and swung it a couple times and sat down again.

The Series opened in New York on a Wednesday, and I pitched and won, and Van Gundy Thursday, and after the Thursday game Bruce went home. "It is practically copped," he said. "I see no sense in trucking all the way out there and back."

"No," said the boys. "Come along for the ride."

"No," he said, "I will see you in the spring. I

will be back in shape by spring," and we said he would, saying, "See you in the spring, Bruce. See you in Aqua Clara."

"See you," said he, and I went with him and his father and put them on the plane. He could barely carry his bags. "Arthur," he said, "send me the scorecard from Detroit," and I said I would.

But then I never sent it. We wrapped the Series up on Sunday, my win again, and I took a scorecard home with me and tossed it on the shelf and left it lay. Goddam it, anyhow, I am just like the rest. Wouldn't it been simple instead of writing a page on my book to shoved it in the mail? How long would it of took? Could I not afford the stamps?

Tuesday I got this letter from Arcturus saying Katie was up there raising holy hell and I better do some sensational explaining. I did not know what in hell to do now. I clipped it in the lampshade, and every night I looked at it. After about 3 nights I seen they took the letter "s" out of Perkinsville and tacked it on the end of Wiggen—

MR. HENRY W. WIGGENS
PERKINVILLE, NEW YORK

I figured one way to start off was bawl the daylight out of them for not spelling, and I hardly got warm when the phone rung. It was his father, and he was dead. That was October 7.

In my Arcturus Calendar for October 7 it says,

"De Soto visited Georgia, 1540." This hands me a laugh. Bruce Pearson also visited Georgia. I was his pall-bear, me and 2 fellows from the crate and box plant and some town boys, and that was all. There were flowers from the club, but no *person* from the club. They could of sent somebody.

He was not a bad fellow, no worse than most and probably better than some, and not a bad ball-player neither when they give him a chance, when they laid off him long enough. From here on in I rag nobody.

Two Dogtown novels by Frank Bonham

THE NITTY GRITTY

If you live in a poor, black slum, you've got to hustle to live, but you've got to have a smart hustle to get out. Charlie Matthews wants to get out of Dogtown but the question is, How? The English teacher says stay in school. His father says shine shoes. When scheming Uncle Baron comes to town with get-rich-quick ideas, Charlie sees a light. He starts raising money to get in on the big deal and becomes a little wiser in the process.

"Real and tough!" —Chicago Tribune

❧«»❧

VIVA CHICANO

"I tried to be straight as an arrow, didn't I? But, man, it's not possible."

Keeny got started on a police record when he was a kid. Things never got much better. His father had taught him pride in *la raza,* but who could think about pride and being a Mexican when most of your life was filled with drugs, gangs, street fights, juvenile courts, and detention homes? When trouble started, people pointed to Keeny. So when he was accused of the murder of his little brother, Keeny ran. But he had to come back for one more fight against a world that didn't understand him.

"Taut and exciting . . . blistering candor."
—Saturday Review

LAUREL-LEAF BOOKS 75c each

Today's
Hangups
and the
Generation
Gap

I'm really dragged but nothing gets me down

by Nat Hentoff
author of *Jazz Country*

Jeremy Wolf is a high school senior whose soul is torn between his responsibility to his country and his social existence. With wit and with rare understanding, this novel examines both sides of the generation gap.

"A taut, highly articulate exposition of today's hangups . . ."—*The Virginia Kirkus Service*

". . . timely and important . . ."
—*The New York Times*

A LAUREL-LEAF BOOK   60c

*Biggest dictionary value
ever offered in paperback!*

The Dell paperback edition of

THE AMERICAN HERITAGE
DICTIONARY
OF THE ENGLISH LANGUAGE

- Largest number of entries—55,000
- 832 pages—nearly 300 illustrations
- The only paperback dictionary with photographs

These special features make this new, modern dictionary clearly superior to any comparable paperback dictionary:

- More entries and more illustrations than any other paperback dictionary
- The first paperback dictionary with photographs
- Words defined in modern-day language that is clear and precise
- Over one hundred notes on usage with more factual information than any comparable paperback dictionary
- Unique appendix of Indo-European roots
- Authoritative definitions of new words from science and technology
- More than one hundred illustrative quotations from Shakespeare to Salinger, Spenser to Sontag
- Hundreds of geographic and biographical entries
- Pictures of all the Presidents of the United States
- Locator maps for all the countries of the world

A DELL BOOK 95c

more good reading in

THE LAUREL-LEAF LIBRARY

If you cannot obtain copies of this title from your local bookseller, just send the price (plus 15c per copy for handling and postage) to Dell Books, Post Office Box 1000, Pinebrook, N. J. 07058.